PRAISE FOR *BLOCK 46*

'A real page-turner … I loved it!' Martina Cole

'A great serial-killer thriller with a nice twist … first rate' James Oswald

'A bold and audacious debut from a very talented writer. Heralds the beginning of a thrilling new series' R J Ellory

'Cleverly plotted, simply excellent…' Ragnar Jónasson

'Viscerally brutal yet delicately beautiful, like blood spatter on fresh snow. An unbelievable debut' Matt Wesolowski

'Gripping … utterly mesmerising. My kind of book!' Thomas Enger

'Harrowing, ambitious, and downright chilling. *Block 46* is not for the faint of heart – and not to be missed' Crime by the Book

'*Block 46* is not for the faint-hearted, nor for those of a sensitive disposition. Johana Gustawsson has written a very impressive and very dark thriller. *Block 46* is her first work translated into English (by the very capable Maxim Jakubowski), and I am quite certain it will be a critical success' TripFiction

'I was so intrigued to see where *Block 46* was going. Yet, after just a few pages, I had to put the book down for a while, needing a break. I desperately wanted to read more, but also didn't. Books don't often have such an impact on me. And not many books make me email a publisher with the expression "OMG"! *Block 46* contains everything I want in crime fiction, including twists, turns and surprises. It totally broke me for a while at the end and is certainly not a book that I'll forget' Off-the-Shelf Books

'Breathtakingly honest and true, *Block 46* really is something unique and special, with a writer who has carved out her own place in the noir genre – French, Swedish, German and her own personal history woven into the mix – and it's a raw, emotional and memorable read' The BookTrail

'With its short chapters and the changing narrative (there are also brief interludes told from the perspective of the killer), *Block 46* is a book that demands your full attention. The threads of the stories are gradually woven together, resulting in a thrilling and shocking denouement. *Block 46* is the best kind of book, it's a gripping psychological thriller with a clever and engaging resolution, but it also does what the most intelligent fiction can do: it reaches into the past and tells us that there are some lessons we must never forget. It's a book that kept me reading long into the night, then I couldn't sleep for thinking about it' Hair Past a Freckle

'Without hesitation this book has already made it to my top reads of 2017. Why? Because it's a rich and harrowing story of the psychology of evil, good versus bad, death versus life; it's complex, fast paced, and disturbing, all the elements that make a crime read stand out from the norm. Gripping from the first page, *Block 46* will keep you on the edge of your seat all the way to its shocking conclusion, that I can guarantee' The Book Review Café

'*Block 46* is the type of book you can't put down. Don't start it at night like I did … as you won't be able to sleep after reading it. Outstanding' @MrsLovesToBake

ABOUT THE AUTHOR

Born in 1978 in Marseille and with a degree in political science, Johana Gustawsson has worked as a journalist for the French press and television. She married a Swede and now lives in London. She was the co-author of a bestseller, *On se retrouvera*, published by Fayard Noir in France, whose television adaptation drew over seven million viewers in June 2015. She is working on the next book in the Roy & Castells series.

ABOUT THE TRANSLATOR

Maxim Jakubowski is a highly regarded translator from French and Italian. An ex-publisher, and one-time owner of the Murder One bookstore, he is also a writer and editor of crime, mystery and erotic fiction, and has published nearly one hundred books. A regular broadcaster on TV and radio, Maxim Jakubowski reviews crime fiction for the *Guardian*. He also contributes to *The Times*, the *Bookseller* and the *Evening Standard* and is the literary director of the Crime Scene Film and Book Festival, held annually in London. For many years, he has edited anthologies of the best British mystery stories of the year and the world's best erotica, which have become bestsellers in the UK and America.

BLOCK 46

JOHANA GUSTAWSSON

translated by Maxim Jakubowski

**ORENDA
BOOKS**

Orenda Books
16 Carson Road
West Dulwich
London SE21 8HU
www.orendabooks.co.uk

First published in French as *Block 46* by éditions Bragelonne in 2015
This edition published by Orenda Books in 2017

ISBN 978-1-910633-70-0
eISBN 978-1-910633-71-7

Typeset in Garamond by MacGuru Ltd
Printed and bound by CPI Group (UK) Ltd, Croydon CRO 4YY

SALES & DISTRIBUTION

In the UK and elsewhere in Europe:
Turnaround Publisher Services
Unit 3, Olympia Trading Estate
Coburg Road, Wood Green
London N22 6TZ
www.turnaround-uk.com

In the USA and Canada:
Trafalgar Square Publishing
Independent Publishers Group
814 North Franklin Street
Chicago, IL 60610
USA
www.ipgbook.com

In Australia and New Zealand:
Affirm Press
28 Thistlethwaite Street
South Melbourne VIC 3205
Australia
www.affirmpress.com.au

For details of other territories, please contact *info@orendabooks.co.uk*

For my parents.
Odile and Jean-Louis,
who gave me a taste for words and hard work.

'There is nothing positive to say about the depths through which I wandered for seven years, surrounded by the blind and the damned who raged like souls possessed against all that remained of human dignity.'

Eugen Kogon

Thursday, 7 November 2013

The light from the three electric torches stripes across the pit.

A perfect rectangle. One metre thirty in length, fifty centimetres in width. Made to measure.

He picks up the spade, gathers earth and spreads it out in the hole. A single shovelful and the legs are already covered; all that sticks out are the toes. Toes as smooth as pebbles, as cold as ice, that make him want to touch them with the tips of his fingers.

Smooth and cold.

He throws another pile of damp earth over the stomach. Some lands just below the thoracic cage, around the navel; the rest slides down the sides. A few more spadefuls and it will all be done.

It had all been child's play.

All of a sudden, he lets go of the spade and brings his muddy gloves up to his ears.

'Just shut up, will you?'

He spits the words out, his jaw frozen with anger.

'No, no, no, no! Stop shouting. Stop!'

He kneels down beside the pit and places his hands against the colour-less lips.

'Shh. Shh, I said…'

His nose brushes across the ice-like cheek.

'OK… OK… I'll do it … I'll sing your little song. I'll sing you "Imse Vimse", but you must remain quiet. Is that understood?'

He stands up and shakes dirt from his trousers.

'Itsy bitsy spider climbs up the waterspout…'

He takes hold of the spade and throws another lot of earth across the torso. It sinks into the wide-open gash running down from the chin to the sternal notch.

'Down came the rain, and washed the spider out…'

A spadeful over the face. The earth spills across the forehead, obscuring the hair, dripping into the eye sockets.

'Up came the sun, dried away all the rain…'

The dirt rains across the marble whiteness of the body to the rhythm of the nursery rhyme.

He packs the final layer of earth tight and smooths it out, then arranges a bunch of brown winter leaves across the top with exaggerated, arrogant artistry. He walks away backwards, his eyes still fixed on the grave, then retraces his steps and kicks a few leaves around with his foot.

He cleans down the spade with his gloved hand, replaces the electric torches in their bag, takes his gloves off, shakes them free of dirt, then one at a time places his tools inside the bag.

Just as he pulls the bag over his shoulder, he hears the chatter of the parakeets. He'd heard somewhere that the exotic birds had escaped from the Shepperton film studios, in Surrey, during the making of Bogart's Oscar-winning 1951 film The African Queen. *But the truth was, no such bird was used on the set, and the film had actually been shot in the studios at Isleworth. So where had the damned birds come from, then?*

He stops for a moment and searches the depths of night for their apple-green plumage. All he can hear is a nearby rustle.

He really needs a second pair of binoculars with night vision. Just can't work by torchlight any more, much too dangerous. He has to get himself better organised and avoid such imprudence.

He pulls one of the torches out of his parka pocket, and, keeping its beam low, gets on his way.

THE FOX WAS BASKING in the solitary band of sunlight that had reached the garden. He'd slipped in through the bushes twenty minutes before and hadn't moved an inch since. Three gardens along, two small girls were running around barefoot, their curling, ginger hair animated by the breeze. It made you wonder how they never caught a cold.

Sitting in her study, its windows overlooking the series of gardens below, Alexis stretched, adjusted the cushion under her backside and switched the tape recorder back on. Rosemary West's monotonous voice spread through the room.

Two months earlier, as she sat facing Rosemary at Low Newton prison, in Northumberland, Alexis had stared at the killer's small, dainty hands; hands that had beaten, strangled, raped. Hands that Rosemary looked down upon, as she told Alexis how she had killed her own daughter.

For a brief moment, Alexis was startled. The blurred features of her parents had appeared on her screen. She paused the recording.

'Can't you see you just don't know how to do it properly?' Her mother was irritable. 'This is where you should click, look.'

The window went blank as the connection was lost. Alexis, with a grin on her face, called them back.

'Hi,' she said, as her father's face filled the screen.

'Oh … be quiet, Mado! Look, she's here now, our baby girl. Alexis, my love, how are you?'

Thirty-seven years old and she was still his 'baby girl'.

'Why aren't you outside, darling?' Her mother took over, her mouth now moving closer to the webcam. 'They say the weather in London is beautiful today. Well, in a manner of speaking, meaning you probably have a couple of rays of sunshine peering through the clouds. If you don't take advantage of it now, you might not have another opportunity this year!'

'She's not outside because she has to finish her book, don't you see! Remember, her publisher is expecting it in two months.'

'But she needs some fresh air. Look at her face.'

Alexis rolled her eyes. *What's wrong with my face? How rough can I look?*

'So, where are my niece and nephew?' she asked, moving the conversation on.

'They're playing with their presents.'

'Presents?' What are you celebrating?'

'The Kings. *Els Reis Mags*,' her father replied in perfect Catalan. 'The youngsters must be taught to remember where they came from. They are, after all, a quart—'

'A quarter Spanish … I know, Dad.'

'No. Catalan! A quarter Catalan. So, baby girl, how's the book going?'

'Five pages further down the road than yesterday, Daddy. I have to leave you both, get on with it, you know…'

'Do you want me to keep some of the *fideuà* I made for you, darling?' her mother asked. 'I can freeze it and you can eat it next time you're over? By the way, when are you planning to be here next? Have you bought your tickets yet?'

'I'm not sure when, Mum…'

'You don't want any of my *fideuà*?'

'Of course I want some of your *fideuà*, Mum, but I'm not sure yet when I can come see you next. I really have to get back to work … Give everyone kisses from me.'

'Don't you want to say a word to your sister and Xavier, at least…?'

'I only spoke to them yesterday, Mum … Anyway, have a lovely afternoon.'

Alexis blew a few kisses towards the screen to interrupt her mother's protests and disconnected from Skype.

She dragged her feet to the kitchen, poured herself another cup of coffee and picked up her mobile phone, which, when she happened to be writing, sat all too temptingly by the fridge. She only allowed herself to consult it whenever she stocked up on caffeine or cheese.

Alexis opened her eyes wide with surprise. Seventeen missed calls from a London landline and four messages. She called the number straight back.

'Alexis Castells, you tried to call me…'

'Alexis, it's Alba…'

Normally, Alba Vidal, a Spaniard whose temperament was as colourful as her apparel, gave you the distinct feeling that she was embracing you as she spoke. But right now her voice seemed to have lost all its warmth. It was dry – splintered with anguish.

'I'm calling from the store phone, I wanted to keep my private line free in case … No, no, no! Keep your hands off that window display!' Alba was clearly in a foul mood.

A few words of protest, mumbled in response to her outburst.

'I'm the damned public relations director, and I'm telling you not to touch the window display, for heaven's sake! So sorry, Alexis … it's total madness here. You try for months to get things properly organised, and on the day it's always the same bloody mess…' Alba sighed heavily. '*Dios mío*, Alexis…'

'What's happening, Alba?'

Germany
July 1944

THE TRAIN SLOWED DOWN as it began its ascent.

With an animal grunt, the prisoner pulled on the wagon door. The others greeted the cold air, stretching their necks, as if this unexpected pool of breath could quench the thirst burning their throats.

He waited for a few minutes, like a sparrow delaying his flight from a branch, then disappeared abruptly into the ink-dark night. As the train came to a complete stop, other prisoners began to jump out, too.

A succession of muted sounds broke out and, all of a sudden, the forest was a blaze of yellow stains: the floodlights positioned on the turrets heralded the manhunt. It broke through the bushes, the tangle of trees, the undergrowth.

'*Ich habe sie! Ich habe sechs von ihnen!*'

The shouts were quickly followed by the staccato ballet of machine guns – the orders shouted out in German mingling with the explosions, until a silence more terrifying even than the barrage of shots surrounded the convoy like a wreath.

Erich Ebner wondered how many men had fallen. How many had managed to escape. How many were slowly dying, in atrocious pain from their wounds. Maybe it was better this way, his erstwhile neighbour had whispered in English. Because, anyway, hell awaited them at the end of the journey. Erich was dubious: how could anything be worse than being in this cattle cart, deprived of air or water as the outside temperature reached twenty-five degrees? The wagons had been designed to carry forty men, or eight horses. There were one hundred and forty-two of them. At any rate, one hundred and forty-two had begun the journey alive.

The old Spanish man had been the first to die, barely a few hours after the convoy had departed. His son had burst into tears as soon as he had realised his father had ceased breathing. He'd wiped the foam from his father's chin and taken him into his arms, moaning, the purple features of the dead man swinging from side to side in a *danse macabre*. The son had then started banging against the wagon's walls, before turning to his neighbour. He took off his shoe and hit the poor guy with the heel. No one moved, barely reacting to the assault. And the fight came to an end as suddenly as it had begun. Exhaustion had overcome the madness.

Since then, others had succumbed, but they were standing so tightly together that the dead passengers were held up by the mass of bodies. Erich couldn't actually see the dead, but he could smell them. The putrid scent of death permeated the wagon, mingling with the smell of sweat and emptying bowels. The pestilential odour of man reduced to an animal state. They only had a single bucket and it hadn't been emptied since their departure, thirty-six hours earlier.

Ebner pivoted on his foot. The prisoner next to him was trying to extricate himself from the tight embrace of those around them. Just before the escape attempt, the very same man had licked the pearls of sweat running down Erich's neck. Erich saw him approach the bucket, inch by inch, and lap the urine spilling from it, his face all the time crumpling with disgust. He was interrupted by the crunching of gravel under the boots of the Nazi soldiers.

Two SS officers stood in front of the now open doors of the wagon. The one on the right stepped forward, a hand on the grip of his pistol.

'*Ausziehen!*'

Nobody moved. Most of the men piled up in the wagon did not speak German.

'*Nackt, verdammte Scheisse!*'

Erich knew that if he translated the soldier's orders, he ran the risk of being shot on the spot. He began to undress as fast as he could manage being stuffed tight between so many other bodies.

His neighbours quickly followed his example. Numb and embarrased, they protected their genitals with their hands.

'*Die Anziehsachen zur ersten Reihe weitergeben!*'

His companions glanced at him sideways to see what they should do now. Ebner passed his clothing along to one of the prisoners standing in front of the officers.

Once the clothes had all been piled on the ground outside the train, the soldier pulled out his Luger, placed the muzzle against the forehead of the prisoner facing him and pulled the trigger. The detonation was masked by the cries of sheer horror coming from the other men as they were showered with pieces of brain matter and bone.

'*Kein Entkommen mehr.*'

The second SS officer closed the wagon door and the train departed again.

‑‑‑‑‑

The convoy arrived in the station the following afternoon.

The shrieking of the brakes melted into the overall clamour – a mix of ferocious barks and orders shouted out in German.

The wagon's door opened and revealed a group of soldiers. Three of them held the leashes of froth-mouthed German Shepherds, aching to rush towards the new arrivals.

'*RAUS! RAUS!*'

The first row of prisoners moved hesitantly forward. Like sudden and heavy rain, rifle butts and thick wooden bats fell across the heads, shoulders and the hands raised in protest. The dogs were set loose on those who were unable to get up again.

'*RAUS!*'

As fast as the prisoners could exit the wagon, the dead fell across the platform like rag dolls. The bodies were trampled by those hoping to survive, and trying to avoid the storm of blows.

The rubber truncheon only made contact with Erich's shoulder and knee; he escaped the dogs and joined the waiting line of survivors.

The walk to the camp seemed to take forever. Erich stumbled along with the column of limping men, five abreast, under the oppressive copper sun, moving to the rhythm of the orchestra accompanying them.

None of this made any sense. The journey. The dead. The cruelty. The music. The naked bodies. No one even tried to conceal their nudity any longer, as if each and every one of them had already abdicated their humanity. And, above all reigned the silence. The silence of unconditional surrender lurking behind the inappropriate music. The guards had not ordered them to be silent, but no one dared to speak. Fear paralysed their senses: it had replaced pain, thirst, hunger and extreme fatigue.

Where were the sons, the daughters, the wives of these men? Where were Erich's parents? And his friends; his university colleagues? What was the destination of this hellish journey? He'd overheard the SS officers mentioning Ettersberg Forest. That meant they must be close to Weimar, in Thuringia; close to the hill where Goethe enjoyed walking amongst the beeches, thinking of Charlotte von Stein.

The soldiers came to a halt in front of a gate. The one leading the column read aloud the inscription carved above the metal doors:

'*Jedem das Seine!*'

To each his own. *Suum cuique.* As if these men, on the threshold of death, were in a position to appreciate the irony of such a philosophical statement.

All of a sudden, someone screeched loudly.

Erich looked to his left and noticed a soldier standing tall, his hand raised. A naked man was moaning, curled up on the ground.

'*Aufstehen!*'

The man remained where he was, his body shaking with spasms.

'*Aufstehen, du verdammte Rastte!*' The soldier's arm fell across his victim.

Erich then realised what the hand was holding: a stone. The Nazi hit the poor man until the stone was lodged inside the shattered skull, then stepped around the body and rejoined the head of the convoy.

The walk resumed, to the enduring rhythm of the periodic beatings and the sprightly music.

Erich tried to swallow down the ball of fear growing inside his throat. He looked down at his bloodied feet, wondering when, if ever, they would be provided with food and drink. He was already salivating at the thought of a stream of cool water running down his throat.

Ten minutes later, they stopped in front of a large shed. Rest must be coming.

But when Erich entered the building, he could see neither the piles of clothes nor the meal they were expecting. He froze in shock, aghast. A prisoner standing behind him nudged him forward towards a brown-haired man wielding clippers. As the implement ran repeatedly over Erich's skull, his delicate straw-coloured hair fell with painful grace to the ground, where it joined the darker curls already spread there.

Finished with Erich's head, the man took hold of a razor and ran it over his armpits, his arms, his torso and his legs. When the blade reached his penis, Erich closed his eyes. The humiliation had drained all his energy. He meekly positioned his head when his ears were inspected. His mouth was held open, revealing his parched throat. His lips were dry and bleeding by now.

He was then led, under a barrage of truncheons, towards a gigantic water tub. A strong kick to his backside pushed him into it. He immediately recognised the smell of phenol. He felt as if his skin was catching fire. He dunked himself under, as ordered by a smiling SS officer, closing his mouth and eyes, then exited the liquid the moment he got the nod. When he reached the jet of cold water that came next, he couldn't help but open his mouth, forgetting how his whole body burned.

The man from the train had been right. It was indeed hell that was greeting them at the end of their journey. But a thoroughly well-organised hell.

ALEXIS PULLED HER SHEATH DRESS up her thighs and almost to the point of indecency, before climbing into the cab with as much elegance as she could muster, considering the dress she was wearing. She was still flustered from having run down the stairs from her second-floor apartment in high heels. Getting into the cab hadn't improved matters. She heaved a deep sigh as she lowered herself onto the seat.

'175 New Bond Street, please,' she called out, adjusting the dress across her legs.

The driver went down Fitzjohn's Avenue and continued along Avenue Road. A few minutes later, they were crossing into Regent's Park.

Alexis peered through the cab window. The outlines of the John Nash white stucco terraces stood out against the soot-coloured sky. By now, the park was darkening and the London winter was taking on a Scandinavian air.

The cab braked to make way for a few women joggers. With admiration and a smidgeon of envy, Alexis followed the passage of the trainer-clad amazons. Striding triumphantly, they braved the damp cold, running through the thin rain which, with grey streaks, shaded the late afternoon. She pulled up the collar of her coat and shivered in reaction. It brushed against her earrings: two pearls set against a red-gold pin designed by her friend, Linnéa Blix.

She had difficulty swallowing and rubbed her throat.

Linnéa had created a collection of jewels for Cartier that was to be launched this very evening in the presence of a handpicked set of exclusive clients. Linnéa had been due to meet up with Alba at the New Bond Street store that afternoon, but had not shown up and couldn't be reached. It was true that Linnéa had, at best, a somewhat elastic notion of time, but she would never have missed a business meeting.

'Miss?'

The cab had come to a halt in front of Cartier's. Alexis settled her fare and disembarked from the vehicle, making a clumsy sidestep to avoid a puddle. She barely had time to set foot on the red carpet leading to the store's entrance before an umbrella was unfurled over her head and sheltered her as she made her way to the door.

Paul Vidal, Alba's husband, was waiting inside, facing another set of doors leading to an impressive staircase. He was nervously moving his weight from foot to foot, like a stilt-bird in a pond, albeit with an elegance that came as a surprise for a man of his size. When he saw her, his smile was radiant and he gave her a short but tender embrace, completed by a quick kiss on the cheek. His 'store manager' persona was already switched on for the occasion.

As they separated, he whispered quietly in her ear, 'She's still not here.'

Alexis' throat tightened again.

Damn it. Where could Linnéa be?

Paul's tone quickly switched to its light-hearted, commercial mode to greet the Russian clients standing patiently behind Alexis.

'Madam, may I show you the way to the boardroom?'

The voice was discreet, clear and crystalline. Alexis turned towards it. A thin-waisted, dark-haired young girl was smiling at her with genuine kindness. Alexis followed her, taking care with every step where she placed her vertiginously high heels.

At the top of the stairs, a mirrored door opened onto a high-ceilinged room. Alexis quickly noticed Alba, in full discussion with an Asian couple.

Alexis wanted to sit down with her friend and with undue, almost adolescent haste, talk of Linnéa – 'gossip away like schoolkids', as Paul often put it, in jest. She wanted to share her anxiety, add Alba's to hers, escalate the worry, dream up ridiculous and melodramatic theories that could put Hollywood to shame; only to then burst out laughing when Linnéa made her appearance, improbably dressed, her mass of blonde hair tightened into a chignon on the top of her head, and madly apologetic at having missed her flight … But, tonight, it seemed that Alba would not be able to spare Alexis a single minute; she moved from client to client – there was no chance of speaking to her. Alexis would have to control her own stress, then. Linnéa would surely show up.

She accepted the champagne glass a sylph-like waitress offered her and took an initial sip as she moved into the conference hall. The delicate bubbles of the champagne washed over her palate.

Alexis took in the room. The expensive furniture, the resplendent, finely chiselled cornices, the heavy curtains brushing against the herringbone parquet floor – it all reminded her of grand old days. As if General de Gaulle was still wandering across this room, which had been, during the war and his London exile, his office. Some even believed his famous 18th of June speech had been written between these four walls.

In the room's very centre, a large cube surrounded by a cloak of red velvet seemed to hang, almost levitating in the air. In all likelihood it was the display unit containing Linnéa's collection. In each corner stood golden, circular birdcages displaying the sumptuous creations of Jeanne Toussaint. After designing handbags for Coco Chanel, the Belgian designer had run Cartier's high-end jewellery range for more than forty years.

Alexis set her empty glass down on a gold platter and stepped towards the birdcage in which the more prestigious pieces from the Panther collection were being exhibited.

'Ladies and gentlemen…'

Paul had begun his speech. Obediently, the thirty or so guests turned to him.

'It's a great honour tonight for Cartier to introduce to you this preview of a new collection, designed and handmade by our new creator, Linnéa Blix, in celebration of the seventieth anniversary of France's liberation. Cartier is not just a witness to history…'

Alexis looked around for Alba. Her friend was listening attentively to her husband's speech. She stood by a stocky, white-haired man whose shape was elegantly flattered by a Savile Row suit. Alexis recognised Richard Anselme, a diamond merchant and Linnéa's very own Pygmalion.

Alexis moved her weight from one heel to another to compensate for her discomfort.

Linnéa must have missed her flight. Twice a year, she exiled herself in Falkenberg, on the west coast of Sweden. She mostly stayed out of touch during the course of these retreats, what she called her 'spoiled brat indulgence'.

Alexis shook her head to banish any alarming thoughts and continued listening to Paul's speech.

'…During the occupation, Jeanne Toussaint displayed a piece the colours of the French flag, and in the shape of a bird imprisoned in a cage, in the window of the Cartier shop in Paris. Unsurprisingly, this audacious gesture attracted the wrath of the occupying forces, and Toussaint had to endure several days in prison. In 1944, Jeanne Toussaint celebrated the liberation of the capital by helping the bird out of its cage. A symbol of a free France.'

Paul marked a theatrical pause and gazed at his audience.

'It's also Jeanne Toussaint who Cartier are celebrating in the new creations we are unveiling tonight. Tomorrow morning, the collection will be introduced to the press in Paris and will go on display in the windows of our rue de la Paix store, where she who was called "the Panther" displayed *The Bird in a Cage* seventy years ago.'

Paul raised his arms with all the authority of a conductor.

'Please.'

The red-velvet cloth spilled down the walls of the display unit with all the quiet arrogance of a wanton woman finally undressing in front of her lover. The crowd rushed forward.

Alexis was about to follow in their wake when she noticed Peter Templeton, Linnéa's partner, standing by the door. His eyes were frantically scanning the crowd.

Alexis' heart jumped so hard she felt she would faint.

PETER WAS SITTING at the table in the dining room of his apartment. His empty eyes moved from his hands to the candle holder sitting in the centre of the table. He'd gone to Cartier to fetch Linnéa. But she wasn't there. She hadn't turned up to the event she had spent months talking about. The evening of her triumph. Maybe she's still in Sweden? Alexis had suggested with a nervous smile. Maybe.

He watched as Alexis, still in her evening dress and holding the mobile phone to her ear, paced an invisible line between the two sash windows. Staring at the floor, she was listening to the police officer on the other end, pinching her lips between thumb and forefinger. As he answered her, her hand ran through the air, tracing shapes like cigarette smoke.

She wedged the phone between her ear and her shoulder, grabbed her notebook from the table and took note of an e-mail address. She thanked the police officer and hung up.

'Peter, do you have a photo of Linnéa that we could forward to the police?'

He looked round at Alexis. His face was twitching. In the space of a few hours, his cheeks had sunk and his normally tanned features had turned grey. He slowly rose, left the dining room and returned with his own mobile phone, which he handed over to Alexis. At the same moment, a bell rang sharply. Peter walked sluggishly to the door.

A minute later, he came back, Alba in his wake.

Alba was no longer wearing her jewellery and had swapped her heels for flats that looked suspiciously like slippers. Her centre-parted brown hair was tied at the back, making her look like a schoolgirl. Her make-up had all the signs of an end-of-evening battle zone: her foundation had sunk deep into the small lines circling her eyes and her mascara was frittering away, highlighting the signs of her fatigue. The short ponytail lengthened her already oblong features, and the tired make-up made her look like someone in mourning. Alba put a hand to her forehead as if checking her temperature.

Alexis greeted her friend with a tense smile.

'I've been in touch with the police,' she said. 'I've just sent them two photos of Linnéa.'

'Have they checked if she was on the passenger manifest for this morning's Gothenburg-to-London flight?'

'They're onto it and will call me back.'

Alba nodded. She slowly walked to the couch, peering around at the surroundings with courteous curiosity. Peter and Linnéa had moved in four months earlier, but neither she nor Alexis had visited their new apartment yet. Her gaze settled on a frame standing on the redwood sideboard – a sketch of Linnéa's depicting a diadem.

Alba looked away and unbuttoned her coat, then kicked her slippers off and curled up between the cushions, drawing her heels back under her body. Peter took his place at the table again while Alexis, like a sleepwalker, continued pacing between the two windows. Each was imprisoned inside their own silence. Like actors frozen on a stage, waiting for the curtain to be raised.

Then, suddenly, the phone in Alexis' hands vibrated and she brought it to her ear.

When she hung up a few minutes later, Peter and Alba were anxiously looking back at her.

'Her flight landed at Heathrow this morning, but she wasn't on board.'

Silence fell on the room like a lead weight.

Alba straightened out. The leather couch beneath her groaned.

'Have they—'

'Yes,' Alexis interrupted her. 'They've checked. She wasn't on any of the other flights that day. Or any of yesterday's either.'

1077.801/AFP

Heathrow Airport, London
Sunday, 12 January 2014, 18.45

ALEXIS BUCKLED UP and took hold of Peter's hand. Normally charismatic, Peter was now like a helpless child. Anxiety had undermined his self-assurance, bowing his shoulders. His eyes were fixed on the plane's window. Hailstones hammered against the wing as if kids with pebbles were using the A320 Airbus for target practice. Alexis looked over at Alba sitting on the other side of the aisle. They stared for a moment, each giving the other a hopeless smile.

The previous evening, the British missing-persons bureau had been in touch with the Falkenberg police, and the Swedes had immediately despatched a patrol to Linnéa's home. No one had answered the door. They had managed to peer through the window, but nothing appeared to be out of order. Swedish police were now about to set in motion a preliminary enquiry into Linnéa's disappearance; then they would decide whether to break in or not.

Unwilling to remain in London awaiting news of his partner, Peter had decided to travel to Falkenberg as soon as possible. Neither Alexis nor Alba had been keen to let him make the journey alone.

They'd had to wait until they could find seats. It was as if all twenty-five thousand Swedes living in London had decided to fly home that same weekend. They were due to land in Gothenburg around ten and were expected at the Falkenberg police station on Monday morning at eight.

Peter's hand held Alexis' in a tight grip.

'What am I going to do?' he asked, his eyes fixed on the tarmac outside. 'What am I going to do if…?'

His mouth was dry and his voice muted. He fell silent.

Alexis stroked his arm to comfort him. She could have reassured him by declaring that she was convinced that Linnéa was OK. But she was tired of reassurances. Riven with anxiety, the words felt untrue. There was still no news and it augured badly. That was the evidence. The mere thought of it was like fingering a scar. Best give him an affectionate touch, Alexis thought. It was less hypocritical.

'That's the way she is, you understand,' he said, his eyes staring at the armrest separating them. 'She enjoys her "me time". When she goes to Sweden, it's to enjoy the rest. She does send me messages from time to time, but … if I'm the one to call … well, you know the way she is when she's there…'

He rubbed his hand against his frowning forehead.

'Do you think I should have been more worried, Alexis? That I should have called the police earlier?'

'No, Peter, not at all. There was no reason to worry. None whatsoever.'

It was the answer he was hoping for. Absolution.

He nodded, reassured by her words, leaned his neck back against the headrest and closed his eyes.

Alexis turned towards Alba. Her friend was dozing, her head nodding from side to side.

She looked at her watch. Just about 19.00. Another thirteen hours to go before they would know. Thirteen hours before any answers might be revealed.

Torsviks småbåtshamn, Falkenberg, Sweden
Sunday, 12 January 2014, 21.00

UNAFFECTED BY THE WIND beating harshly against his face, Kommissionar Lennart Bergström was rushing down the snowy dune two steps at a time, his path lit up by his torch.

Further down, frozen and empty, the small pleasure marina was as unrecognisable as an old friend who'd long lost contact: winter had scared the boats away and swallowed up the banks of reeds. Huddling against a wooden shed, a wide white tent had been erected. Two police officers stood on either side of it. The picturesque landscape of the *småbåtshamn* was quite spoiled by this intrusion.

Björn Holm, the head of the SKL, the scene-of-crime police, awaited the Kommissionar at the foot of the dune.

'Good God, Lennart … I've never seen anything of the sort,' he muttered, nervously plucking ice from his moustache.

Bergström cleared his throat.

'Is the pathologist here?'

'Not any more. He was called over to Gothenburg.'

'Damn … Have you made a start?'

'We've had a brief look at the body and replaced the *snipa**** as it was. I wanted the guys to start looking at the hull and then around the boat, although I strongly doubt if we'll find anything, what with all this snow.'

Bergström slipped on his protective clothing, pulled on similar

---

* A *snipa* is a wooden boat

covers over his shoes, then blew into a pair of blue latex gloves before putting them on.

'You go first,' Björn said, as he moved aside.

Two arc lights threw a fierce, naked light across the interior of the tent. In its centre a small wooden boat lay upside down, the red line of its hull pointing upwards.

The three technicians momentarily looked up from the *snipa* as the Kommissionar entered and acknowledged his presence with brief hand gestures.

'We need another couple of minutes,' the smallest of the men said from behind his mask, his gaze not moving away from the specific area he was examining.

'What have you done with the two kids who discovered the body?' Björn asked the Kommissionar.

'I left them at the station, with Olofsson. They were quite shaken up.'

'I gather they were dead drunk. But in a terrible state of shock, all the same. Frozen to the spot, I heard. What the hell were they doing in Torsviks småbåtshamn in the middle of the night?'

'Probably came here to drink in peace. They'd stolen a couple of bottles of vodka from their parents and thought they'd found the ideal hiding place.'

'Looks as if they weren't the only ones…'

'Right, that's it, we're done,' said one of the technicians. 'Now we can move the *snipa*.'

Björn and Bergström both stepped back while the other two technicians began to move the small boat.

The hull had clearly survived years of harsh weather and torrents of spindrift; it reminded the Kommissionar of the nutshell Thumbelina had used as a cot in the Andersen fairy tale. *What a strange train of thought*, he reflected, as he watched the boat being raised like the lid of a box.

A naked woman lay underneath. She was on her back, her arms alongside her body, her legs tight against each other.

Bergström kneeled down by the body. Under the film of frost, you could see the skin had turned blue from the severe cold. Her thick, blonde hair was carefully laid out, reaching down to her shoulders. Her pubis had been shaved and the letter X carved into her left arm. Her eyes had been pulled out. The ocular cavities were empty, dark and unnaturally large, like a huge stain in the delicate landscape of her face. Her throat had been slashed vertically from her chin down to her sternal notch, and the skin of her neck yawned like an open shirt. Her trachea had been sectioned.

The Kommissionar rose and exited the tent. He discarded the protective clothing and picked up his mobile phone. It was time to summon the troops, and fast. He had the uneasy feeling that a Pandora's Box had just been opened.

THE BITING COLD took Alexis in its grip. For a few seconds, her anxieties faded away. All she could feel were the icy tides rushing through the soles of her shoes and rising up her legs. She even managed to enjoy this momentary pause in the dark flow of her thoughts. To be able to feel and not have to think. As if her brain had been disconnected. Deliverance. But it didn't last.

She was soon hopping up and down, waiting for Alba and Peter to get into the cab, then followed them inside and closed the door behind her.

The flight had been silent. Unending. Alba had slept all the way. Peter had alternated between sleep and wakefulness, muttering incoherently most of the time.

Alexis had hoped the busy clamour of the airport would help banish all thoughts of Linnéa. But the atmosphere in Landvetter was soporific. In the arrival hall, an anonymous mass of blonde heads greeted the travellers with an apathy that was anything but welcoming. Alexis had walked out into the cold determined to rid herself of all this negative energy. Now, however, she was confined to the interior of the cab for an hour and a half.

The three friends sank into contemplation of the white blanket of snow covering the plain outside, a soft blue light spreading across the night. Wedged between Alba and Alexis, Peter stared at the road, listless. Alba had her nose stuck to the window, like a moody child.

The driver had the radio playing quietly. The unexpected grace and musicality of the Swedish language felt like a lullaby to Alexis. She closed her eyes and massaged a temple with the tip of her fingers. She'd never actually heard Linnéa speak in her native tongue, or even talk about Falkenberg and what she did there. Linnéa always studiously avoided answering questions about her sojourns in Sweden, waving her hands in the air almost Mediterranean-style, before quickly changing the subject.

'I'm sorry … How long until we get there?'

Alba had asked the question, her voice almost a whisper, her eyes fixed on the road ahead. They'd been driving for more than an hour already.

The driver answered, his English rough, with almost German intonations – in sharp contrast to the natural softness of his voice: 'Five minutes.'

Peter was pulling nervously at his seatbelt, as if attempting to escape its tight embrace. 'I just can't,' he gasped. 'I can't wait until tomorrow morning. We must go to Linnéa's. Right now!'

Alba threw a panicky look at Alexis, who then took Peter's hands into hers to calm him down.

'We haven't got any keys, Peter. And, anyway, the police have already been to Linnéa's place. There's nothing we can do.'

'It's crazy. They didn't even bother to break in and look inside the house, damn it! Maybe she felt unwell and she's waiting … waiting for…'

His breathing was becoming frantic. He bent forward, his hands against his open mouth in an effort to staunch a flow of tears.

Alexis dug out her mobile phone, her hand unsteady, and gave Linnéa's address to the driver, who was throwing them nervous looks in his rear-view mirror. His head now buried in the hollow of Alba's neck, Peter no longer bothered to hold back his tears.

The cab slowed down then turned right onto a narrow path, shuddering like a boat about to go to sea. Alexis' phone began to vibrate. She took the call, steadying herself against the front seat as the car navigated the rough terrain.

'Alexis Castelli?'

She ignored the incorrect pronunciation of her name and abruptly confirmed it was she.

The man at the other end of the line introduced himself, then spoke briefly in perfect English. Her eyes wide open, her forehead balanced against the front seat, Alexis asked him to repeat what he had just said. All of a sudden, fear and pain surged through her stomach, crushing her lungs, her throat becoming unbearably dry.

Yet again, death had come visiting.

The driver came to a halt in front of a stately yellow-wood house. Snow peppered the sky, forming a curtain of white netting. In the distance, flashing lights were dancing busily.

Alexis was biting her lips in an effort to prevent herself shaking. A body had just been discovered in the small marina nearby. That's what the Swedish policeman had told Alexis on the phone. They had come across a *body*. He knew Alexis was on the way to Falkenberg – had been informed of the fact by the missing-persons bureau – but he hadn't realised she was now just five hundred metres away from Linnéa's place. The policeman had stuttered, hesitated, exchanged a few words in Swedish with another man with a drawling voice, then requested Alexis to ask the taxi to drop them off at another address, not far away.

Alexis had hung up and closed her eyes, fear overcoming her fatigue, so she could barely breathe. She hardly had time to absorb the terrible piece of information before she knew she would have to repeat it. She didn't go into any details; didn't use fancy words. She just impassively passed on the gist of the conversation to her friends.

Peter had nodded and fallen into a deathly silence. Alba's eyes had widened briefly, and then her gaze had returned to the snowy spectacle outside the cab's window.

A body had just been discovered.

The door of the yellow house opened and a broad-backed fellow

wrapped up in a snow-splashed red parka appeared on the threshold.
As Alexis opened the door of the cab, a cloud of snowflakes rushed in
and whipped across her face. She screwed up her eyes to shake off the
shards of snow stuck to her eyelashes and exited the vehicle quickly,
followed by Peter and Alba.

As they walked towards the porch, the man moved to one side to
allow them in, and began to speak, but his words were swallowed
up by the roar of the wind. The sting of the cold faded as soon as he
closed the door behind them. Shedding her coat, Alexis asked the
man to repeat what he had said.

'I'm Kristian Olofsson, a detective with the Falkenberg police
force. We spoke on the phone just a few minutes ago.'

'Yes, of course…'

Alba and Peter stood behind her, like lost children.

'This is Stellan Eklund.'

A man stood in the arched vault that led to the kitchen on their
right. He nodded briefly in their direction.

'Stellan will look after you while we wait for Kommissionar
Lennart Bergström to arrive.'

'Is…'

But the detective didn't give her the chance to finish her question; he pulled his phone out of his pocket and moved away, into
the corridor.

Stellan welcomed the new arrivals, asking whether they wanted
coffee.

'There's something I have to ask the detective, then I'll come and
join you,' Alexis said.

She followed Olofsson and asked, without pausing, 'Do you have
a description? A photo? Any information about the person you've
just discovered?'

Surprised, Olofsson turned towards her. Staring at Alexis, he finished his phone conversation and hung up.

'I can't—'

'Listen, all I'm asking is for you to share any information you have, even if you haven't identified the … body … yet.' Grief tightened her throat.

'There's nothing I can tell you. I haven't been given any of the details.'

Alexis rolled her eyes and sighed with frustration.

Olofsson kept on speaking in his monotonous voice. 'Kommissionar Bergström sent me here, to Eklund's, and asked me to have you wait. He should be here any minute.'

'Can you at least tell me who Eklund is and why we're in his home?'

'Stellan Eklund used to be with the Falkenberg police.'

A door slammed.

'That must be Lennart,' Olofsson stated, moving past Alexis towards the front door.

As the door opened, Alexis caught sight of a particularly large individual with a short, greying beard. In his marine blue oilskins, his features chiselled by the seasons and his hair still damp with melting snow, Lennart Bergström looked more like a sailor than a police officer.

'*Hej, Lennart,*' Olofsson greeted him. '*Det är Alexis Castelli, Linnéa Blix vän. Hon Kommer ifrån…*'

'*Ja, ja, ja, visst Kristian.*'

Bergström looked straight at Alexis and held out his hand. 'Hello, I'm Lennart Bergström, Kommissionar of Falkenberg police.'

His grip was firm, but he placed his other hand on Alexis' shoulder with surprising tenderness.

'I am so sorry…' he said.

Alexis' legs gave way and Bergström just about managed to catch her. An abominable sadness surged over her, eating away at her soul like a hungry beast.

Bergström helped her sit down on one of the chairs lining the wall of the corridor. He sat down next to her.

Her back bent, staring down at her knees, Alexis listened to the words she had feared hearing.

KRISTIAN OLOFSSON SERVED HIMSELF some more coffee. The tall, skinny woman, whose name he had forgotten, handed him her cup as if he were common muck. He couldn't stand these big-town chicks. This particular one stank of money, with her handbag perfectly matching her belt and her shoes, and that look of superiority on her face that said 'My bracelet alone cost the same as you earn in six months, you fucking peasant'.

He filled the bourgeoise's cup while gazing over at the other woman, Alexis, the pretty one. Stellan was busy with her. No surprise. After her fainting spell in the corridor, she'd taken a deep breath and had walked over to impart the bad news to the pretty boy, who'd promptly collapsed in a heap, like the gutless piece of shit he no doubt was. Just another guy who'd lost his balls; maybe she'd stolen them ... she sure looked fiery. She and Horseface had given him some pill to calm him down and had put him to bed in one of the spare bedrooms. In the meantime, Bergström had explained that this Linnéa Blix who'd been found at Torsviks småbåtshamn – starkers and her face in a mess – was something of a celebrity. Kristian had never heard of her, though.

'Kristian!'

Talk of the devil ... The Kommissionar had been keeping a close eye on him ever since he'd moved here from Gothenburg.

'Yeah?'

The fat-arsed cunt was always on the case. And now, for once, something had actually happened in Falkenberg; it probably gave him a hard-on.

Olofsson set his coffee cup down and stepped over to join Bergström next door.

'The forensics team have finished at the victim's home. I'll need Peter Templeton taken there to check nothing is missing or has been moved; or even added.'

'He's asleep. They gave him a pill.'

'Oh … Well, go and see if either of his two friends can help until he's back in circulation.'

Olofsson nodded and returned to the kitchen. Sure, they could be of assistance. But there was no way he wanted the tall, skinny one along; he'd take the pretty one – give them time to get to know each other.

◆◆◆◆◆

Things didn't turn out the way Olofsson had hoped. The snobby bitch had turned ugly at the suggestion of looking over Linnéa's home. She found the idea inappropriate while they were still reeling from the news of her death and, anyway, it would be useless, as neither of them had ever set foot in the house. The hottie had then argued her side of things, saying that they should do anything for the sake of the investigation. They might not know their friend's Swedish home, but they had been intimate with her and they might see something random that could prove useful: the presence of something or some missing object, maybe. She'd made a good case, concluding that it was something they should do, notwithstanding their feelings.

Horseface had reluctantly accepted her friend's logic and calmed down. But, as usual, shit happens, and the useless pretty boy had then woken up, so Olofsson had to take all three of them along. A bloody nuisance. Add to this the fact he was getting damned tired; it was four in the morning and he was dying to get his head down.

The detective slammed the car door and shivered. No one had

said a word since they had left Eklund's. The mood of the party was downright sinister. Despite the polar cold and the heavy pall of night, which seemed to adhere to their skin, every single one of them would much have preferred to remain outside.

The cop left on guard duty opened the door for them, switched the lights on and stepped aside to let them in, closing the door behind them. Alexis briefly felt like she was part of a group of tourists being hurried along by their guide.

Her tired gaze travelled over the hallway's walls which, to her surprise, were covered in an orange-coloured flowery wallpaper. By the door leading to the kitchen stood two odd chairs, alongside a pale wooden chest of drawers, over which were scattered a few woollen hats, a tube of lipstick, an assortment of coins and some leaflets.

The kitchen was decorated in the same colours as the hallway, aside from some psychedelic-patterned tiles and a Formica-topped table. Alexis had trouble believing this house had ever belonged to her friend. It didn't feel right at all. Linnéa always had a brand name to match any of her belongings: a Philippe Starck chair; an Arne Jacobsen table; a Ron Arad shelf.

As if echoing her thoughts, Peter's pained red eyes searched around questioningly. He ran his fingers across the edge of a table still littered with breadcrumbs, then walked out of the room.

Alexis followed him into a narrow bathroom. Linnéa's toiletry bag stood on a stool next to the shower cubicle. A brush and a mascara compact peered through the opening, as if they had just been used.

'I don't understand,' Peter whispered. 'This is all so unlike her…'

Alexis could only agree, but she remained silent. She led Peter along to the next room.

As they went, they heard the loud sound of Alba's voice behind them, by the front door. 'No, no, no, no, no!'

Olofsson ran towards her, Alexis and Peter on his heels.

'Have you found something?' the detective asked.

'What the hell are you expecting me to find?' she answered, her voice tearful. 'The killer's business card? There's just nothing that resembles Linnéa in this house! Nothing at all!'

'But you haven't yet been upstairs,' Olofsson protested.

'I've had enough of all this! We're exhausted and had to bear enough horror already today, don't you understand? We can't put up with any more. Take us to the hotel.'

Alba was right, Alexis thought: this day couldn't end soon enough.

Buchenwald Concentration Camp, Germany
August 1944

THIS MORNING, it was the cosh that had woken them up. Repeatedly crashing down on their skulls alongside the litany of the officers' insults.

Erich pulled himself out of the bunk, in time for the morning roll call. The two men with whom he shared the straw matting weren't as fast as him and were both repeatedly hit in the ribs. Watching their bony bodies climbing down from the wooden cradle that served as their bed felt like gazing at the living dead escaping from a columbarium.

Erich discreetly exercised his joints. He'd only been here for a few weeks, but already the terrible tiredness was taking its toll. Night was never long enough to compensate for the hellish days. They slept head to toe, on their sides, squeezed against total strangers, surrounded by the collective miasma – the rattles of pain, the moaning, the nightmares and the cries; the effluents of dysentery spilling all over the thin matting; the flea bites, the bedbugs and the lice swarming under their bodies. The nights were as inhuman as the days.

One of his acquaintances on the block – a man who'd swallowed his wedding ring before being inspected on their arrival and kept retrieving it again and again from his excrement – had called it 'dehumanising the prisoners'. Erich felt that was an understatement. Like identifying an illness but ignoring its symptoms. Not only were they dehumanised, they were dying of thirst and hunger, were exploited, tortured, degraded. Buchenwald was a never-ending waltz with Death. Everything they did, every single task, every step, was part of the dance.

Erich hadn't seen the cold yet, though. A Pole whose torso had been riddled by ulcers said the wind rushing across the camp was as deadly as an SS Luger; the 'devil's breath' he called it. The guy cried aloud when he evoked the winter, when he mourned his comrades frozen on the ground, who he'd had to gather up.

The cosh went into action again to encourage them out of the block. It was wash time. Erich only had half an hour to make his bed, clean himself, dress and swallow down his breakfast.

When the signal for gruel rang, he always seemed to be queuing for the latrines. If he didn't reach the block in time, he'd forfeit his ration. He ran towards the sinks. But, for the sixth day in a row, he gave up on cleaning himself and rushed away again.

He set down the piece of stale bread and the bowl full of what approximated coffee on the corner of the wooden table. He broke the bread into small pieces and began to eat it, softening it with his saliva prior to chewing it slowly, before trying to wash it down with the ersatz coffee. As the final crumb of this thin morning gruel hit the back of his throat, he thought back to the summons he had received towards the end of his previous day's work at the quarry. After the roll call, he was to present himself to desk number two. He had no idea why.

He wetted his forefinger with the tip of his tongue to try and retrieve the four orphaned breadcrumbs lodged in a gap in the wood, and then left the block. Hunger raging inside his stomach and fear holding his throat in a tight grip, he walked over to the roll-call area. There was a strong possibility that the coming hour, standing with his companions in misery, listening to an SS officer count down the camp's occupants, might well be his last. He was surprised to actually feel some form of relief. The guy who had thrown himself, the previous evening, against the barbed wire, knowing all too well he would be cut down by the SS machine guns, had probably made the right choice.

'Caps off! Caps back on!'

Erich was familiar with the next shouted order. Fear accelerated his heartbeat.

'Summoned prisoners to the big door!'

He walked jauntily over to the second desk. He had to demonstrate he was in good condition, healthy, therefore still useful.

'Work commandos, assemble.'

He watched the lines of skeleton-thin bodies gather in groups of five to the sound of the lively music from the orchestra.

'20076!'

Erich turned round. A pot-bellied soldier was consulting a sheet of paper he held between his swollen fingers.

'Yes, sir.'

The officer scowled at him as he took note of the inverted red triangle sewn into Erich's shirt. He came closer.

'Bloody hell … You're actually German…' He took his cap off, scratched his forehead, then put the cap back on. 'You know what, you fucker? As far as I'm concerned, you're the worst of them all. Traitors to your own country. No better than if you'd tried to kill your mother, you fucker. Do you understand?'

His drink-soaked breath almost made Erich sick.

'Yes, sir.'

'Take your pants off, you bloody traitor.'

His hands unsteady, Erich let his trousers slip down to his ankles.

'Lean forward, you fucker.'

The gummi smacked ten times against his backside. Erich gritted his teeth and swallowed the bile rushing up his throat.

'That's the thrashing your mother should have given you.' Out of breath, the officer put the club back into his belt. 'But I'm not going to damage you too much. No reason you shouldn't be able to enjoy your next treat: you're expected at the ovens, arsehole. Your turn to be roasted.'

LENNART BERGSTRÖM HANDED A cup of coffee to Stellan.

'So how long is it since you spoke to or saw Linnéa Blix?' the Kommissionar asked, sitting at his desk.

'Last November. We dined at my house. I wasn't aware she was planning to come to Falkenberg this month.'

'Did she come here often?'

'Two or three times a year, I'd say. For two, three weeks at a time. Sometimes a whole month, in summer.'

'Alone?'

'I don't know. All I can say is, she never brought anyone when we ate together.'

'Did she normally warn you when she was visiting?'

'Yes. We always took advantage of her visits to see each other.'

'Were you fucking her?'

The question came as no surprise to Stellan.

'We'd known each other for almost thirty years, Lennart. If we'd ever wanted a roll in the hay, we'd have done it long ago.'

'I see.'

'We just enjoyed good meals together. She was always there for me when … well, you know…'

Stellan's voice deepened. Bergström concealed his embarrassment by sipping at his coffee.

'Did she ever talk about her partner, Peter Templeton?' he asked, as he rose from the desk to fill his cup again.

'I knew they were together, yes, and that he worked in human resources or something of the sort. But she mostly talked about her own work.'

'And on Friday, when you returned from Stockholm, you didn't see any lights in her windows?'

Stellan shook his head.

'Or a car in the drive? Damn, I've just realised I haven't had time to check if she actually had a car,' the Kommissionar remarked, as if speaking to himself.

'She didn't that I know of. She usually took a cab from the airport. Around here, she used to walk or cycle.'

'OK … Well, Olofsson will take down your official statement. You understand I can't get directly involved.'

Bergström hugged Stellan – more an impersonal Scandinavian gesture of affection that anything intimate – and opened the door to his office to show him out.

Walking through the station, Stellan noticed Alexis exiting the interview room with Olofsson on her heels. She was nodding mechanically in response to the detective's continuous monologue, while taking in her surroundings. Her pale-blue eyes examined everything carefully, as if she didn't want to miss anything important.

Olofsson finally moved away. When she noticed Stellan, the young woman gave him a tired smile.

'*Hej*, Alexis. How is Peter doing?'

The question came as both a surprise and a relief to Alexis. She couldn't pretend her shoulders were wide enough both to offer support to Peter and to console Alba – and also to reassure her own parents, who were deeply disturbed by the knowledge that their daughter was involved in such a dreadful story. By asking her for news of Peter, Stellan had unwittingly offered her a hand.

'He's devastated, of course. Exhausted, too. He's giving his statement right now.'

'You've made yours?'

She nodded.

Olofsson returned, holding a cup in each hand, and positioned himself between the two of them. He'd taken off his woollen jacket and was displaying a strong set of abs under his tight pullover. The hound couldn't have chosen a worst moment to parade his wares, Stellan thought, as he took the cups from him. He offered one to Alexis. Taken by surprise, Olofsson had no choice but to give up his amorous ammunition.

'Isn't it my turn to answer some questions, Kristian?' Stellan said, sipping from his cup. 'Shall we?'

Olofsson gave him a dirty look.

'It's what the boss wants.' Stellan raised his left hand to make his point.

His intentions defeated, Olofsson gave Alexis a crooked smile and asked Stellan to follow him into the nearest interview room. Stellan winked at Alexis, drawing a smile, then obediently followed the detective.

Alexis set her handbag and coat on one of the chairs lining the corridor wall and slowly drank her coffee, her hands cradling the cup in a familiar and reassuring fashion.

Linnéa is dead. Linnéa has been killed. Linnéa is dead.

She repeated the words to herself over and over, as if hoping she would become accustomed to them and the heaviness in her chest would subside. She knew that time would provide no balm; at best it would help her to live with this new reality. She had to move forward and confront it if she was to overcome this awful feeling.

She had suggested to Bergström that she should identify her friend's body, so that Peter was spared the task. Bergström had swallowed hard, then explained in his deep, drawl of a voice that the tattoo on the victim's ankle and the birthmark below her left breast left her identity in no doubt. The answer shattered Alexis' equilibrium. She closed her eyes and tried to banish all the awful images her brain was racing to manufacture.

'*Ursäkta!*'

A uniformed police woman was pushing a board on wheels

towards her. Alexis shifted sideways and the cop continued on to a
set of heavy doors, which she pushed open with her hip. The doors
remained open a brief moment, just long enough for Alexis to notice
the photographs thumbtacked to the wall inside the room. Just long
enough for her to recognise the long, curling blonde hair flowing
from the mutilated body, shot from every conceivable angle. A naked
body where two dark tunnels now replaced the eyes, and a bloody,
dark-red gash extended all the way down from her neck.

Just as the door closed, Alexis noticed that Bergström was in
intense discussion with someone she recognised instantly, and whose
presence was anything but good news.

The young woman closed her eyes and took a deep breath, like a
swimmer returning to the surface after a lengthy dive.

~~~~

'Where should I leave it, Kommissionar?' the cop asked as she
wheeled the board in.

'Put it over there,' Emily Roy ordered, pointing towards the
room's only window.

The cop silently sought Lennart Bergström's approval. With a
slight nod of the head, he indicated she should follow their guest's
suggestion. The female cop reluctantly did so then left the room, not
before throwing Emily a dirty look.

Although Bergström was Swedish and a strong proponent of
equality between the sexes, when Jack Pearce of Scotland Yard had
warned him he was sending over his best profiler, he had to admit he
hadn't expected a woman. Not that Emily Roy was particularly femi-
nine: she was short, athletic thin but robust; and rather intimidating.

'You told Pearce she was found in a marina?'

Her back to the Kommissionar, Emily was firing questions at him
while moving the photos from the wall to the board. Her slow, eco-
nomical, precise gestures reminded Bergström of a martial-arts master.

'Yes. Torsviks småbåtshamn, in the Olofsbo quarter. Quite a rustic and isolated area. *Småbåtshamn* means "a port for small boats". It's mostly used by summer residents who own houses in Olofsbo.'

'Who discovered the victim?'

'Two boys.'

'How old?'

'Fourteen and fifteen.'

'Who owns the small boat where the body was hidden?'

'It belonged to an Olofsbo resident who died back in 2004. He had no living relatives. His house was sold and the *snipa* had been hanging around next to the *småbåtshamn* information kiosk for more than ten years.'

'I presume the kiosk is closed in winter.'

Bergström concurred.

'And no weapons were found in the vicinity?'

'None whatsoever.'

There were a few seconds of silence between them, the police station's hubbub continuing in the background.

'Have you anything to hand to make notes in?' Emily asked him peremptorily as she contemplated the patchwork of photographs.

Her demanding tone surprised Bergström, but he meekly executed the order, like a good schoolboy.

'I will require aerial shots of the area where the victim was found and a scale map of the immediate surroundings, with everything clearly marked: houses, apartments, schools, fuel stations, supermarkets, shops, everything in the neighbourhood. I'll also need the video that was taken when the body was discovered…'

'We have photographs, but no vi—'

'…the preliminary police report with all the possible clues uncovered by the scene-of-crime team, any information relating to the body's discovery, and statements from all witnesses and neighbours, as well as any socio-economic information about the precise spot where the body was discovered – i.e., what type of people live in and frequent the area. I also require the autopsy report and its toxicological and serological tests, the conclusions and thoughts of the pathologist, and autopsy photos with a clear view of the wounds once they have been cleaned up.'

Bergström looked up to the ceiling. Falkenberg wasn't London, for sure, but he felt insulted by the assumption he had no clue as to how a proper investigation should proceed.

'I'll get busy building a profile of the victim. What's the actual address of the marina?'

'We can drive you there, if you want.'

'No need. I'll make my own way.'

Bergström gave her the address, and watched the profiler slip on her padded jacket and backpack with catlike movements.

Emily left her host behind without a further word and quietly closed the door behind her.

'Well, I do hope that not all Canadians are that rude,' said Bergström out loud. 'It's sure going to be a pleasure working with Miss Emily Roy.'

<hr />

Emily adjusted her cap so that it covered her ears. The fiery cold made her feel alive. All of her senses awakened, she gazed at the expanse of Torsviks småbåtshamn. Now empty of boats, the *småbåtshamn* was just an icebound, snow-covered wilderness. The pontoons just about indicated the borders of the white expanse – the tentative rectangle opening out onto the North Sea, like a trench carved into the Olofsbo dunes and its rocky beaches.

To the south, on the left, white fields extended to infinity, their trees tamed by the wind into eternal submission. The first dwelling stood about four hundred metres away. An old L-shaped farmhouse with a dark-red facade: Linnéa's home. Further inland, two hundred metres to the east, was a small agglomeration of four yellow buildings. To the north, on the right, a dune of unkempt grass stood like a wall between the marina and the camping grounds. That was the way Emily had come. She'd driven to the car park by the beach and followed the shortest path, skirting the camping grounds, winding round the side of the dune before reaching the marina. A two-minute walk; four or five at most, for someone carrying a body weighing forty-seven kilos.

It was the most obvious way for someone in a car, in a hurry and wishing to not be seen. Crossing the snow fields all the way from the main road, three hundred metres to the west, was unlikely: a car parked by the side of the road would have attracted undue attention. Wading through the fields all the way from Linnéa's house, from the group of yellow houses or from the lighthouse's car park, two hundred metres north of the camping grounds, was unthinkable. The killer could have reached the marina from the beach, but it would have proven a long, tiring and dangerous walk, what with the frost and snow making the pebbled path so slippery. No, the killer must have come the same way she had.

Emily retraced her steps and walked by the Torsviks småbåtshamn information kiosk. This was where Linnéa's body had been found, concealed beneath an abandoned boat situated between the yellow wooden hut and the dune. A boat the SKL, the scene-of-crime team, had towed away.

She pulled a large, stiff envelope from her backpack and took out a series of photos, which she quickly glanced at. Eight of the shots showed details of the boat in which the body had been found. The profiler examined the snow-covered ground under her feet. Nature had already washed the horror away, burying the bloodstains, the clues, and the activity of the police under several layers of white powder. Nature had restored peace. Emily tried to imagine the whole scene that might have unfolded earlier beneath the spotlights illuminating the interior of the white tent.

Latex-gloved hands pulling the boat away. Beneath it, the body is naked, the skin blue, with a thin film of frost. Emily can't smell the rancid scent of death, which has been blown away by the cold. The silky blonde hair frames the face, all the way down to the shoulders. The arms have been placed alongside the body. The pubis is shaven. The eye sockets are empty, black, dried blood highlighting their circles. The incision made to enucleate the victim is visible and tidy. The throat is cut wide open. The gash is deep, flaps of skin hanging on both sides of it. The trachea has been sectioned and pulled out.

Emily looked up, her hair disturbed by the wind, and stared out to sea. She couldn't understand. But if it made no sense to her, it certainly did for the killer. She had to think as she usually did – move on from the bare facts of the case at her disposal to the essence of the killer's fantasies, the keys to unlock his crime; move from logic to lack of logic, analyse the bloody work confronting her in order to understand the artist at play here.

ALEXIS COULD NO LONGER SIT still in her hotel room. She'd resolved to clear her mind by walking over to Bratt, a restaurant in the old town where she had a dinner meeting planned for later. She'd have a drink, and, if all went well, she'd also obtain some answers to her questions.

This first day without Linnéa in her life had seen her thoughts move between sadness and utter exhaustion. She had attempted in vain to hold onto passing dreams, as if surreal illusions might briefly banish reality. But, as Alba had once told her, death was not an absence but, on the contrary, a secret presence. For Alexis, however, this secret presence was proving even more unbearable than the abyss of vacancy.

The waiter set a glass of rioja down in front of Alexis. She stared at the wine's elegant coat of purple reflections.

That morning, as they had been leaving the police station, Peter had informed his two friends that he would have to remain in Sweden for a few more days to sort out Linnéa's affairs. With one voice, they had firmly objected. Alba had reminded him of their painful visit to Linnéa's in the early hours of morning, which had come to a sudden halt before they'd been able even to move upstairs. Alexis had insisted they should bear the burden of the tragic events together, all three of them. She had volunteered to complete an inventory of the house. Peter had seemed to mentally collapse when she suggested this. So Alexis had proposed that she remain in Sweden alone, and had insisted that Alba and Peter return to England. There was a lot for them to do in London, too. She reckoned it would take her two or three days to complete the task at Linnéa's and then she would go home.

Pressured by his two friends, Peter had ended up accepting. He'd left for the airport with Alba in the middle of the afternoon, leaving Alexis to her demons.

'What are you drinking?'

Alexis jumped, even though this was said in more of a whisper than a loud voice.

'Emily! Just a glass of rioja, thanks. So how are you?' Alexis attempted a feeble smile and thought she caught a spark of irony in the fixed gaze of the profiler.

Emily pulled off her woollen hat and her padded jacket, placed her backpack on the chair, hanging it by its straps, and sat facing Alexis.

'You can interrogate me properly once we're eating. Shall we order?'

It was a purely rhetorical question. Alexis grabbed the menu by her plate.

She had met Emily three years earlier, while she was working on a project about the Scottish serial killer, Johnny Burnett. Scotland Yard had put her in touch with Emily, one of the five profilers on their books – or Behaviour Investigative Advisors, as they were called in the UK.

A transfer from the Royal Canadian Mounted Police, Emily had been the only one to establish any sort of close relationship with Burnett. Alexis had interviewed Emily at length, and Emily had finally agreed to introduce her to the killer. They hadn't seen each other since that day at Full Sutton prison.

The waiter brought their dishes. Emily, still silent, immediately dug in. She carefully forked each piece of gravlax into her mouth, barely chewing, and keeping her eyes fixed on her plate.

Alexis opted to respect her companion's apparently deliberate silence and gulped down her own saffron-flavoured risotto with little appreciation of its taste or smell.

The photos depicting Linnéa's mutilated body dominated her mind, banishing all the other light-hearted thoughts she'd previously tried to conjure up about her friend. It felt awful. In order to get rid of these lingering images, she knew she had to act, grab some answers to all the questions crowding her brain. She had, as a result, suggested to Emily they should dine together, hoping this would help her extract from the profiler some information about the enquiry.

Alexis observed the regular movements of her fellow diner, wondering all along how and when to phrase her initial question. She knew there was no point in trying to be clever with Emily; she would see right through you if you tried any tricks and would just walk out in the middle of the meal.

'What is it you want?' the profiler said out of the blue as she sipped her wine.

Alexis' throat tightened. She'd always disliked the prickly tone often present in Emily's voice. And today of all days she was unwilling to deal with it.

'I saw the photos of Linnéa at the police station,' she said, curtly. It was as if they were now imprinted at the back of her mind. In just that fraction of a second, her brain had memorised every single pixel. 'I saw you discussing them with Bergström,' she added.

Emily speared a piece of salmon and a slice of potato with her fork, dipping them in the dill sauce spread across one side of her plate.

'Was Linnéa the victim of a serial killer, is that it?' Alexis continued.

Emily raised her head and, with cold determination, looked back at her. Alexis couldn't tell whether she was judging her, was angry or just staring at her with indifference.

'That's why you're here in Sweden?' she continued, sustaining Emily's gaze.

'Correct,' Emily answered, placing the knife and fork on either side of the plate and wiping her mouth.

Alexis blinked as if a rush of wind had slammed against her face.

She'd prepared herself to fight it out with Emily. She'd carefully rehearsed every argument. But she'd never believed she would get a direct answer.

'...in London too.'

'Sorry, I didn't hear what you just said,' apologised Alexis, connecting again with the conversation.

'Bodies with identical mutilations have been found in London.'

Alexis' eyes opened in horror. She swallowed once, her tongue rampaging inside her mouth.

'But no one ... well, I haven't heard about that...'

'Because we haven't informed the press,' Emily responded, pouring a glass of water.

She pushed it across the table towards Alexis, who picked it up and obediently drank from it. The first sip cooled down the fire raging in her throat.

'Thank you,' she said, less for the glass of water than for the trust Emily was conferring on her – something she had not expected.

Emily silently waited for Alexis to empty her glass of water.

'But how did you ... know about Linnéa?' Alexis asked once she'd gathered her thoughts again.

'Bergström called his colleagues at the Rikskriminalpolisen in Gothenburg to find out if any other victims had been discovered with similar mutilations anywhere in the region or the country. There was nothing. So he'd contacted the Interpol offices in Stockholm, who put him in touch with the Yard.'

'How many?'

'Two in London. And now Linnéa.'

Alexis nodded, filing away the information.

'And ... you think it might be the same person? Or do you think there might be two of them?'

Emily's face darkened and, for a moment, she appeared to be lost in her thoughts, her eyes fixed on something behind Alexis.

'I just don't know,' she said at last. 'And that's exactly what the problem is.'

He switches the engine off, opens his rucksack, picks out the binoculars and peers through the minivan's tinted windows. Just as she begins to undress by the sash window, as if she has been waiting for him to arrive. He likes her small, round, high breasts.

She climbs on the bed, crawls forward on all fours, like a dog. Why the hell does she insist on doing that, every single time? It doesn't get him hard, no way, to see a human being act like an animal. There is nothing exciting about it. Submission? Wasn't this concept of dog and master somewhat hackneyed? So why? Voyeurism? Displayed like this, her breasts flop limply like hanging pears, her stomach loses its tautness and you can't even see her pussy. The guy isn't even looking at her, anyway. He's sniffing the cocaine the other girl has spread across her nipples.

All of a sudden, the door opens and Logan appears. His mother doesn't even notice; she's too busy with her nose between the other girl's thighs. Logan stands still for a few seconds, puts his thumb inside his mouth then departs, closing the door behind him. He knows that tonight he will not be sleeping in his own bed – at any rate, the one he shares with his whore of a mother. Sorry, Logan, Mum has guests. You should know the way it works by now.

He focuses his binoculars on the other room in the house. He is aware that Logan will walk to the fridge and get himself a drink, which has been bought along with his ready meal on the way back from school, will park himself on the settee and switch the TV on. Later, he will wet himself in his sleep, and his mother will chide him, slap him, all the while holding his soiled clothing right in front of his nose in an effort to shame him. There's something about this woman and dogs. It's the same, over and over.

He takes a look at his watch. The mother and her girlfriend always charge per half-hour. This is the fourth customer in a row, and it appears this one is going to stay for a whole hour. In twenty minutes, if all goes well, he will leave and the two friends will go out onto the street just ten minutes' walk away, to attract further business. Later, they will end the evening at another girl's place. The mother will return to the house at 3 a.m. and will collapse onto the bed without even taking a shower or checking out how her son is.

It will be around eight, when she wakes up in the early-morning light, that she'll finally deal with Logan and beat him until he manages to escape and lock himself inside the bathroom. She will knock on the door for five whole minutes, until she gives up and leaves the place, slamming the door behind her, like a teenager having a hissy fit.

But, tomorrow, when she awakens, her pupils still dilated from the coke she's been stuffing into her nose all night long, her little Logan will no longer be there.

Falkenberg Police Station
Monday, 13 January 2014, 22.00

EMILY TOOK THE PHOTOGRAPHS out of the padded folder. Each one was marked with a 1, a 2 or a 3, depending on the crime they related to. She pinned them to the board, grouping them by themes, then sat herself down at the large conference table, facing the board, her notepad open, eyes staring at the story that the pictures told, a story the first chapter of which had been written in London just a few weeks earlier.

On that Saturday, the 14th of December, Emily had been woken up by the ring of her mobile phone at 5.50 in the morning. She'd put it on speaker and dressed while listening to Sergeant Scott, from the Metropolitan Police. He explained to her that she was expected at a crime scene on Hampstead Heath and that Detective Chief Superintendent Jack Pearce had asked him to collect her. She had thanked him, but, before hanging up, she had asked him for the GPS coordinates of the crime scene. The obedient sergeant provided them with little argument. Whatever DCS Pearce had ordered, there was no way she was going to sit around waiting for someone to escort her there.

Emily had slipped on her trainers, zipped up her parka and put her hood up. She dropped a small black box into the front pocket of her backpack and left her home, her mobile phone in her hand.

She ambled up Flask Walk at a trot, ignoring the damp cold that made the early-morning air quite unwelcome, continued onto Well Walk, crossed East Heath Road and entered the woods, better known as Hampstead Heath, with her torch in her hand.

Fog embraced the claw-like trees and the thorny bushes with its streams of cotton tentacles, and drifted over the carpet of dead leaves spread across the ground. Emily checked her phone: she wasn't far from the crime scene now. She took a muddy and twisting short-cut to her right and walked down it with a lightness in her step, indifferent to the brown, earthy stains beginning to spread across the bottom of her trousers. Fifty metres east, she caught sight of a ballet of electric lights. A few seconds later, she was sliding under the white-and-blue ribbon the police had unfurled, brandishing her warrant card and shouting out 'BIA Roy!' to an overzealous sergeant who already had a hand on his truncheon to halt her progress.

He quickly apologised, red-faced, trying to explain that, with her stained trousers, her mud-splattered shoes, her cap and backpack, he'd mistaken Emily for a homeless person.

'Where's Sergeant Scott?' she heard Superintendent Pearce ask. And before the embarrassed officer had a chance to respond, he said, 'Bloody hell, Emily! Why didn't you wait for him?'

The boss stood facing her, his untidy mop of grey hair uncombed and wild.

Already intent on seeing the body, waiting for her just ten metres away, the profiler didn't reply, or even glance at Pearce.

Pearce shrugged, giving up.

Emily pulled a sealed plastic bag from her backpack, tore it open and slid out a flimsy protective suit, a hair net, a face mask, gloves and shoe covers. She adjusted everything over her own clothing, her eyes narrowing in deep thought.

'It's OK, Emily, I asked the crime-scene guys not to touch the body until you got here,' Pearce informed her, as if reading her thoughts. 'They're about to set the tent up. The body was discovered by a dog,' he went on, 'belonging to a retired music teacher, seventy-two years old.'

She turned towards Pearce and gave him a dubious look.

'It's an enormous German Shepherd. I guess she's not scared to go out alone at night with that beast. She lives close by and takes a walk on the Heath every morning around 5 a.m., summer and winter, normally sticking to the paths. She got worried when her dog disappeared for a moment. She followed its barks and found it moaning, trying to dig something up. She approached and noticed the top of the skull just emerging through the dirt. She went straight home and called us.'

Emily nodded at this information, adjusted her latex gloves and moved towards the burial site.

The muddy earth was littered with brown, soggy leaves, scattered here and there by the rain. First she noticed the hole dug up by the dog, then, as she kneeled down, some strands of curly hair stuck in the wet ground.

She gave a sign to the technicians. The tallest one acknowledged her with a similar gesture of his thumb, spoke to his colleagues and the whole group joined her on the edge of the improvised grave. They quietly greeted the profiler with a 'Hello, Em', then meticulously began to rake the patch of earth in front of them.

First they freed the face and the brown hair from the earth, then the forehead and the tiny snub nose. The empty orbs were unnaturally large. The lips barely open. The throat was slit vertically, from the chin all the way down to the sternal notch. Maggots were slithering inside the narrow nostrils, peering out from the ocular cavities, crawling across the lips and the borders of the gash that extended all the way down the neck.

The technicians gradually cleared away the dark blanket of dirt, revealing a body already deformed by putrefaction. Once the earth covering the upper half of the cadaver had been removed, Emily leaned across the grave and delicately took hold of the child's left arm, being careful not to damage it.

Brushing some dirt away, she had found the mark she was seeking. An identical Y to the one found on the body of another little boy discovered just a month earlier, barely one hundred metres away from this very spot.

‑••••‑

Emily stood up, stepped around the conference table and moved nearer to the photographs she had pinned to the board. Three victims who had never known each other. The parents of the first two victims had been categorical: their children had never met, and neither had any of them ever come across Linnéa Blix. Three enucleated victims, whose throats had been carefully slashed from the chin to the sternal notch, and who had had their tracheas sectioned. The letter Y had been carved into the arms of both little boys, and the letter X in Linnéa's. The X had been a much deeper cut. Did the killer mark his victims according to their sex? An easy assumption, but it was possible. He had shaved Linnéa's pubis and had savagely cut into her arm; did this signify he was angry with women? Did he have a compulsion to eliminate little boys before they reached the age where they could be perverted by the opposite sex, which he considered noxious? But then, what was the link between London and Falkenberg? The chances of Linnéa's case being a copycat murder were almost non-existent: neither the public nor the press yet knew about the killings committed in London.

Emily stared at each photograph in turn.

Could it be there were two people involved? A pair acting in tandem, but with different tastes: the one in London having a taste for little boys, while the one active in Falkenberg preferred women?

Emily sat on the edge of the table. None of these explanations satisfied her. The pieces just didn't fit. She would have to forget these speculations and keep on gathering information. She would reach some form of conclusion later.

Her next step would be to visit Linnéa Blix's home the following morning; find out more, refine her profile of the third victim. For now, there was only one piece of knowledge that was certain: whoever had abandoned Linnéa Blix's body under the boat knew the area well.

Buchenwald Concentration Camp, Germany
August 1944

THE SS OFFICER FOLLOWING right on his heels, Erich crossed
the roll-call ground, moving towards the square-chimneyed building that spat out its thick black smoke night and day. He would
not be the first to be burned alive. Josef, the eldest man in their
block, had spoken of a convoy of four hundred children. According
to him, they had been incinerated alive by the young SS officer with
the stammer who sometimes enjoyed throwing babies in the air and
then shooting them like clay pigeons.

Erich could no longer feel the lacerations the cosh had left on his
backside; adrenalin was blotting out the pain. He had been tempted
to hasten his own death by provoking the SS officer in some way:
making the Nazi pull out his Luger and shoot him in the head. But,
in Buchenwald, you never knew how you would die. If a soldier
preferred to torture you for days rather than kill you on the spot,
maybe being burned alive was one of the better alternatives on offer.

The potbellied SS guard abandoned him by the crematorium,
handing him over to a scar-faced prisoner.

Following him inside, Erich found himself in a high-ceilinged
room. Red-brick blocks, each two and a half metres tall, which
housed the three incinerators, stood in the centre of the room.

'I've just finished off what the cadaver conveyor, the *Leichenträger*
as you would call him, brought me yesterday night, just prior to roll
call,' the man with the speckled face said in English; he had a faint
French accent. 'What's your name?'

Fear formed a knot in Erich's throat. He tried to swallow. It felt as if he had pins lodged down there.

'Erich,' he murmured.

'I'm Alain. I don't know what they've told you about the crematorium, but if I had a choice, I'd run back to the quarry. Anyway, I'll quickly explain how everything works, then we can get on with it; the *Leichenträger* will return soon.'

Erich gave Alain a puzzled look. So the crematorium was to be his new assignment: he was to work here, not be thrown in alive! He began to sob, hands pulled up to his lips. Relief flooded his body and awakened the pain radiating through his thighs and midriff. He greeted it like an unexpected gift.

Alain slapped him amicably on the back.

'It'll be OK, mate; it'll be OK. We'll make our way out of here eventually … Come on, we'll begin in the strangling cellar.'

Alain led Erich to the basement.

'Today, all we have to do is retrieve bodies from the strangling cave. They've left nothing to collect from the torture chamber or the dissection room. Well, for now … Be careful where you step, young friend. And breathe through your mouth.'

The stairs ended in a rectangular hall. Erich froze when he reached the last step.

The narrow paths, the blocks, the latrines, the SS – wherever you looked, Buchenwald stank of death. But this room embodied the very essence of the camp's horror, the final resting place towards which herds of men, women and starving and wounded children advanced, thinking all the way of just one further step, the minute beyond the present; any more and they would succumb to madness.

Facing Erich, scores of bodies, naked, or clad in meagre rags, were hanging on hooks fixed just a few centimetres from the ceiling, like slabs of meat. Their faces, twisted by fear and pain, still appeared alive.

'We have to move them to the carts, then into the lift,' Alain continued, seemingly unconcerned. 'But it's going to take a couple of journeys: the lift will only accommodate between twenty-five and thirty bodies. Normally, it's only eighteen, but what with the camp's general diet, we can fit many more.... Come on, give me a hand. I'll grab this one by his legs and you, as you're taller, you get hold of him from the top, under the armpits. No need to cut the rope off his neck.'

Erich stepped round the puddles of urine, excrement and blood, and unhooked the first man. The body's weight came as a surprise, and he stumbled backwards, just about righting himself by spreading his legs. The cadaver fell against his chest, its head buried against his neck as if seeking to huddle into him. His stomach shuddered with disgust, more in reaction to the pestilential smell than this parody of an embrace.

'Are you OK, young friend?' Alain asked as he helped him straighten himself out. 'They're heavier than they first appear, aren't they? Don't let go of him. I'll get the feet. OK? Ready?'

Erich nodded imperceptibly and they carried the body to the cart.

Once the forty-five bodies had been transported to the floor above, they piled them up by the oven. Alain opened the first incinerator's heavy, half-moon-shaped door. A scorching heat was released. He took off his striped shirt. Erich copied him.

'I'll show you how to do it first,' Alain said handing Erich a pair of long-handled anvil tongs. 'You pull them along by their feet with the pincers, and then I'll take hold of their necks and stuff them into the oven. OK? Then we'll move on to the other ovens. We can't waste any time.'

Erich's gaze was lost within the mass of tangled bodies, his eyes resting a brief moment on a cyanotic face, its hanging, swollen tongue and eyes seemingly popping out of the bruised head.

'Hey, German guy, step on it.'

Erich followed Alain's instructions. Holding the heavy tongs, he seized the cadaver's ankles and they threw him into the oven. Then they moved on to the next body. Just after they had dealt with the twelfth prisoner, a sharp shriek reached them from inside the oven.

Erich froze, his heart rising to his lips.

Alain closed his eyes and gritted his teeth. 'It happens sometimes. Let's just continue.'

'Damn it, you still haven't got rid of all of your cargo?'

The *Leichenträger* stood at the entrance to the room, his outline framed by the door. His stocky silhouette towered over them. He had addressed Alain in French.

'You're running late this morning, my Belgian friend! And with the new supplies I've brought you, you've still a lot on your plate. Who's this with you, there? One of yours?'

'No. He's a Kraut.'

'Hell. Poor guy.'

The *Leichenträger* continued in English: 'How old are you, shorty?'

'Twenty-four.'

'That's a hell of a tattoo, there,' he said, pointing to Erich's shoulder. 'You know, if you'd arrived in Buchenwald a few years back, there's a good chance you'd have ended up as a lampshade in Himmler's drawing room.'

Erich gazed at him, not quite understanding what he had been told.

'You've never heard of the Bitch? Kommandant Koch's wife?'

Erich shook his head.

'Hey, Alain, you're going to have to educate the kid!' The *Leichenträger* clapped his powerful hands together. 'That Ilse Koch whore had every prisoner with fancy tattoos put down like a rabid dog. Then she used their skins to have lampshades made, or bindings for books, and canvases for the drawing rooms of her friends. End of lesson. Now, back to our cargo, it's all outside. And these are just the bodies from Block 50, so you've a long day ahead of you.'

Alain and Erich followed him outside, each pushing a cart.

Erich gazed at the mountains of bodies piled up like logs by the entrance door. They looked like split-open rag dolls.

◆◆◆◆

By the time Erich left the crematorium to attend the evening roll call, the smell of carbonised flesh was stuck to his skin.

The twenty thousand deportees arranged themselves in groups of one hundred to the sound of the music. Behind the slow procession of the orchestra, two prisoners were pulling a cart along on which stood a naked prisoner, his face cast down. The tired fingers of the musicians played *J'attendrai*, and, for a brief moment, Erich almost thought he heard the seductive voice of Rina Ketty.

Two SS soldiers escorted the deportee to the gallows that stood at the centre of the grounds.

The roll call began with the man's body still jerking around like a puppet on the end of the rope.

For four full hours, an SS officer called out each registration number in turn. During this time, fifty-five men, who had reached the end of their tethers, collapsed. They had to be held up by their nearest companions until the officer finally reached the end of his list.

Once Erich and his comrades made it to their block, Josef, the eldest prisoner, pulled a canvas bag onto the table. His ribs were almost peering through his thin skin, but his pale features looked triumphant.

The denizens of the block knew what he had brought back from the kitchens. They were already salivating with impatience as they sat in front of their half-full plates of clear soup in which floated random, minuscule pieces of rotten potato.

Josef distributed a handful of peelings to all and sundry. Some dipped them into their soup, others kept them separate, next to their bread, alternating a spoonful of soup and a meagre bite of potato peel.

Michal, a Czech, waited until his comrades left the table before he began his harvest. Tonight, it was his turn: the breadcrumbs and whatever else had been left were his.

Erich joined Josef and the group of inmates sitting at the ends of their bunks.

'Do you know, we didn't expect to see you tonight, Erich?' Josef said, with a tentative smile.

'I've been transferred to the ovens.'

Josef grimaced.

'I'm sure you'd rather be working with us at the quarry.'

The Pole with the chest covered in ulcers shook his head. 'Well, I, for one, would happily swap places with you and work in the crematorium. Today there was a guy who just couldn't stand up any more and they buried him alive.'

Erich thought back to the cries of agony of the man they had burned alive.

'Do you know what's happening in Block 50?' he asked, his mind still haunted by the screams.

'46 and 50 are the medical experiment units,' the Pole explained. 'Where we poor suckers are used as guinea pigs in order to prolong the life of the superior race. You must have noticed Block 50 when you wandered by on Sunday afternoon. It's the one where the windows are all whitewashed. According to one of the guys who works there, they're studying "exan-something typhus".'

'Exanthematous typhus,' Erich corrected him.

'Yeah, that's it. There's about sixty people working there, each stark naked and shaven down. They say it's that other madman, SS Sturmbannführer Ding-Schuler who's in charge. But Block 46, on the other hand – I have no idea what's happening there, and neither does anyone else.'

'Block 46 is the antechamber to death,' Michal intervened, having just walked away from the table. 'Anyone who walks in there never comes out.'

ALEXIS WAS BURROWING through her bag, while moving from foot to foot in an attempt to combat the cold seeping through her jeans. Despite Olofsson's reminders, she had left her passport at the hotel. She managed to find her driving licence and showed it to the policeman in charge at Linnéa's house.

Silently, for a minute that seemed to go on forever, the young cop compared the young woman's features with the identity photo, then checked her name against a list supplied by his superiors. He finally allowed her to pass. Alexis thanked him, drawing on all the politeness she had managed to absorb in her seven years living in London, and entered her friend's home.

To be inside Linnéa's place without her around felt bizarre, and unpleasant. Alexis was almost expecting her to come rushing down the stairs when a voice made her freeze.

'Alexis!'

She turned around. Emily was looking out from the kitchen, at the other end of the hall.

'Bergström told me you were planning to do an inventory of Linnéa's house today. It's a good thing, because I have some questions for you before I return to the police station,' the profiler said, disappearing into the room.

Shaking her head, Alexis followed Emily into the kitchen. How could the woman be so devoid of tact and empathy; it was beyond belief, worrying even. She must have no social life, surely, to treat people the way she did.

Emily stood behind the kitchen counter.

'What sort of woman was Linnéa?' she asked.

'Can't we do this somewhere else, Emily? Maybe at the police station?'

'The faster I have answers to my questions, the more rapidly my investigation can move forward.'

Straight away, Emily was making Alexis feel guilty. All things considered, she was a crafty psychologist, Alexis thought. She stood in the centre of the kitchen, unwilling to sit or lean against anything.

'Linnéa was dynamic. Obsessed by her work. Funny. An extrovert. She could talk all night, even to a wall.'

'Did she often come to Falkenberg?'

'Twice a year, maybe, for two or three weeks at a time.'

'Did she come with anyone?'

'Alone. Always…'

Emily seemed to frown.

'And when she was staying here, she was never in touch much. Even with Peter. It was like a retreat for her.'

'How long had she owned this house?'

'She'd bought it two or three years ago, I think.'

'Did she have any family in Sweden?'

'Not that I know of.'

'So what exactly was Linnéa's profession?'

'She designed high-end jewellery for Cartier in London.'

'How did she spend her days?'

'She … she drew; sometimes she worked with the salespeople at the store, meeting clients who were interested in special creations.'

'How long had she been in the job?'

'Less than a year. It was a big step forward in her career. She was about to unveil her first collection three days ago, last Saturday,' Alexis said, her voice filling with tears.

'And what did she do before?'

Alexis cleared her throat. 'She worked for another jeweller, but she wasn't allowed to sign her creations.'

'How long had she lived in London?'

'Oh, a long time. She originally went there to study at Central St Martin's.'

'And before that?'

'She lived in Sweden, but I'm not sure where.'

'How long had she been with Peter Templeton?'

'Two years.'

'Did they live together?'

'For the last four months.'

'Was it an exclusive relationship?'

'Yes, I think so…' Alexis' gaze was fixed on a spot in the distance, behind Emily. 'As a matter of fact, she never said much about the relationship … She only really talked about her work.'

'What were they like together?'

'Peter was attentive, tender.'

'And her?'

'She…' The trace of a smile moved across Alexis' lips as the memories flowed back. 'She appeared happy.'

'Did she have any enemies? Had she recently met any unusual new people? Unsettling acquaintances? Anything out of the ordinary happened?'

Alexis shook her head in response to every question.

Then a thought occurred, and she began to frown.

'Sorry. I almost forgot to mention it: Linnéa had an ex-husband. A Swede. He moved to this area just a few months ago.'

KRISTIAN OLOFSSON CLOSED the door to the conference room, still biting into his *kanelbulle*.

'Miss Roy, Kommissionar.'

Bergström distractedly pinched the top of his nose and briefly closed his eyes. The detective was late for their morning meeting once again.

'May I help myself to a cup of coffee?'

Emily's face remained calm and expressionless.

Olofsson settled down next to the Kommissionar, setting down his breakfast on the table.

'Who is this Svensson you're talking about?' he asked, brushing some specks of sugar from his shirt.

'Linnéa Blix's ex-husband,' Bergström answered, his voice unemotional. 'He's been living in Falkenberg for the last few months.'

'Never heard of him,' Olofsson said, still sipping his coffee. 'Falkenberg ain't no Rörö*, Miss Roy. There are twenty thousand people living here; no way we could know every soul. And do you know how many Svenssons live in the whole of Sweden?'

'Kristian,' a tired-voiced Bergström intervened, 'we're referring to Karl Svensson, the sculptor.'

'The one who lives in the big house on the beach and who earns a living assembling shards of broken bottles? Damn it, it's a small world...'

---

* Rörö is a small island of 269 inhabitants on the west coast of Sweden, in the Bohuslän province.

'So, as I was saying to Emily, we are indeed aware of Karl Svensson. He's a well-known artist and…'

'…a hell of a party animal, with a taste for drink and an eye for girls a third of his age,' Olofsson continued, swallowing the final bite of his pastry.

Emily, who had been silent since Olofsson's arrival, looked over at Bergström.

'Yes, that's about it. He's been arrested for driving under the influence. He's been found several times with female minors…'

'How old?'

'Between thirteen and fifteen.'

'Has he ever been arrested for sexually assaulting a minor, or for rape?'

'The fucker's always managed to slip through the net,' Olofsson declared, holding his cup aloft, a dismissive smile curling his lips. Bergström shot him an angry gaze, which he didn't even notice. 'He's never been arrested. And no one has lodged a complaint against him.'

'And who is Stellan Eklund – aside from being Linnéa's neighbour?' Emily asked, her voice neutral.

'That's such a good question!' said Kristian, with a hint of laughter, twisting in his chair.

'*För guds skull*, Olofsson!' the Kommissionar shouted.

Olofsson sank back in his chair. Emily had no need for a translation.

Bergström loudly sighed.

'Do you want a coffee?' he asked, now getting up.

The profiler shook her head.

Bergström served himself in a night-blue Hogänäs mug, adding a spot of milk.

'Stellan was one of ours,' he said as he sat back down. 'He used to work for me, here in Falkenberg. Then he was moved to Gothenburg to investigate a trafficking affair. A few months later, his partner, his partner's wife and their two daughters were all murdered by the East European mafia gang they were investigating. Right in front of Stellan.'

Home of Linnéa Blix, Olofsbo, Falkenberg
Tuesday, 14 January 2014, 14.00

LEFT ALONE following Emily's departure, Alexis had begun sorting out the contents of the study, setting invoices and irrelevant documents aside, then inspecting the kitchen and the drawing room. All Peter wanted to keep were Linnéa's sketches. He'd asked for the rest – the furniture, books, crockery, clothes and trinkets – to be given away to charity.

She had not been looking forward to completing this inventory. She was aware of the pain it might cause her. Every single object had the potential to revive the person she had loved so much; might give Alexis the feeling that she was sinking into Linnéa's lost embrace. In effect, however, what with the kitchen's orange wall tiles, the drawing room and the living room's psychedelic tapestries and the unmatched furniture, she felt as if she was not truly in her friend's place at all, and this made the task easier. The police had left few traces of their presence: just, here and there, white and black flecks of powder across the wooden floor, on the door handles and on the light switches, which gave the impression of random touches of minor artistry dotting loud patterns of the place.

Upstairs, the guest room was barely large enough to fit a bed and a narrow set of drawers; however, it offered an unmissable view of the beach and the lighthouse. Linnéa's bedroom had a curiously rural feel to it for a place bordering the sea. The bed had a flowery patchwork cover, and the walls, whose lower halves were panelled, displayed a wallpaper of bucolic tones, which stretched all the way to the ceiling. Lively yellow curtains framed the windows. A novel by Harry Martinson and another by Jan Guillou sat on the right-hand bedside table, while on the left was an empty leather wallet. A fitted white-wood cupboard faced the bed.

As she opened the cupboard door, Alexis could feel her heartbeat pounding: a red coat, silvery Louboutin shoes, a silk blouse and a pair of pin-striped trousers – the outfit Linnéa had no doubt been planning to wear for the Cartier evening. Alexis moved the hangers from one side to the other. The clothes were so delicate she had the feeling she was looking through a child's wardrobe. Small and slight, Linnéa's height didn't conform to Swedish standards, only her blonde hair and pale eyes betraying her origins.

Alexis suddenly frowned. Two pairs of trousers, a couple of T-shirts and a pullover – all much too large to fit her friend – hung in the far right of the cupboard. She checked the labels: the jeans in a 42, the tops L.

Alexis sat down on the edge of the bed. A man's clothing. But Peter had never set foot in this room.

'Miss Castells?'

She jumped. The duty cop had popped his head round the open door.

'There's someone downstairs who wishes to see you. Name's Stellan Eklund. I'm not allowed to let him in as he's not on the list of permitted visitors the station gave me for today. I'm sorry, but I'm new to this; not supposed to make any mistakes, you'll understand…'

'That's OK. Thank you.'

A wave of lassitude taking hold of her, Alexis sighed and gave a final look in the cupboard. She followed the cop out of the room, feeling as if she was abandoning Linnéa's unknown lover there alone, unobserved.

Stellan was waiting for her outside, indifferent to the gusts of cold wind buffeting his face and inflating the hood of his anorak.

'*Hej*, Alexis. I went by the police station and Bergström told me I'd find you here.'

'Do you have some news about the enquiry?' she asked, worried.

'None at all, I'm afraid … Just wanted to offer you something of a coffee break, let you breathe a little. I can drive you back here as soon as you want to get back on the case again.'

It was true – Stellan had come at exactly the right time. Alexis needed to inject a new perspective into her thoughts.

She picked up her handbag in the hall and stepped into the car. One minute later, they arrived at Stellan's.

Alexis' heart tightened as she walked into the house. She recalled following Kristian Olofsson through this corridor, then meeting the gentle giant Bergström, who had informed her of her friend's death. She briefly closed her eyes and imperceptibly shook her head, forbidding herself to dwell on this recent memory.

'Come, we'll be better in the kitchen,' Stellan proposed.

Her gaze fascinated by the wide glass windows, Alexis slowly moved towards the breakfast counter. The house had been built on the edge of the beach, just far enough from the sea that you could embrace its splendour, just close enough to appreciate its power. Black, foaming waves washed over the snow-crowned shingles, forming the prelude to the imminent sunset.

Stellan handed a cup to Alexis and sat down next to her. They watched the night fall across the beach in comfortable silence.

A few minutes later, a second cup of coffee in her hand, Alexis asked Stellan Eklund how he'd originally met Linnéa. And, while he was telling her about the summer when he was fourteen, she wondered whether the men's clothing abandoned in the bedroom cupboard belonged to him.

EMILY WALKED FAST along the cycle path bordering the snow-covered road. The wind was animating the snowflakes, sending them dancing like a swarm of small flies. Her body felt tight, her thoughts confused, frustration spreading like poison through her veins.

Bergström had handed over most of the files she had requested: the aerial views of the area where Linnéa Blix had been discovered; the scale map of the immediate surroundings; the preliminary police report containing all the information about the circumstances in which the body was found, as well as the relevant socio-economic information about the Olofsbo area. But she was still waiting for the autopsy report; and of Linnéa's neighbours, only Stellan Eklund had been interviewed.

Eklund: a retired cop with a zealous reputation who now worked in real estate. Unusual and uncommon enough for her to ignore and not wish to meet Eklund in the flesh.

The profiler broke into a steady run in an attempt to get rid of some of the tension that was building up inside her.

The investigations, both into the murders of the children in London, as well as into Linnéa's death, cast more shadows than light at this stage. Information filtered through in no particular order, spoiling her attempts to forge any form of profile of the killer. This latest death had added fresh elements, but nothing that enabled Emily to start separating the wheat from the chaff.

First she should focus on Linnéa Blix. Alexis Castells had painted an interesting picture of her and, furthermore, Emily had made a fascinating discovery at the victim's home that very morning. She was now eager to hear what the ex-cop, Eklund, would be able to tell her about Linnéa. Or reveal about himself.

She slowed her pace, regulated her breathing and rang Stellan's bell.

She hadn't warned him she was coming over. She preferred to take people by surprise, catch them in the midst of their day-to-day activities, not allowing them enough time to compose themselves.

Stellan Eklund opened the door, a cup of coffee in his hand. Emily remembered catching sight of him as she arrived at the police station. Tall, square shoulders and jaw, pale eyes; the sort of guy you couldn't help noticing.

She quickly introduced herself, walked inside and, to conform with Swedish habits, took off her shoes. Following Stellan into the kitchen, she came across Alexis, leaning against the American-style counter. She nodded towards her, careful not to betray any surprise.

Alexis felt like a child caught lying. Her cheeks reddened as she cleared her throat and responded to Emily's greeting.

'I'm sorry to disturb you at home, Stellan,' the profiler said, a candid smile spreading across her lips. 'I'm attempting to draw up a profile of the victim and I need your help…'

Alexis, shocked, threw a glance at her. She'd never witnessed Emily be so tactful and gentle.

'I'll leave you to it,' she said, getting off her stool.

'I'm not bothered if you want to stay,' Emily said, then turned to Stellan: 'As long as it's OK with you.'

Alexis opened her eyes wide. This was unbelievable. Emily on a charm offensive.

Stellan, totally relaxed, nodded his head.

Emily accepted the coffee she was offered and they all sat at the living-room table, facing the sea.

Delighted to be allowed to stay, but in a state of discomfort, Alexis left a chair between her and her host and concentrated on her cup.

'Linnéa Blix and you had known each other for a long time, am I right?'

Emily's voice swam with empathy. Alexis had to prevent herself looking up to the sky in sheer amazement.

'We knew each other as teenagers,' replied Stellan. 'We spent our summers in Båstad, with our parents. It's a town on the coast, a bit further to the south.'

'You lived in the region?'

'No. I lived in Stockholm. And Linnéa in Norrköping.'

'How did you end up in Falkenberg?'

'My first posting, twenty years ago. I liked it here, so I stayed on.'

'And Linnéa?'

'Linnéa left Sweden some two decades ago. She only came here on vacation. If I remember correctly, she bought her house almost three years ago. Prior to that, she stayed with her parents, in Båstad. Following their deaths, she sold their villa and acquired this farm – her "psychedelic chalet" she used to call it. She didn't change a thing inside. She was waiting to come into some money and summon up enough energy to deal with the place properly. We'd planned to set to work on it this year, in the spring.' He frowned as he said this, his eyes looking down at his coffee cup.

Pain flowed through Alexis. How did everyone else find it so easy to talk about Linnéa?

'You were going to renovate the house together?'

Stellan looked at Emily in silence for a few seconds. 'No. Linnéa had asked us to do the work.'

'Us?' Emily's eyes had shrunk, making her look somewhat suspicious.

'I deal in real estate,' he explained as he rose from the table.

He moved behind the kitchen counter, picked up the coffee pot and returned, serving all three of them again.

'I manage a building company dealing with renovations.'

'Are you familiar with Linnéa's ex-husband?'

These sudden changes of subject enervated Alexis. Stellan, on the other hand, didn't appear bothered.

'Yes. Karl was part of the group of kids we spent our holidays with.'

'And have you stayed in touch with him?'

Stellan straightened. 'No.'

'What type of man is he?'

'Angry. Full of himself. A notorious pervert.' Every single word was spoken sharply, like a sword cutting through the air.

'Do you know Peter Templeton?'

'I once had dinner with him and Linnéa in London. And we came across each other the other evening.'

'What did you make of him?'

'I liked him. Back in London I found him sympathetic, open. Although, on Sunday, he was more like a man torn apart by his partner's death.'

'Did Linnéa ever talk to you about her relationship with him?'

'She would never discuss her personal life with me.'

'Do you know if she was sleeping with anyone else?'

Stellan made no sign of being surprised or shocked by the question. 'I really don't know. If that was the case, she didn't confide in me.'

Of course, Alexis thought. There was no doubt Emily had also noticed the items of male clothing in Linnéa's cupboard. And the profiler was asking the very same questions she herself would have asked.

THE HEAVY CURTAIN OF NIGHT hung like a cloud of ice, the cold turning into something even fiercer.

Emily energetically advanced along the field bordering the Olofsbo beach. Alexis had difficulty keeping up; she was nowhere near as strong, nor did she possess the right equipment for this sort of romp, with the snow and frost pulling the temperature down to minus 15 degrees. The cold was clawing all the way down to the bottom of her lungs, insinuating itself through all her layers of clothing, breezing across her skin. But she had no one else to blame but herself: she was the one who'd insisted, on leaving Stellan's place, that she accompany the profiler to the small pleasure harbour. Emily wanted to see the *småbåtshamn* again, now she had the scale map of the area and the aerial photographs in hand.

A wave of questions about Linnéa's murder swept through Alexis' mind, and Emily was the only one who could provide answers. She was not looking forward to this dialogue – having to endure Emily's brusque mannerisms and misanthropic attitude, but it would be worth it, she knew. She'd return to Linnéa's to complete the inventory tomorrow.

Emily's torch beam swept across the ground, illuminating their path as they moved along to the sound of their shoes struggling through the snow.

Alexis gritted her teeth to divert the pain. With every step, she had to raise her knees almost halfway to her waist in order to extricate her legs from the frozen grip of the snow. Her thigh muscles soon tired, reminding her how unfit she was.

Emily, on the other hand, moved with surprising agility. Alexis watched her conquer the fields of snow with a demeanour that was simultaneously feline and warrior-like. She was thinking back to how sycophantic the profiler had been when interrogating Stellan, almost seductive in fact. Had she taken a fancy to him, or what? And why not? Alexis pondered.

They finally left the field and reached the small marina, if she was to believe the presence of the pontoons isolated in the midst of the icy esplanade. They swerved to the right to avoid the pontoons, and finally came level with a small wooden hut braced against the dune.

Alexis pulled a bottle of water from her bag and greedily drank the whole half-litre in an attempt to soothe the fire raging in her lungs.

'Do you want some more?' Emily asked, reaching for her rucksack.

Alexis whispered a 'no', wiping her mouth dry with the back of her hand.

'I've never known you to be so considerate,' she said. 'You surprised me at Stellan's, earlier.'

'I'm told people respond well to this sort of approach,' Emily answered with assurance, then gripped the small torch between her teeth.

She pulled a thick cardboard folder from her backpack, and from the folder took a set of photographs, which she placed under the circle of light from the torch. Alexis noted these were aerial views of the bay and the beach. Photographs of the area where her friend's body had been found, abandoned.

Eyes strained with anguish, she looked away, staring at the desolate landscape. She was treading the same ground as Linnéa's killer. Her feet were standing on the very ground across which he had probably dragged the naked, mutilated body.

It wasn't as if Alexis was not accustomed to crime scenes. To document her books, she had looked at countless blood-splattered and horrifying photos. She'd examined them with cold eyes, with the detachment of someone who hadn't been involved, and had not experienced the suffering. With two exceptions: one particular murder seven years earlier, and now Linnéa's.

Her heart was beating frantically inside her chest and she felt the sudden urge to vomit. She leaned forward to expel the bile rising up her throat, spitting it out. She had to swallow hard a couple of times to repel the horrible taste spreading across her palate as she bent forward; it was as if even gravity was conspiring against her, and she felt her nerves jangle.

A hand brushed against her shoulder: Emily was encouraging her to just let go, expel the pain and the anxiety. Alexis allowed a wave of sadness to submerge her thoughts and feelings. Tears welled up in her eyes, threatening to drown her. She forgot the cold surrounding her, the snowflakes burning her face and hands, hanging onto her hair, her eyelashes.

Finally, the spasms became less frequent, then faded away. She straightened up, wiped her face, gulped down a sharp gust of cold air as if it might negate the sorrow, and followed Emily, who had begun climbing the dune. On the other side was the car park where they had left the car.

Inside, Alexis curled herself up, waiting for Emily to switch the engine on and the heating to begin working.

They drove in silence to the hotel.

Standing in front of the door to her room, Alexis couldn't help thinking over and again about all the questions going round in circles in her mind. But Emily anticipated her thoughts.

'Go and have a rest,' she said. 'We'll talk about it tomorrow.'

He lowers his hand to the top of the child's head and, with his fingers, combs the rebellious strands into place. His hair is soft, much too long for a small boy.

He leans down and buries his face in the untidy curls obscuring the child's forehead. The smell has become slightly acrid, but he knows that if he breathes in deeply enough, his nostrils will inhale a touch of sweetness, with a hint of vanilla.

His inhalations are noisy and greedy, and the little one's hair is tickling the end of his nose. He smiles. A smile full of tenderness, overflowing with pride.

He continues to caress the child's head, his mouth nearing the perfect and divine oval-shaped ear.

'I know you don't want to have a bath.'

His worried eyes move from the steel slab to the tub. This is the part he never likes. The bath. And the rest. Takes too long. Fastidious.

'But not quite right now. You can lay here a little longer, you know.'

His tongue moves across his dry lips.

He now has to summon all his courage and inform the Other that it's now his turn to make the rules of the game. His chest swells. His ribs stand out against his shirt. Yes, this is it. It's his turn now, his alone, to make the rules. He will tell him tonight. Tonight.

He moves even nearer until his lips are grazing the tiny earlobe.

'He's not going to be happy about it, but I've decided I'm not going to bathe you either.'

With the tip of his nose, he traces an imaginary line from the corner of one eye all the way down to the boy's chin.

'I'll just prepare you and then ... then we'll allow nature to take its course. What do you say?'

He slips off the pyjamas and the dirty pants and slides them down the skinny legs, unveiling the white skin, speckled with blue stains.

Then his whole body freezes with apprehension. It's always at this particular point that he hears them. They all moan in unison. As if they'd simultaneously agreed to form a whole choir of supplicants. They're not sobbing; no, they're screaming.

With the back of his hand, he caresses the sole of the foot. It's soft, still supple to the touch, its curve a sheer delight. Maybe this one will stay quiet? Maybe he will understand why...

Suddenly, his features distort in pain.

The child's screams pierce his mind, strident, unbearable. His plaints, like steel claws, are tearing at his eardrums. They are lacerating, slashing away, eviscerating him.

And now, all the others have joined in.

ALTHOUGH SHE WASN'T REALLY HUNGRY, Alexis kept on eating, if only to dull her stomach's complaints and repel the persistent migraine she was suffering from. She'd just swallowed a cinnamon-flavoured *pain au raisin* and was now biting into some other treat, with an unpronounceable name. It was difficult to rival the good old *made-in-France* butter croissants, but these delicate Swedish morsels weren't bad either, she reckoned.

Between sips of tea, she had agreed to go with Emily to see Karl Svensson, Linnéa's ex-husband. The profiler was to meet her at the patisserie.

The day had not begun well. She'd woken at dawn, feeling nauseous, a knot of sadness lodged at the back of her throat. How could she have collapsed into such a heap of tears the day before? At least Emily's reassuring presence and solid strength had proven helpful. Maybe that was the very reason she had allowed herself to be submerged in the pain, knowing Emily was present and there to assist.

A scalding shower had brought her back to life and she had then taken a cab to Linnéa's to complete the sorting out. Four hours later, she had finished, her stomach hollow and her head about to burst open. She had decided it would be best to catch a bite in town before returning to her room.

After she'd spoken to Emily, her phone had rung again. Alexis swiped her grease-covered screen and readied herself for the call.

'Alexis, I've told him you were the one to call, OK?' her mother

whispered. 'Bert, BERT! It's your daughter! She's calling you to wish
you a happy birthday! See!'

Alexis had totally forgotten her father's birthday.

'Hello, my baby girl!'

'Happy birthday, Dad,' she said, trying to sound happy.

'Thanks, my baby girl. How are you? How's it going there…?'

Her mother took the phone away from him. 'Where are you? It's
noisy. Are you with someone?'

'I'm at the Ritz, a—'

'You're at the Ritz? At the hotel? Why aren't you at home?'

'Mum—'

'I've told you, I always want to know when you're travelling, or I
begin to worry. So you're in London? When did you get back?'

'Mum—'

'Have they found out who did it? It's a terrible story; truly terrible.
You know it's even all over the newspapers back here.'

'Mum, I'm not at THE Ritz. I'm at the Ritz Patisserie. I'm still in
Sweden. I'm having breakfast.'

'A patisserie? In Sweden! Wow, you're adventurous: Swedish cakes
must be so heavy on the stomach! At least it means you're eating,
darling. That's not a bad thing.'

Her mother fell silent for a moment. In the background, Alexis
could hear her niece's squeaky little voice asking to speak to her
auntie. Alexis smiled. Her lips parted wide.

'Auntie?'

'Hello, little chick.'

She closed her eyes, listening to her delightful niece tell her all
about her day. She could imagine her, phone stuck to her mouth,
manically pulling her skirt in all directions or attempting to undo
the ribbon with which her mother was always trying to keep her hair
tidy. The child explained that she had decided to become a boy so
she could pee standing up, like her brother did, but the problem was
that it would mean she could no longer wear dresses, as boys were
not allowed to. Sometimes they wore skirts, like the 'Scotties', but

they had to be checked and she only liked flower patterns. And heart shapes. And polka dots too. But not green ones. Definitely not green dots. They looked like green peas. And she hated green peas.

For ten serene minutes, Alexis wallowed inside her niece's universe, and then her nephew's – a soft, comforting world full of warm kisses.

She finally hung up, having promised them she would come back with some authentic Swedish snow.

Buchenwald Concentration Camp, Germany
October 1944

ERICH PULLED UP HIS SHIRT COLLAR as he passed the dying oak tree.

The Nazis had deforested the Ettersberg and chosen the slope where the wind blew strongest to build Buchenwald. The only tree to survive had been this one, retained in homage to Goethe and the many visits he had made to this particular hill. What a strange idea it was to have surrounded this symbol of German culture with barbed wire ... A striking and ironic image, which had certainly not occurred to the camp's architects.

On the 24th of August, the oak tree had partly burned away during the bombing. Its forlorn silhouette now echoed those of the inmates inhabiting the alleys of Buchenwald.

'*Schweinehund!*' an SS officer suddenly began screaming at a prisoner crossing his path.

Erich increased his pace. Hitler had poisoned everything. Erich's own mother language now offended him – so full of barbarity.

Silently, he began to recite to himself verses by Theodor Storm. He tried to remember parts of *Immensee, Die Stadt* and *Der Schimmelreiter*, lines his memory had preserved; his tongue savoured every word, like gourmet food.

He reached the latrines, his head now bursting with the most refined music. Andreas, Jonas and Wilhelm were waiting for him, conversing next to a bunch of haggard prisoners who seemed to be on their last legs.

Greeting his comrades, he couldn't help noticing the frozen, pain-ravaged eyes of one of the poor guys. His backside still soiled following his visit to the latrines, his bones sharply visible beneath his grey skin, he wandered barefoot through the disgusting mud – a mix of faecal matter and urine – that bordered the sanitary pits.

Erich had met Andreas, Jonas and Wilhelm, three Norwegians who, like him, had been medical students, one Sunday afternoon in August, during the course of the only weekly break they were allowed.

They had chosen this abominable place for their Sunday get-togethers, as the SS never set foot here.

As usual, they jested with Erich about his lack of progress in learning Norwegian, before the conversation resumed in English.

'You should have chosen any other language than ours, mate. The Swedes would understand you, but they'll laugh in your face!' Andreas joked, winking at him. 'Do you really want to settle in Sweden after you get out of here?'

'*If* I ever get out of here…'

'Of course we'll get out, old man! But instead of exiling yourself, would it not be better to stay and help rebuild your own country?'

'My country is rotten to the core, Andreas. How do you explain the existence of this camp? This hell on earth? Designed so that the ceilings in the cellars are high enough to hang men up as if they were slabs of meat. With ovens constructed to accommodate and burn three bodies at a time. This mad project of expanding the realm of the Aryan race isn't Hitler's alone; many, many other Germans follow him and contribute to all this.'

'But there are still Germans like you, mate. Germans who had the guts to say no to the Nazis and Hitler's delirium. Many have died because of what they said. And others, like you, are locked up here or in other camps, all waiting to become the artisans of the renewal, when things finally change.'

Erich failed to answer, his thoughts wandering well beyond the barbed wire.

'You'll freeze your arse off in Scandinavia, anyway,' Wilhelm added. 'Your Weimar winters are a joke compared to ours.'

'Where exactly was your mother from?' Jonas intervened, pulling on his shirt sleeve.

Sorrow passed like a veil in front of Erich's eyes. His parents had both died during the journey to Buchenwald. He swallowed hard to fight back the sadness gripping his throat.

'From Jönköping, in the south.'

'And your father also had a Swedish background?'

'No, he was German. Born in the Brandenburg region, in Falkenberg.'

'Falkenberg? That's a hell of a coincidence! Did you know there's a town on the west coast of Sweden that's also called Falkenberg?'

Erich rubbed his hands together. 'That, guys, is a sign from fate!'

But Andreas' features had frozen.

A surge of terrible pain washed over Erich, then he fell unconscious.

━━◆◆◆◆━━

A web of atrocious, radiating agony, paralysed him from his shoulders all the way down to the tips of his fingers. With difficulty, Erich opened his eyes. Two SS officers were dragging him along the gravelled ground like a dead animal.

He slowly turned his head to the left, fighting the involuntary spasms that ran through his neck like an electric current. They were approaching a series of huts. He recognised them in a flash: the *Revier*. The camp infirmary. The soldiers must have taken a path inmates were not allowed to use.

Two metres from the entrance, they dropped him into the mud.

'Take your shoes off, you pig!'

Erich looked down at his bloodied feet. He wasn't wearing any shoes.

The soldiers mimed disappointment. 'Oh, what a damned pity!' said one. He knew how difficult it would be for Erich to obtain another pair. 'The Doktor is waiting for you, arsehole,' he went on. 'Tell him Hauptscharführer Hess is delivering the parcel on behalf of Sturmbannführer Fleischer.'

Hess lit a cigarette and his companion shoved Erich inside, hurrying him along with his cosh.

Like every Sunday, the infirmary was jam-packed. A nauseating smell rose to the ceiling; he felt as if he was about to retch.

Erich provided his registration number and passed on Hess's message to a thin man whose neck appeared to float inside his yellowing smock. The nurse, no doubt an inmate too, in view of his meek response and lack of insults, asked him to remain where he was, sitting on the floor, facing a bed that was occupied by a man enveloped in wet sheets.

The Doktor arrived three hours later. Erich was awakened by the cries of the suffering inmates, kicked aside by the medic's boots as he made his way as if through a tunnel of cordless puppets.

The man stopped in front of the bed opposite Erich and unswaddled the poor inhabitant, whose teeth were chattering loudly and repeatedly, in between his piercing screams. His shin displayed a lengthy, open gash full of pus. The Doktor instructed the thin-necked nurse to clean the wound, and then he began digging into the opening with a scalpel.

The patient began to scream but then quickly fell silent. The poor guy had probably fainted with the pain. The Doktor continued to forage inside his skin for several minutes, then left it to the nurse to close up the wound.

'20076!' he barked as he washed his hands.

Erich rose. The Doktor gestured with two of his fingers, instructing him to undress.

Shedding his garments, Erich realised how servile the constant threat of terror had made him. He hadn't even thought to ask why he was here.

The surgeon's cold hands examined him in the same detached and brutal way the nameless overseer had inspected him on his arrival at

Buchenwald. But it felt different now. The daily routine of the camp had eliminated any possible sense of privacy. Within the barbed wire, there was no way you could be shy or hold anything back; you were too busy trying to survive.

Following his summary inspection, the medic jotted down a few notes on a sheet of paper which he then handed over to Erich, ordering him to deliver it to Hauptscharführer Hess.

Erich warily slipped on his clothes again. They were still wet and covered in excrement following his earlier fall in front of the latrines.

He left the *Revier* and passed the paper over to the SS officer, who had been waiting outside all along, following orders; Erich hadn't dared unfold or read it.

'Come on, arsehole, time for us to go back. Now that you're awake again, we'll have to take the path reserved for pigs. And, do you know what, arsehole? You're going to do the journey on all fours, and I want to listen to you oinking all the way, like the pig you truly are.'

The officer burst out laughing. His companion did the same.

Erich knew the path threaded between the infirmary and the camp. It was a field of mud, a gutter of muck, traversed by knotted roots and dead tree trunks.

He got down on all fours and began the painful journey, accompanied by the strikes of the cosh and his own, animal sounds.

When they finally emerged from the woods, the soldier ordered Erich to stand. Covered in mud, overcome by cold and fear, Erich continued along the path, shivering uncontrollably, his back, the palms of his hands and the length of his legs bruised and full of cuts, his throat on fire.

The two SS officers took him past the roll-call area and stopped in front of the large box standing at its centre. Cries of agony echoed inside. Behind the small opening, barred with sharp wire, Erich could see a man curled up on his haunches. Long nails emerging from the wooden walls dug into his skin with every movement he attempted.

A stream of urine pearled down Erich's leg. What sort of fate did his tormentors have in wait for him? Was he to take the place of the man in the box?

The two soldiers gave the box a few kicks and insulted its occupier before moving on. The prisoner's terrible cries wouldn't leave Erich's mind until the soldiers finally came to a halt in front of another building.

Noting the number on the door, fear gripped his guts. They were facing Block 46.

Block 46, the antechamber to death.

EMILY PARKED ON THE WIDE, paved driveway that led to the grand, typically Swedish, yellow-wood villa.

The previous day, Karl Svensson had refused to open his door to Olofsson. Emily had had to visit a sour-faced judge to get the right to interview Linnéa's ex-husband. So he was now aware of her visit and had had time to prepare, which Emily didn't appreciate in the slightest. However, she had no choice in the matter.

When he opened the door, Alexis found it difficult to conceal her surprise: she had assumed he would be youthful and good-looking – not the quiet and conservative man who stood before them.

They followed him into the house. Inside, it was as modern as its exterior was traditional, and even had a winter garden that over-looked the endless sandy beach.

Karl settled himself in a sleekly designed armchair.

The two women sat down opposite him on a deep-seated settee on which three large leather cushions were scattered.

'So?' he asked curtly.

'We'd like to offer you our condolences, sir,' Emily responded.

Karl's features remained impassive. 'Thank you,' he whispered, with total insincerity.

Emily paused before continuing.

'Could you tell us about Linnéa, Mr Svensson?'

'Do you think I'm the right person for that?' he asked, curling his lips.

'You have known Linnéa since she was young. You were her artistic mentor, in a manner of speaking. You—'

'Oh, I wasn't only that. Did you know she originally wanted to be an air hostess? Of all things…'

He's a snob, thought Alexis, *on top of everything else.*

'It's true I inspired her. I uncovered her innate talent.'

He stood up, served himself some water from a thin glass decanter and sat himself down on the seat's arm-rest, stiff like an '*i*', looking down on his female guests, as if in an attempt to dominate them.

'She was fascinated by my mother's jewellery. She was always making pencil drawings of it. So I suggested she should try and create some, not just copy the pieces, and that's how it all began. We went to London to study at St Martin's – both financed by my father – and we were about to return to Sweden when she was offered a job at Anselme, the jewellers. My sculpture studio awaited me in Stockholm – I already had a fair few commissions. We did get married, although our relationship was already under strain. I came back here; she stayed there. You know the rest.'

A pretentious snob and an idiot, noted Emily. All she had to do was flatter his ego and he had presented her with what she needed on a platter.

'Did you know she had acquired a house in Falkenberg?'

'Of course. But that's not the reason I came to live here. I would say it was more her who wanted to be close to *me*. She was aware that my father was paying an annuity on this villa and that it wouldn't be long before he could get his hands on it. In fact, the old guy who sold it to my father finally passed away last year. He still lived here, you see, even though my father owned it.'

Alexis had to bite her tongue to avoid speaking.

'Were you on good terms with Linnéa?' Emily continued.

Karl's jaw tightened. His lips curled downwards. 'We were not on speaking terms.'

'Had she tried to contact you?'

'No.'

'And how about you?'

'Contact her? Why would I?'

'And your studio: is it in the house?' Emily cleverly changed the subject, her voice neutral.

There was a flash of childish excitement in the artist's previously vacant eyes. 'It's in the barn next door.'

'Could we take a look?'

Karl's features froze again. 'In order to do that, ladies, you'd have to come back with some official papers.'

++++

Emily hadn't spoken since they had left Karl Svensson's house.

Her nose stuck against the car window, Alexis was watching the landscape unfurl. The sky was low and heavy, and gave her the impression the day hadn't yet begun. The trees were bending under the weight of the snow, like an old man overcome by the burden of the passing years.

'What did you want to know?'

Alexis jumped. Emily's voice had stolen her away from her lyrical dreams. She collected her sparse thoughts.

'I'm sorry I interrupted your inspection of the marina yesterday evening…'

'No harm. I went back this morning. What was it you wanted?'

'I'm not sure you'll be able to answer me…'

The profiler remained silent, her eyes drawn to the road they were driving on.

'Tell me about the other women. The two London victims.'

'They were two young boys.'

'Two b…'

Alexis had assumed all along they were women, between thirty and forty, blonde like Linnéa, even with long hair. Not this. Not children. She closed her eyes for a while in an attempt to digest this new information.

'The same wounds…?'

Emily nodded.

A wave of pain coursed through Alexis' chest. Thinking of the abominable agony the children must have endured. The unbearable sadness of the parents, the families. Her mind went to her nephew and niece, and a ring of nausea encircled her heart, dismay washing over her. But she had to remain strong. She couldn't break down a second time in front of Emily.

Alexis opened her side window a little; a rush of cold air swept across her, returning her to the present.

'Are you thinking of two separate killers with the same signature, but different *modus operandi*?' she continued, her voice strained.

'Maybe.'

'And Linnéa might have surprised them?'

'Surprised or recognised,' Emily continued, still unwilling to take her eyes off the road.

Alexis felt cold sweat run down the back of her neck.

It was clear the police were suspicious of anyone close to Linnéa.

He sets the scalpel down on the steel tray. The blue absorbent paper shrivels when the blade and the blood-spattered handle make contact with it.

Earlier, the walls were sweating. Those who had been transformed were vomiting their fear and anxieties. Their tears, the size of rain drops, dripped all the way down to the floor. When they finally stopped crying, he gazed at their accusing, horrified eyes.

But no longer. Now, all is silent. A comforting, pleasing silence. The child is quiet and terror has left his eyes.

He wraps gauze around the sockets and the opening he has carved into the child's neck. With an antiseptic cloth, he cleans the forehead, the nose and the marbled cheeks. Then the shoulders, the torso and the navel, on which he delicately places a cotton pad to absorb the blood. He throws the soaked pad away and completes his cleaning with a small, thin towel that he has rolled round his fingers. He uses it to delve into the depths of the ears, to wipe the sides of the nose and the skin on the child's stomach.

He takes off the white overalls, the mask, the shoe covers and the cap holding back his hair, and steps into the small kitchen he has set up by the study. He picks up an olive lying in an earthenware ramequin and, nibbling away at it, slices through one of the green lemons he has left by the sink. He drops the slice into his glass and drowns it in sparkling water. He takes a sip and closes his eyes. The bubbles wash over his tongue, running down his palate.

Dear God, was he thirsty!

OUT OF BREATH, Alexis pushed through Bratt's doors. Although the restaurant was only a stone's throw from the hotel, the short distance had frozen her from head to toe.

She'd gone out with the intention of picking up a pizza she could then eat in her hotel room, but had changed her mind. She'd recalled the generous bread basket and the soothing light of the candles, and her plans had changed.

The restaurant was almost empty. She sat herself at a small, round table. She ordered a glass of Pouilly Fumé to complement her scallop carpaccio when Bergström, accompanied by a woman who was almost as tall as he was, walked in.

Noticing her, the Kommissionar greeted her with a nod. Alexis responded with a wave of her hand, then concentrated again on her Pouilly, glad not to have to share it with anyone.

She was about to bite into the final rye bread roll from the basket when, out of the corner of her eye, she realised that Bergström's companion was moving towards her table. Lithe, a welcoming smile illuminated her features.

'Good evening, Alexis. I'm Lena, Lennart's wife.'

Obliged to neglect her piece of bread, Alexis shook hands with her.

'Why don't you come and join us? I hear it's your last night here, and we can't have you eating on your own, can we?'

Alexis had no choice. It would be impolite to decline the invitation. She tried to appear pleased, and reluctantly left her small, round table behind.

'Stellan should be arriving any minute now. I hope you don't mind,' Lena added, sitting next to Bergström, who was halfway through a telephone conversation.

This is getting better and better, Alexis reflected, feeling increasingly less sociable. The previous evening, she'd almost fled Stellan's, convinced he had been Linnéa's lover. And now she was going to be stuck at a table with him!

'I'm sorry, Alexis,' Bergström said as he hung up. 'I couldn't convince my wife to leave you alone. She's not easy to persuade...'

Lena smiled and patted her husband's hand, then called a waiter over and ordered the same wine Alexis had been drinking.

Stellan made an appearance while the Sauvignon Blanc was being poured. He said '*hej*' to everyone present and sat himself next to Alexis, facing the Bergströms.

'I found this lovely lady on her own,' Lena explained. 'I knew right away she would be much better off sitting with us. Where were you?'

'With Molin,' said Stellan, puffing his cheeks out slightly, in a show of indifference.

'What did he want?'

'He wants us to start work on the country house in the summer, instead of Christmas.'

'This summer? But we're already busy with two sites in Stockholm and one overseas!'

'He won't listen to reason,' Stellan said.

Bergström began laughing loudly. 'Poor Alexis hasn't a clue what you're talking about!'

Alexis remained silent.

'Lena and Stellan work together. I can't begin to tell you all the problems that come up when a brother and sister disagree...'

Alexis widened her eyes with surprise.

'Oh, you didn't know that either? Your friend Emily really isn't into gossip, is she?'

'I'm sorry, it's my fault,' Stellan intervened. 'I should have thought of telling you…'

'Welcome to our family dinner,' Lena joked, winking at Alexis as she poured another glass of wine.

Grand Hotel, Falkenberg
Wednesday, 15 January 2014, 20.00

A TOWEL DRAPED around her waist, Emily came out of the bathroom and sat down on the bed, her body still dripping with water. In front of her she'd laid out a dozen photographs and her notepad.

When Pearce had arrived at her house, around midnight on Sunday, she hadn't expected him to tell her that a body discovered in Sweden displayed the same injuries seen on the Hampstead victims. Normally, killers were territorial. But the details passed on by the Falkenberg police – a sectioned trachea; enucleation; and a letter carved into the arm – left no doubt: the murder of Linnéa Blix, some thousands of kilometres from London, was connected to her existing cases. The new death changed everything about the direction of her enquiries. She'd have to start from scratch.

Emily picked up an oat biscuit from a packet on her bedside table and chewed away at it in silence.

Returning from Karl Svensson's, she had dropped Alexis off at the hotel and then visited the police station to get hold of the autopsy report and the notes about the neighbouring area, which had been written in English at Bergström's request. As she had half expected, there were no real surprises. The medical examiner's conclusions, however, were in Swedish. Emily and the Kommissionar had sat themselves down in the conference room and, without protest, Bergström had translated the report for her, page by page.

According to the medical examiner, Linnéa Blix had died approximately one week before her body had been discovered. Which placed

her death on the weekend of the 4th and 5th of January. Linnea's
mobile-phone records had provided no useful clues, as Linnéa hadn't
used it once following her arrival in Sweden.

Like the children found in Hampstead, she had died of asphyxia.
The medical examiner had found traces of glue, originating from
some kind of adhesive band, which had been placed around her
neck. His theory, which was similar to his English counterpart's, was
that the victim's head had been wrapped inside a bag, which had then
been taped tightly around the neck.

The enucleation, the sectioning of the trachea, the carving of the
letter into the arm and the cleansing of the body, had all taken place
post mortem, as they had with the London victims. The incisions
around the eyes and the neck had been made with a scalpel in a
precise and tidy manner in all cases.

The Kommissionar had ventured to suggest that the use of a
scalpel and the surgical aspect of the wounds might point to a criminal with a medical background. Emily had shaken her head. A killer's
anatomical knowledge seldom had anything to do with his day-to-
day work. Sociopaths and psychopaths often had strange hobbies.

There were no signs of sexual activity, either with the children or
Linnéa. The only fibres found on her body almost certainly origi-
nated from the clothes she had been wearing when she had been
killed. As with the two previous victims, the killer had left no trace
that could point in his or her direction; not a single clue.

Emily stared at the three scene-of-crime photos spread out across
the bed. They all echoed each other, even Linnéa's shaven pubis
which, aesthetically, matched the hairless genital areas of the small
boys.

Emily knew from experience that, when it came to comparing
crime scenes, it was best to concentrate on the similarities rather
than the differences. But here she just couldn't dismiss the diver-
gences: in Linnéa's case, the sex and age of the victim, an X rather
than a Y carved into her arm, and this so much deeper than the
others. The fact that Linnéa had not actually been buried could be

attributed to the sheer hardness of the frozen ground in Falkenberg, which might explain why her body had been hidden out of sight under the boat.

Emily shed her towel, pulled her legs up under her and stretched her back. With one finger she slid the photo of Linnéa lying in the snow towards her. The killer had not covered her face, and he hadn't cut her hair. Could this mean he felt no anger towards her, had no wish to punish her? This in no way, however, excluded the possibility that he might have known her.

Emily stepped off the bed, switched on the kettle and dropped a tea bag into a cup.

These changes in the *modus operandi* were leading her towards a variety of theories.

The first was that there were two killers involved, one of whom was dominant over the other. The criminal identity of the Swedish killer hadn't yet fully evolved; he was merely borrowing elements from the working methods and fantasies of his London inspiration.

Emily filled the cup with boiling water and went back to sit on the bed.

Her second theory was that there was only one killer – the London one; he had links with Sweden and hunted there at random. Linnéa Blix, a perfect stranger, had happened to cross his path.

The third possibility was that there was only one killer, but Linnéa knew him and they had come across each other in Sweden.

In the last two instances, the killer had followed his usual procedure, but had had to deviate from it in that his victim was a woman and he had been unable to bury her.

Emily carefully sipped the steaming drink.

At any rate, the criminal or criminals always took the time to clean up the corpses after they had been mutilated, then provided them with some form of burial. A proof, if needed, of a kind of remorse, but maybe also respect.

Emily rolled her shoulders to release the tightness in her muscles. Her gaze moved from the slit throats to the dark, empty orbs, and lingered on the letters carved into the victims' left arms. The direction of the letter was different on each body. Compared to the shoulder-hand axis, Linnéa's X was straight, seeming to point north, while the first victim's Y veered to the right, indicating north-north-east, and the second one pointed towards east-south-east.

These spatial indications, however, provided her with no clue as to where the next body might be discovered, the potential victim's place of residence, nor the identity of any victim who might follow. Emily could think of no explanation for the variations. Pearce had had scores of people studying the matter, but no one had come up with anything.

The signification of the trachea being removed represented less of a problem: the killer, who certainly suffered from hallucinations, was preventing his victims from speaking or screaming. The enucleation could be interpreted in several ways: either the murderer could not bear to watch the victims' look of panic, which mirrored his own cruelty, or he was hoping to shield them from the painful truth by blinding them. Which theory was correct? Right now, Emily had no clue.

She picked up her notebook and read her most recent notes. They concerned Linnéa's ex-husband. Not once had he referred to his ex-wife by name. He'd always said 'she', indicating some form of disapproval. Here, the profiler could only agree with Stellan Eklund: Svensson was a narcissist – he'd been so excited when the location of his work studio had been mentioned. Arms crossed, gritted teeth, eyes shaded, his whole posture betrayed the fact that he was a narcissist who had something to hide. When Emily had asked him if she could visit his workspace, Svensson had immediately gone on the defensive, clearly feeling threatened.

However, as things stood, according to Bergström, the judge was unlikely to grant them a search warrant on the grounds of suspicion alone.

She would have to wait. Wait for the next victim.

She picked up the photographs and locked them away, together with her notebook, inside the room's safe. She then quickly brushed her teeth and slipped between the sheets.

Before switching the light off, she opened the small black box she had set down on the bedside table and briefly peered inside before looking away.

EMILY CLIMBED THE STEEP PATH that led to the Holly Bush in three hearty steps. With a nod of her head, she greeted Bridge, the bouncer standing by the door, who responded with a 'Hello Em', his voice rough from years of heavy smoking.

The profiler made her way to the back of the pub and entered a small room to the right. Sitting at a round table was Detective Chief Superintendent Jack Pearce, two foamy glasses of beer of different colours marking out his territory.

'Just in from Heathrow?'

She took off her parka and sat down facing him.

'I just dropped my case off at home.'

She took a mouthful of the black beer and looked at her boss.

'We're still combing through the passenger manifests,' Pearce said, his face expressionless.

Emily slowly nodded her head.

'Look, you know all too well how much work that takes – seven airports in Sweden, and Copenhagen to boot. Are you aware of the number of flights connecting London to Sweden and Copenhagen in a week? That's a hell of a lot of names to check up on; it takes time.'

The profiler kept on sipping at her Guinness as if it were a vintage Bordeaux.

Pearce leaned back and continued, now in a lower voice: 'For now, we haven't found anything. No one close to Linnéa appears on any of the passenger lists. And all the alibis are solid: Alba and Paul

Vidal were in London, as was Alexis Castells. Peter Templeton was in Lausanne and Anselme in Berlin. We've checked the flights departing Lausanne and Berlin for Scandinavia, and they don't appear on any list. So nothing on that front. What about you – anything about the Swedes?'

'Stellan was in Stockholm, alone, and Karl Svensson was at home in Falkenberg, with a young woman who has confirmed his alibi.'

'Svensson was close by. Eklund could have made the journey by car.'

'The same applies to our London friends. They could even have taken a ferry to get to Sweden.'

'I know, Emily. I know.' Pearce downed some more of his lager. 'Stellan Eklund is Bergström's brother-in-law, isn't he?'

She nodded silently.

'He's the ex-copper?'

A similar gesture.

'Do you think he was Linnéa Blix's lover?'

Emily's head began to move.

'Please, Emily,' begged Pearce, 'say something. I'm not into sign language.'

'No, I don't think he was Linnéa Blix's lover,' she calmly answered, looking straight into his eyes.

'Have you got time for a bite?'

'I'm not hungry.'

Pearce finished his beer and rose. He waited for Emily to slip her parka on, and then followed her out of the pub. There was a slight drizzle, and they walked silently through it to Hampstead High Street, where Pearce had parked his car. Saying their goodbyes, Emily walked home to Flask Walk, just a stone's throw away.

Once her front door had closed, she leaned back against it, slipped a hand into her pocket and took out the little black box. She opened it, stared inside it for a few minutes, then closed it again and lowered it to the sideboard, next to her keys.

Now, she was hungry.

A STRONG WIND had cleared the sky of clouds and it was now lit with an almost summery glow. Delighted to be able to shed their umbrellas, Londoners crowded the streets of the West End, taking advantage of the more clement weather.

Alexis had installed herself at Hush's heated terrace, just a few steps away from Alba's office. She waved to her friend, who was cautiously making her way down the gentle but still-wet slope.

Joining Alexis at her table, Alba hooked her handbag over the back of the chair and unbuttoned her coat. 'I'm just getting away for a quick snack and everyone looks at me like I'm decamping to the end of the world, can you imagine?' She sighed loudly. 'How about you? Are you OK – not too tired?' She took a grissini stick from the bread basket.

'All fine. I had Peter on the phone this morning. It's a good thing he's able to stay at yours for a bit.'

'My God, it's awful, just awful, this whole story … He's totally wrecked. Paul encouraged him to get back to work. I'm not sure that was the right thing to suggest, but then … We couldn't just let him stay in the flat he shared with Linnéa. It was absolutely out of the question.'

Alba raised a forefinger in front of her face for a moment, as if she was pausing a metronome. Seeing her sign, the waiter came over to take their order. They both chose a burger with chips, with Diet Cokes to wash them down.

'Any news about the investigation?' Alba continued, nibbling away at another grissini.

'No,' Alexis lied, smoothing out the white serviette folded on the table.

Alba shook her head. 'I just don't get it,' she said, shaking the bracelets on her arm. 'You know that silly expression, "Pinch me, I'm dreaming"? Well, that's the way I feel. It's all so monstrous it feels unreal. I still get the feeling that Linnéa is about to run into my office, skipping along, crying out *"Hola Sangria!"*, the only two words of Spanish she knew…' Alba closed her eyes and bit her upper lip in a bid to hold back her tears.

Alexis slumped in her chair, her back heavy with shame. Her friend was badly in need of a comforting embrace, but she just didn't have the energy. It was as if trying to help Alba would only serve to increase her own burden of sadness.

Alba opened her eyes again and expelled a theatrical sigh. Then began speaking again, loudly this time. 'If you could only see the office, Alexis! People sniffling in every corner; it's unbearable. All these girls who are turning it into their own personal drama and moaning non-stop when they barely even knew Linnéa – it's making me sick.'

The waiter brought their hamburgers. Alba pecked at a few fries with no sign of an appetite.

'Did you know they've told Peter they have no idea when they will be able to release Linnéa's body? She's still in Sweden, you realise. We can't even bury her. How can we be expected to have any form of closure? How can poor Peter ever get over this? Will *we* ever get over it?'

'I don't think anyone does,' Alexis said curtly.

Alba looked up, clearly realising how selfish and tactless she had been.

They both began eating, one mouthful at a time, not saying a word. The silence became as weighty as a stormy sky.

Alexis finally broke the atmosphere. 'What's this you mentioned in your text about a memorial?'

'Little House Mayfair contacted Peter; well, it was Paul who took the call. They want to organise a function tomorrow evening in honour of Linnéa's memory. I wanted to know what you thought of the idea.'

The Little House Mayfair members' club had almost been Linnéa's second home. Alexis had often lunched and dined there with her friend. The last time she had met her, they shared a few glasses of mulled wine there, just before she had left for Sweden.

'It's an excellent idea, Alba.'

An evening to honour Linnéa, in her favourite place, with her friends, her colleagues … and maybe even her killer.

HESS PUSHED HIM through the door and into Block 46.

Exhausted, Erich fell to the ground. The SS officer's baton immediately thundered against his back.

'That's enough!'

A younger voice, full of authority, made itself heard, sharp as a bullet hitting a wall. Erich looked up and noticed a man wearing white overalls standing by a grey steel door at the end of the corridor.

'That will be all, thank you, Hauptscharführer Hess. You can leave number 20076 with me.'

A grimace of contempt curled the lips of the SS officer. He walked down the corridor and handed over the form the Doktor had given Erich at the *Revier*.

'Sturmbannführer Fleischer,' Hess said, with a military salute, and turned on his heels.

With a wave of the hand, Fleischer invited Erich to follow him.

The room Erich entered was as large as the crematorium; its walls were painted white and the floor was covered with brown tiling. A strong smell of formaldehyde rushed towards his nose.

Fleischer stood in front of four shiny dissecting tables. He unfolded the piece of paper and read it attentively. His blond, elegantly slicked-back hair was in total contrast to this room, marked by the presence of death.

'It appears you are in good health,' he said, his pale-blue eyes settling on Erich. 'Well, at any rate, you were last time you were in the infirmary. I see Hess has messed you up a little on the way here.'

He gazed at the bloody, torn, mud-stained rags Erich was wearing.

'You smell of shit. Throw those tattered garments into the incinerator behind you.' Fleischer's chin was pointing to the other end of the room.

Erich turned round. When he had walked in he hadn't caught sight of the oven, the dissecting tables having seized his immediate attention. The oven was small in size, just large enough for a single body. It couldn't compare with the industrial ovens in the main crematorium.

Erich painfully hopped over to the incinerator and undressed as fast as he could manage, as if Hess was still hurrying him along.

'Wash yourself with that hose over there, by the cabinet.'

Frozen to the spot for a moment, Erich stared at the piece of black soap which lay on an upturned bucket. He switched on the tap and sprayed his face. As the water ran over his lips, he opened his mouth wide and swallowed whole gulps of it, pacifying the soreness of his dry throat.

'I said wash yourself. Use the soap.'

Even though the water was ice-cold and his cuts burned like hell, Erich managed to enjoy every single second of this unexpected shower, washing away months of accumulated filth, regaining a semblance of humanity.

'Use the sheet to dry yourself.'

Fleischer's voice made Erich jump. He had totally forgotten he was there. He picked up the sheet, which hung from a stool, and carefully unfolded it. It was white. Clean. Thick.

Leaning against one of the dissecting tables, Fleischer watched Erich dry himself.

'You know it wasn't easy to have you brought here, Erich. Not simple in any way. I was wondering why a brilliant medical student and surgery intern had landed in the quarry, then the crematorium. You should have been assigned to the *Revier*, to Block 50, or at least to the pathology block. But no. Someone preferred to have you sweating in the forest or facing the ovens.'

Erich set the sheet down on the stool. Fleischer straightened his jacket collar.

'You must appreciate the irony of the situation, no? A man trained to save the life of his own kind finding himself having to burn them instead. And I'm well aware you haven't just been burning the dead. The news goes around, you know. It was only last week that I got the answers to my questions. I was dining, in the camp, with Doktor Ellenbeck. He explained things to me. What a truly stupid set of circumstances ... But these are the sort of things that happen in times of war, no? A mistake that can change the course of a man's life ... SS Sturmbannführer Ding-Schuler had offered his colleague sets of paperweights. But your father, Doktor Reinhard Ebner, didn't appreciate the gift. He was even bold enough to become rather angry.'

A knot of pain and sadness tightened Erich's chest.

'I must confess it was a tasteless sort of gift: the paperweights in question were made out of human heads, or at any rate, Jewish ones – mummified, boneless and shrunk by methods once used in some islands in the Pacific, then fitted onto marble stands. So, naturally, when Ding-Schuler learned that Doktor Reinhard Ebner's son had miraculously reached our camp, he was busy arranging the best possible welcome for you.'

A door slammed, probably the one allowing entrance to the block.

'Sturmbannführer Fleischer!' The loud voice echoed through the corridor. The SS always carried such an extraordinary weight of anger in their voices.

'Come in, Hans.'

A wide-shouldered SS officer walked into the room, followed by an inmate pushing a wooden cart ahead of him.

With his finger, Fleischer indicated one of the dissecting tables. One by one, the man pulled four bodies from the cart, then carried them across his back and, avoiding eye contact, delicately laid them out in the centre of the steel tables.

Fleischer indicated that Erich should approach.

Erich moved towards the tables and saw the bodies of four children, all terribly broken following abominable violence. He gazed at the inhuman wounds that had been inflicted on the small boys.

'Thank you, Hans,' said Fleischer.

The officer gave the obligatory regulation salute, then took off at a rapid pace, with the inmate and his cart at his heels.

Fleischer expelled a tired sigh. 'The Reich does not believe in my research. All they've provided me with is this laboratory in Buchenwald and free labour I have to pick from a bunch of weaklings and cripples. It's not as if I'm asking much. Between you and me, I don't give a damn if my assistant is German, French or even Jewish. All I need is someone with the right skills for what I am hoping to achieve here. Now, I have to check if my choice has been the right one.'

Fleischer picked up a stainless steel tray and handed it to Erich. On it lay a scalpel.

'Show me what you can do, Erich.'

ALEXIS DELETED THE PARAGRAPH she had just written.

The afternoon had proven anything but productive. Whatever she did, the words were dislodged by her thoughts; like a swarm of bees hounded from their hive, they scattered erratically, unable to organise themselves. They converged in the direction of Torsviks småbåtshamn and the photographs of Linnéa's mutilated body, then they fluttered above the chapter she had to write about the teenage years of the killer Rosemary West, only to drift back to Hampstead and the bodies of the two children buried in the woods, so close to where she lived.

She shook her head from side to side in an attempt to banish the parasitical images and distractedly picked up the cup standing by her laptop. She grimaced as she swallowed a mouthful of the cold milky tea, and rose irritably to walk to the kitchen to warm up the drink yet again.

If only she could switch off and ignore all these irrelevant thoughts that were laying siege to her mind. But she couldn't help herself experiencing a terrible and unhealthy obsession with the murders that had taken place around her. It was as if thinking about them, and perhaps assisting with the investigation, she would ultimately be able to leave behind her the sorrow and the pain caused by the loss of her friend.

She went back to sit at her desk, the cup of now-steaming tea held in her hand. She read again the pages she had written in the morning, consulted her notes and closed her eyes in frustration. She wouldn't be able to write any more today.

There was no alternative but to allow her thoughts free rein.

Following a day when the sun sat in a sky of cerulean hue, he didn't expect a starless night. Compact. Opaque.

As early as dusk, he picks up his equipment and goes for a stroll.

Darkness had already taken hold of Hampstead Heath an hour ago and the humid cold runs through his running gear, turning his thighs to ice.

He enters the park from the north-east, near Highgate, and begins to run like all the other determined joggers, hood down over his face, ergonomic bottle in hand. Few people venture into the woods on such a dark night, but he has no wish to take unnecessary risks.

In the initial weeks following the discovery of Cole's body, Scotland Yard posted staff close by the scene of the crime in the hope of catching him, should he return there to pay Cole and Andy a visit. He calmly installed himself, unseen, for hours on end, just yards away from the plodding cops who were supposed to keep an eye on the area. Not for a second did the idiots suspect his presence. They neither saw nor heard anything. All he had to do was wait until they gave up their vigil to begin his recce again.

He stops behind a line of thick trees, takes his night-vision binoculars from his backpack and raises them to his face. Tomorrow he will be bringing his fresh little one along, but he hasn't yet decided where he will bury him.

He zips up his bag and gets on the move again. He's going to treat himself to a small visit. To please himself. He makes his way through the bushes, steps round two enormous tree trunks draped across the ground and cautiously descends the muddy path snaking its way to his right. He stops behind two leafy trees, just twenty metres away from Cole's grave.

Of course, he would rather the small boy was still where he left him, peaceful and quiet. Gazing down at his burial place, outlined by the white-and-blue police tape, is terribly exciting, nevertheless. His grave looks like a stage. A grandiose stage with the Y-shaped trees leaning against each other, springing from the earth like titans, reaching up to tear at the sky. A crown of spines for his defunct little prince.

All of a sudden, his heartbeat accelerates wildly, banging against his chest like a prisoner struggling against the bars of his cell. Alexis Castells is there, as if admiring what is left of his work, her torchlight slowly washing across the contours of the grave. She's accompanied by another person whose face he can't see, hidden under a loose hood. She, too, is gazing at the resting place of his treasure.

Excitement courses through his body, dilates his pupils, hardens his sex.

He will tell the Other of the interest he is stirring up. He will tell him how much his work is appreciated. Maybe then he will be allowed to continue his journey in peace.

THE FREEMASONS ARMS was crowded, hushed conversations and muted laughter just about reaching Alexis' ears. The sandstone fireplace and bruised leather fabric of the chairs gave the pub the feel of a comfortable and welcoming country cottage.

Alexis set the two glasses of Mouton Cadet and the potato crisps down on the low table. She opened one of the packets, offered it to Emily, who turned it down with a shake of the head, and began to chew indifferently on the crisps.

Two hours earlier, having exhausted every single scenario, she had resolved to call the profiler and ask to be taken to Hampstead Heath and the crime scenes. Much to her surprise, Emily had immediately agreed. She was on her way there herself, and had even suggested she come round to pick Alexis up.

Alexis had never envisaged going there after dark, but there was no point in being awkward. She'd dressed warmly and stepped into her wellies, in readiness for a trek through the mud, the cold and even the rain, if that regular London companion were to manifest itself again that night.

Equipped with powerful torches, the two women had walked for twenty minutes until they had reached the first grave, where Andy Meadowbanks had been found. Emily had told her the whole story, her light moving between the photographs she was holding and the actual pit. She had gone through a similar process as they stood at the edge of the second grave, that of young Cole Halliwell.

They had then crossed the Heath and come out onto Downshire

Hill. Frozen to the core, Alexis had suggested they have a drink before returning home. Once again, Emily had accepted.

Swallowing a mouthful of Bordeaux, Alexis reckoned she had finally managed to regain her composure. While Emily had been detailing the tortures inflicted on the young victims, Alexis had found she was able to render the horror abstract, concentrating on the technical and factual aspects of the murders. She was also able to keep the seven-year-old images that flashed before her eyes, ugly and painful, at a distance. Her 'investigative' mode was switched on at last and was holding her memories at bay, blocking her emotions.

She looked up. The profiler had set down her glass and was staring at her, frowning.

Alexis again recalled the heat of her hand on her back a few days earlier. A hand that had felt reassuring and motherly, providing consolation and comfort.

'My partner died seven years ago. Almost eight now,' she whispered.

The words had crossed her lips, out of her control. But it felt good to have said them.

'He was investigating a serial killer, and the man murdered him,' she added, her voice flat and unemotional.

She put her hands down on her lap and her eyes moved from one leg to another, as if comparing them.

'It's why I've become so interested in mutilated, tortured, raped bodies, and the twisted sort of folk who perform the mutilations, inflict the tortures and commit the rapes.'

She leaned over and took hold of the glass she had left on the table.

'I can't even pretend I'm being altruistic or have any form of empathy, because I'm certainly no use to the victims. I don't contribute to the capture of their killers, I do nothing to stop these freaks of nature. All I do is write the victims' stories. I suppose you could say my job is to distract people by narrating the pain of others.'

Emily kept on staring at her, her forehead creased.

'Don't get me wrong,' Alexis continued, her tone almost sarcastic, 'I know my curiosity might seem unhealthy, but I think it acts as a balm for my own pain. I guess I'm no great representative of the species, Emily: I wallow in the unhappiness of others to forget my own.' She attempted a thin smile. 'Well, "forget" might be the wrong word. Things just heal a little, for a few hours, and that's good enough. I don't believe I can ever truly forget.'

ERICH OPENED his eyes.

A fetid, unpleasant smell reached his nose. He looked around. His senses seemed to be failing him.

He was no longer sharing his bunk or his blanket with anyone. No neighbour was squashed against him, no feet rubbed across his face in the night. No cries of pain and agony. No longer the awful sound of rumbling, diseased stomachs. Solitude and quiet. A soft form of silence in which he sheltered for a few seconds more every single morning.

The first few days he had woken up in a cold sweat of guilt. Josef and Alain must believe he was dead. His two former comrades, along with the thousands of other damned denizens of Buchenwald, were still mired in the daily hell from which he had miraculously escaped.

He glanced at the alarm clock Doktor Fleischer had given him: 04.40. He rose, folded the blanket and stowed it away on the floor beside his straw mattress. He picked up his trousers and shirt, which he now washed once a week and dried next to the stove, and slipped them on.

The day following his arrival in Block 46, he had shaved his head and pubic hair to get rid of the lice. The hair on his arms, in his armpits and on his legs had not grown back since it was first shaved off back in July. His body no longer itched. And he smelled clean. Every night, around midnight, when the Doktor left the block to return to the quarters reserved for the SS, Erich washed himself with the hose. Using soap. Particularly his hands. The blood he dipped them in most of the day was beginning to colour the skin around his nails, turning it a pale shade of brown. After washing, he dried himself by the stove, which was kept working day and night to ward off the polar cold that now reigned over Buchenwald.

Every day, after he rose and before he went to bed, Erich had developed the habit of peering briefly outside the door of the block, shrouded in his blanket. He breathed in the cool air for a quarter of an hour, in order to relieve the pain in his lungs, which were becoming affected by the formaldehyde fumes. This week, however, he had not done this. The wind was so fierce he could have caught his death.

Slipping his shoes on, he realised he hadn't seen a glimpse of the sun since October. Its pale light breaking against the whitewashed windows was barely recognisable.

He sat by the stove and slowly breakfasted on the piece of stale bread he had set aside from the previous night's dinner. The size of his food portions had changed: now he ate at midday as well as at night, and was even allowed a bowl of real coffee. He was given a square of margarine every day and drank from the hose whenever he felt like it. He had suffered terribly from thirst before, and the pleasure he now took from drinking was still as intense as ever, even after two months spent inside Block 46.

Doktor Fleischer had laid down the rules on the day of his arrival, after he had passed his 'exam'. This entailed Erich performing autopsies on three bodies while answering Fleischer's specific questions. The children's skin was still warm to the touch, and Erich had felt as if the shadow of death was spreading across their bodies while he worked. He had never conducted an autopsy on a child before, and had to keep careful control of his movements. Doktor Fleischer had insisted on tidy, regular incisions. Erich had only managed to maintain his concentration by thinking of his own survival. It was just another test. An opportunity. With every movement of the scalpel, though, he had felt the passion that had animated him back at the hospital in Munich. Despite the terror he felt, the hazy memories of his craft carried him through the exam.

As he began to work on a fourth child, however, the little boy had opened his eyes. Erich had briefly seized up, and Doktor Fleischer, who was as surprised as he was, had agreed to spare the child. The lively little brat was now serving them dinner. His name was Theodore. *Theodoros*, the gift of God.

That same day, Hans, the Doktor's SS guard-dog, had informed Erich what his work timetable would be. He would be working seven days out of seven, from 5.30 to midnight, in order for the research to progress as quickly as could be managed. The Doktor had a straw mattress and a blanket brought over and, to Erich's amazement, had allowed the stove to purr all night.

Now, Erich had even reached the stage of allowing himself a few liberties, such as the brief morning and evening excursions outside to breathe in the fresh air, or the use of the second WC located by the entrance door. The Doktor must have been aware of these, but said nothing. Many things worked that way with him.

Erich chewed and swallowed his final mouthful of bread. He then wetted his forefinger with saliva, picked up the remaining crumbs that had fallen to the ground and tasted them with his eyes closed.

The work wasn't physical and his nights were better, so his body was regaining its strength. He felt less tired, more alert. But hunger remained. It twisted his stomach and cramp regularly paralysed his muscles. He couldn't afford to waste a single breadcrumb. It would be another seven lengthy hours before he could ingest anything else again: lunch was brought along around midday and dinner at 18.00 sharp.

Erich ate and slept on the floor, in the room where they worked, next to the cadavers laid out on the dissecting tables. The smell of formaldehyde masked all the other putrid odours lingering around the block, and allowed him to digest his rations without experiencing too much nausea. Doktor Fleischer took his meals in the adjoining office. Erich could smell their unctuous odour as he swallowed his turnip soup. Meal breaks lasted twenty to thirty minutes, depending on how many despatches from the Party or from Herman Pister, the Buchenwald KZ-Kommandant, Doktor Fleischer had to respond to.

'Erich!'

He heard the Doktor's voice in the corridor, immediately followed by the sound of the door slamming. He entered the laboratory in a hurry, holding his coffee thermos in one hand.

'The time has come for me to show you what I'm hoping to achieve here. Follow me.'

FOR HALF AN HOUR already, Alexis had been shaking hands and greeting people with at least a semblance of warmth. The guests would share their anecdotes about Linnéa, moving between tears and laughter, and washing them down with sips of champagne. The atmosphere was light-hearted and jovial, just as her friend had once been.

She was struck by the notion that all this jollity might not be in the best of taste. The newspapers had provided some clues as to the degree of violence the death had involved, but every single person here appeared to be ignoring it. Only Peter, Alba, Paul and she knew the true extent of Linnéa's torture.

Alexis noticed Emily making her way through the throng of guests. Cleanly parted in the middle, her straight, brown hair fell like a shroud across her shoulders and all the way down to her elbows. The profiler had switched from her practical sports gear into a black T-shirt and skinny jeans tucked into a pair of laced-up boots. Random eyes turned towards her, attracted by the compactness of her body.

Emily stopped to contemplate one of the portraits of Linnéa hung on the wall of the private members' club. Alexis was about to join her when Alba grabbed the microphone and, with a nod of the head, beckoned Alexis over. The young woman apologised to the people around her and joined her friend by the grand piano at the other end of the room.

Emily took advantage of this to step through to the bar, where she sat herself down on a free stool. She hadn't expected so many people to attend this celebration evening. She'd thought there would be around thirty at most, but there were at least a hundred or so listening to Alba Vidal's speech. It didn't make her task any easier.

She quickly scanned the crowd. She recognised Peter Templeton from the photos she had been given. His face downcast, he stood between a man manically tearing a paper napkin to pieces – this was Paul Vidal – and another stocky character with unreadable features and white hair – Richard Anselme, the jeweller.

After finishing their short speeches, Alba and Alexis joined the three men. Emily slid off her stool and made her way through the crowd, sorry Pearce couldn't be with her now. There were four people here worth investigating and alone she was bound to miss some details.

'BIA Roy,' she announced, shaking Peter's hand firmly. Ninety-nine percent of the population had no idea what a 'BIA' was, but the authoritative tone she used was enough to silence anyone.

Peter nodded back at her, his eyes begging Paul Vidal for help.

'I'm investigating your partner's death. I'm sincerely sorry for your loss, Mr Templeton.'

'This evening is a celebration of Linnéa Blix,' Vidal complained. 'Can't your investigation wait until tomorrow?'

'I'm not investigating, Mr Vidal,' she said, smiling in apology. 'I've just come to introduce myself and offer my condolences. That's all.'

Emily briefly glanced at Alexis, who was standing back, allowing her the floor. She noticed Anselme's lips almost curling; the jeweller instantly concealed his reaction by simulating a cough.

'Paul, please,' Alba intervened, laying a hand on her husband's arm.

Vidal immediately stepped back.

Emily was about to press on with the conversation when her phone buzzed inside her jeans pocket. It was Pearce. She excused herself and took the call.

PEARCE LIFTED THE BLUE-AND-WHITE plastic tape to allow Emily out.

'Do you think he was in a hurry this time, or maybe was interrupted?' he asked.

She took off her mask, her cap and the latex gloves, her eyes still firmly fixed on the body of the small boy lying across the muddy piece of ground.

This time, the killer had failed to bury his victim.

'I think he's just getting bolder.'

She stepped out of her protective outfit, rolled it up, threw it into the black bin by her side and looked around her.

The third grave in the serial killer's own little London cemetery was now crawling with cops and technicians. The teenagers who had stumbled across the corpse stood waiting just ten metres away. They had initially thought it was some form of prank and had contaminated the whole crime scene with their footsteps, and then with their vomit, when they realised it really was a corpse lying there.

'It's too busy.'

'I know, Emily.' Pearce closed his eyes and rubbed the end of his nose. 'And it's going to get busier. One of the youngsters who discovered the body is the daughter of Geri Plummaker – you know, the morning-show presenter on ITV? It's only a matter of time before the place is crawling with journalists. And, to cap it all, Hartgrove will soon be here. He wants to meet you.'

'All three graves must be kept under watch.'

'We're doing that, Emily. One man is assigned to each crime scene, hidden somewhere close in the bushes. We've had them there for three weeks. But the killer hasn't shown himself.'

'He did return, but your men didn't see him.'

Emily squatted down, opened her rucksack, took out her bottle of water and drank almost half of it in one go.

'BIA Roy?'

She looked up. Leland Hartgrove, the new head of the London police force, stood before her, his crisp uniform all sharp creases.

'Commissioner,' Pearce said, shaking hands with him.

Emily straightened up and did the same.

'So, where are you at, Miss Roy? I've already been contacted by journalists from the *Guardian* and the *Daily Mail*. With the press now involved, things are going to get complicated.'

'Haven't you read my reports?'

Hartgrove's eyes opened wide. Pearce, stunned, formed an O with his pursed lips.

'No, Miss Roy, I was busy perusing page three of the *Sun*,' Hartgrove replied, his voice quite steady. 'So where are you at?' he repeated, his tone severe.

'Nowhere.'

Pearce threw a deadly look at Emily. She completely ignored it.

Hartgrove nodded, a half-smile appearing across his lips.

'Do you think it's the same man in all three cases?"

'As far as the London victims are concerned, yes.'

'You don't believe he also killed Linnéa Blix?'

'I don't know.'

'You think there might be two killers?'

'I'm thinking a lot of things, but, right now, I'm not certain of much.'

Pearce threw a nervous glance at Hartgrove.

'So, why don't you share your thoughts and any certainties with us, Miss Roy?'

Emily looked straight into the commissioner's eyes. 'The London killer is a man between thirty-five and forty-five years old. Athletic, cultured. Organised. Meticulous.'

'I know this already from your rep—'

'The degree of sophistication of his murders – that is to say how the victims are chosen and carefully hunted down; the instruments he uses to mutilate the bodies and then how he gets rid of them; the precision of the incisions and the ablations and subsequent cleaning of the bodies – all demonstrates we are dealing with an accomplished expert, who has been practising his art for some time. The ablation of the trachea confirms this particular point: he's been torturing and killing people for a while and can no longer bear to hear his victims cry out with fear and pain. The London victims are the first he has displayed and is sharing with the world. I predict the frequency of the murders will increase. The next victim in Sweden will reveal more about him or them.'

'Why in Sweden?'

'Because that's where it all began.'

Emily pulled the rucksack onto her back and moved away between the trees.

Hartgrove smiled as he shook his head and gave Pearce a friendly pat on the back.

'I don't know how yours feel after all these years, Pearce, but she sure as hell busted my balls there in five minutes flat. Good luck, and keep me in the loop.'

New Scotland Yard, London
Sunday, 19 January 2014, 09.00

PEARCE YAWNED LOUDLY as he stood in the lift. He hadn't had much sleep. He hadn't got home until 1.30, and had been woken at 5.00 by an overzealous colleague in a rush to advance the investigation. He'd taken a quick shower, slipped on a suit, jumped into a cab and arrived back at the Yard before six in the morning, having only left the previous evening at 21.30 to visit the woods at Hampstead where their third London victim had been discovered by a group of drunken teenagers.

He walked down the empty corridor and stepped into his office to pick up some documents. Once again, his gaze confronted the photographs pinned all over the wall. The horror of it all was a wound to his soul.

He piled up three folders and swiftly left the room.

This was like fighting the Hydra: as quickly as they put a killer behind bars, monstrous new ones emerged.

He went down a flight of stairs, crossed the corridor and found Emily waiting in front of the interview room. He opened the door, letting her go ahead of him before he stepped inside.

Wearing an anthracite grey tweed suit and a midnight-blue tie, Richard Anselme was sitting with his legs crossed, gazing at the walls as if a set of invaluable paintings was displayed there.

'Mr Anselme, this is Miss Roy. I'm DCS Pearce.'

'I already know Miss Roy. We met yesterday evening.' Anselme leered at Emily. 'What does "BIA" stand for, Miss Roy?' he went on.

'Behavioural Investigative Advisor. I'm a profiler,' she replied in a formal tone.

The jeweller nodded, giving her a rictus smile.

Emily and Pearce sat down facing him.

'Mr Anselme,' Pearce took over, 'your name was found on a flight manifest of passengers travelling between London and Gothenburg a few days prior to Linnéa Blix's murder.'

Although his posture didn't change – relaxed to the point of provocative – Anselme remained silent.

'Can you tell us why you went to Sweden?'

'Business.'

'Did you meet Linnéa Blix while you were there?'

'Of course.'

'When?'

'I can't recall the dates precisely. You'd have to check with Paula, my secretary.'

'Approximately?'

'Two or three days after I arrived there.'

'So it could actually have been on the day of her death,' Pearce added, with a touch of mischief.

'How would I know?' Anselme replied abruptly, his lips tight.

'What did you get up to together?'

'We attended an evening function.'

Emily briefly frowned. Hadn't Alexis referred to Linnéa Blix's sojourns in Sweden as 'retreats'?

'Where?'

'Gothenburg, but I can't remember the name of the place.'

'What type of function?'

'Cocktails, canapes, pretty women.'

'At someone's home?'

'No. In a club.'

'Did you leave together?'

'No. I left before she did. I had a plane to Berlin to catch the following morning.'

'What time did you leave the club?'

'I don't know. Probably after midnight.'

'Is there anyone who can confirm all of this?'

Anselme wetted his lips. 'I can't provide you with any names.'

'What time did you see Linnéa for the last time?'

'I have no idea. I had better things to do than to check my watch.'

'There was no incident, argument – anything of note?'

'Not that I know of.'

'Do you often travel to Sweden, Mr Anselme?'

'It happens, yes.'

'Gothenburg? Stockholm?'

'All over the place.'

'Was that the first time you met up with Linnéa in Sweden?'

'No. If we happened to be in Sweden at the same time, we generally arranged to see each other.'

'And what happened during these meetings?'

'We had dinner, went out.'

'In Falkenberg?'

'No, always in Gothenburg.'

'Have you ever visited her place in Falkenberg?'

'No, never.'

'Were you lovers?'

The jeweller burst out in loud laughter as he straightened his tie. 'If only!'

'When did you see her for the last time, Mr Anselme?'

'That evening.'

'What were the last words you exchanged, what did you talk about?'

'As I left the function, I wished her well, hoping she would enjoy herself.'

'What sort of mood was she in that evening?'

'She appeared quite vivacious.'

Emily noticed the eyes of the witness lighting up with a touch of amusement.

'One final question, Mr Anselme…' Pearce examined his notes.

There was a knock at the door, it opened and a man with short blond hair looked in. The DCS immediately fell silent. Emily continued staring at the jeweller, keeping her attention on him.

'Yes, Durham?' said Pearce.

'Logan Mansfield's mother is here, Sir.'

Richard Anselme adjusted his shirt collar and smoothed out his expensive jacket.

'Good, thank you, Durham.'

'Mr Anselme, we'll leave you with Inspector Andrew Durham. He will ask you some further questions so we can trace Linnéa Blix's whereabouts prior to her death. Thank you for coming to see us.'

'The pleasure was all mine, BIA Roy and DCS Pearce,' the jeweller replied, a note of irony in his voice.

Buchenwald Concentration Camp, Germany
February 1945

ERICH STILL WOKE UP with nightmares of the dreaded roll calls lingering in his mind. Some of the inmates feared it even more than the day's exhausting work, as so many of them ended up dying at the evening call.

At breakfast, Doktor Fleischer had informed him that yesterday's early-morning roll call had lasted nineteen hours. Nineteen hours. Three inmates were missing, so the SS had taken turns to count and recount the prisoners. During the night, the thermometer had fallen to minus 7 degrees.

Erich knew that his erstwhile companions, cold coursing through them, would have no way to warm up their numbed bodies; they would have had to remain standing, motionless lest their skulls be assaulted by boots or blackjacks. If it had been raining or snowing, they would have been wet to the bone. Some blocks didn't even have a stove, so there would have been no opportunity for their rags to dry once they had been allowed to break rank, and they would have been obliged to dress in them again, still wet. The weakest amongst them, those who had not succumbed already to the infernal roll call, might now be on the way to dying of pneumonia.

Since his arrival in Block 46, Erich had escaped the two daily roll calls. The Doktor had obtained his exemption. Every day, he signed a document confirming that Erich was by his side. Hans then handed it over to the Kommandantur.

Erich pushed his two blankets aside. He dressed, drank some water from the hose and set to work.

By selecting him as his assistant for his research work, Doktor Horst Fleischer had changed the course of his life. Erich had emerged from the larval state in which he had laid dormant since his arrival in Buchenwald. He no longer just put one foot in front of the other, thinking only of survival: he was now part of a grand project. Something larger than anything he had ever been involved in.

Some months earlier, the Doktor had ordered him into the room adjoining his study. Erich had been rendered speechless by what he was allowed to witness. He had so often been told that the so-called Nazi medics were imposters, barely able to handle a stethoscope … Erich had told the Doktor how his research would change the world and how honoured he was to be chosen to partner him in his mission. The Doktor had been visibly touched by his words; Erich had seen the sincerity in his eyes. He'd even briefly smiled at him and given him a gentle tap on the shoulder.

'Good morning, Erich.' Fleischer set down two jugs of coffee and some buttered slices of bread on the shelf he had installed by the dissecting tables.

'Good morning, Horst.'

They each filled a mug and paid a visit to the room where the bodies were kept. Doktor Fleischer had explained why he had chosen only to work with the bodies of children: aside from the fact that their organs and tissues were in perfect condition, they deserved a share of eternity.

Erich followed the Doktor through his morning inspection. For about twenty minutes, they examined each respective body, noting what hadn't worked and what could be improved. They then wolfed down their breakfasts and set to work again.

'Have you given any thought to my proposal?' Erich enquired, without looking up from the thigh he was dissecting.

The Doktor had asked Erich to call him by his first name, but it wasn't an easy habit to acquire.

'Which one?'

'The one concerning my friends, the medical students.'

'You mean the Norwegians? The ones who were helping you with your Scandinavian language skills – preparing you for your new life in Sweden?' the practitioner commented with a wry smile. 'Yes, I've thought about it. And I don't believe it's a good idea. Why show them our research? The two of us work perfectly well together, you see, and we've made such progress already. The more there are of us, the more complicated it all becomes. And I don't wish to run the risk of them getting hold of our results and taking them to Ding-Schuler or Ellenbeck.'

The Doktor was right, Erich thought; they had to remain on their guard. Too much openness was risky.

He nodded his approval, set down his scalpel and stepped over to the formaldehyde pump, which had begun to stutter like a badly oiled engine. He checked the tube he had connected to the child's aorta, then the pump's supply, switched it off, waited patiently for a few seconds and switched it back on again. The noise had gone.

He walked across the room to the vat that stood by the incinerator, checked the state of the two other pumps, threw a quick glance at the body immersed inside it and returned to the corpse he was working on.

They set down their respective scalpels around midday, when Stan, the guy from the kitchens, brought them lunch.

They moved to the office and silently ate their first bites of stuffed chicken.

The first time Doktor Fleischer had invited Erich to join him at his table, they had shared the same meal. The Doktor had asked him to bring his bowl and had filled it with creamy potato gratin. Erich could still recall the taste. He had closed his eyes and allowed the potatoes to melt, butter and cream teasing his taste buds as if with effervescence. He'd been sick a few minutes later, his stomach no longer used to so much food, or its richness. He'd had to increase the quantities gradually and, three weeks later, Stan had arrived with two separate portions of the same food. Two hors d'oeuvres, two main courses and two desserts.

The Doktor interrupted the silence. 'Gross-Rosen has been evacuated.'

'And two weeks before that, the liberation of Auschwitz,' Erich commented, his mouth full.

'Hermann Pister was screaming his head off yesterday evening, at the extraordinary meeting. We have to complete our work, Erich, before we're booted out of here.'

The Doktor shuffled through his mail as he finished his chicken. Erich nodded, his eyes fixed on his plate.

The meal came to an end in an unusual silence. Stan cleared up and left with the remains of the poultry, which he'd no doubt stuff down his throat on the way back to the kitchens.

That afternoon Horst and Erich continued to work in a dull but productive manner. They managed to complete a new corpse.

When little Theodore arrived with dinner, they had just begun to clean a new body. The boy ignored Erich and set the table. Since Erich had begun sharing meals with the Doktor, Theodore had been throwing him hostile looks and no longer spoke to him. How could the little brat ever understand? He could not appreciate that the faith the Doktor had in Erich had provided him with a reason to live again.

AFTER A FEW DAYS of respite, the rain had returned to London with a vengeance. The raindrops felt as large as marbles and crashed against the windscreen, slowing cars down to a crawl.

Sitting in the front of Pearce's car, Emily was thinking back to Anselme and his deceptively relaxed attitude. Pearce had planned Inspector Durham's interruption: he wanted to see how the jeweller would react to hearing the name of the third victim. Anselme had clearly been perturbed and it had taken some time for him to regain his composure, but Emily wasn't sure how to interpret this. Of one thing she was certain, however: Anselme had found the whole process oddly amusing.

Pearce broke the silence, his eyes fixed on the road ahead. 'I spoke to Bergström before we left. He's going to check the information we were given by Anselme. He's sending someone to Gothenburg today.'

Emily nodded her head in approval. She was eager to know more about Linnéa's escapades in Gothenburg.

Pearce turned left. If the robotic voice of the GPS was to be believed, they had reached their destination. He parked in front of number 43, the house where young Logan Mansfield, seven years of age, had lived with his mother.

A uniformed young woman opened the door for them. 'Hello, Sir. Hello, Miss Roy.'

'Are the scene-of-crime technicians still here, Burrows?'

'They left half an hour ago, Sir.'

'What have they found?'

'No evidence of forced entry, but the locks on the two sash windows are broken, Sir, so they can be opened from the outside. And as the flat is on the ground floor, it would be easy to enter through the windows. They found lots of prints inside the house – too many to be of any use, according to the techs. They found nothing outside, though.'

Pearce found it unlikely that the killer, until now so cautious and meticulous, would have used his bare hands.

'There are traces of cocaine all over the place, Sir. The poor kid lived in a real pigsty … To think that some people can't have children while others treat them in such a terrible way…'

'Please keep your opinions to yourself, Burrows.'

'Sorry, Sir, I…'

'Where is Miss Mansfield?'

'In her room with the psychologist. This way, Sir.' Burrows indicated the door to their right.

After knocking twice, Pearce walked in, followed by Emily. The smell of stale tobacco reached out to them.

Katie Mansfield couldn't have been older than twenty-five. She was sitting cross-legged on a bed so large it filled the room. She threw a listless glance at the two visitors.

'Good day, Miss Mansfield, Jack Pearce. We spoke on the phone this morning…'

She silently acknowledged him, pulling the edges of her thick dressing gown across the sweater she wore underneath.

'And this is Emily Roy, my colleague. We'd like to talk to you for a bit.'

She nodded again in reply.

The psychologist left, closing the door behind her.

'When can I see Logan?' the young woman asked in a strangulated voice.

Emily smiled at her, demonstrating some form of empathy. 'Very soon, Katie. May I?' Emily pointed at the bed.

The young mother agreed.

Emily sat on the edge of the bed. They were now at the same level. It should put Katie Mansfield at ease, Emily thought.

'Katie, tell me about Logan. What sort of little boy was he?'

The mother's lower lip began to tremble. She sniffed and clenched her jaw so hard her lips froze.

'I always had problems with him, one after another: he broke plates and glasses; burned a saucepan; wet himself … But at school, they said he was shy – not talkative, according to his teachers. If only he had been like that at home, instead of messing up the place and turning it into a battleground!'

'Katie, can you tell me about the moment when you realised Logan had disappeared?'

'It was the beginning of the week. I'm not sure if it was Monday or Tuesday. The police know the precise day. I work at night, and I don't have anyone to look after Logan, so he was by himself. I didn't have a choice…'

'I realise how difficult it is to raise a child on your own. I'm sure you do it to the best of your ability, Katie. I truly am.'

Pearce wondered how, when faced with interviews, Emily seemed to find just the right words to put people at ease, while, during the normal course of things, she did anything but.

'It's just that … it's easy when you have a husband or a grandmother nearby, or a good job … I've got no one, and I don't have any skills apart from…' Her eyes were fixed on the bed. She lit a cigarette and took a few, avid puffs.

'Katie, what time did you leave for work that night?'

'Around ten or eleven. He was watching the telly. I got back later in the night – I'm not sure what time, probably around four in the morning – and I fell asleep on the couch. I woke up a bit later than usual, somewhere around ten. But as he's usually at school by then, I thought there was nothing to worry about. Then he didn't come back from school. I mean, by five in the afternoon, he still wasn't home.'

Pearce and Emily were aware that the police had found Logan's bag in the front room, which indicated with some certainty that he had been kidnapped from his home between 10 p.m. and 4 a.m. But going over the timetable with the mother might elicit some further important clues.

'I went for a walk around the neighbourhood, because he often likes to play around the square down the road. I've told him a thousand times to always come straight back home from school, but he never listened, always went his own way. Pig-headed. He wasn't easy, I can tell you.'

She stubbed her cigarette out in the overflowing ashtray that lay on the bedside table.

'Anyway, he wasn't in the square. So I waited a bit longer, until, I think, around eight, and then I called the police.' Her lower lip was trembling. She went on talking, her voice shaken by tears. 'But I still thought he'd been mucking about and was afraid of coming home because he thought I'd be annoyed.' She angrily wiped away the tears staining her cheeks.

'Did he ever mention any new friends or teachers at school?'

'No. The only friend he ever talked about was Kim. They were at school together.'

'Did you meet him?'

'Yes – a Chinese or maybe Japanese boy, I'm not sure. Slant-eyed, you know. They were friends since their first year in school.'

'OK,' said Emily gently. 'I think that'll do for now. We'll be in touch soon.'

As they were leaving the flat, Pearce called out to Burrows. 'Call Logan Mansfield's school and get the address for Kim – a boy who was in his class. Pay him a visit and find out if Logan mentioned anyone new in his life recently – a new playmate, a neighbour, anyone…'

'Will do, Sir.'

Pearce exchanged a few words with the two other cops who were present and the psychologist assigned to keep Katie Mansfield company, then he joined Emily in the car.

Face turned to the window, Emily remained silent for the whole journey. Jack guessed what she was thinking about: what Burrows had said about people who were unable to have children and the curse of others who mistreated them. God just hadn't done his job properly…

Emily was thinking about the three London victims: Andy Meadowbanks, Cole Halliwell and Logan Mansfield. Three boys aged between six and eight, all living in the north of the city, all in one-parent families, all neglected and abused, as shown by the bruises and marks on their bodies, their state of malnutrition and the unhealthy environment in which they had lived.

Logan's murder had transformed some of her speculations into certainties. It was the 'rule of three': two similar victims could prove coincidence; three was part of a plan.

ALEXIS WALKED DOWN Duke Street, her steps regular and robot-like.

Unable to control her curiosity any longer, she had called Emily to find out the reason for her hasty departure from the party the previous evening. Emily had held nothing back: a new murder had been committed; the murder of a child.

Alexis hadn't expected the media to find out so quickly: little Logan's mother was already on every channel. However, no journalist had yet thought of linking the case with Linnéa's death.

· This time around, the killer had abandoned the body on the ground, rather than burying it. Alexis was aware that this represented a change in the killer's *modus operandi*; he was now becoming more audacious, more confident, mastering his art. It seemed inevitable that another new body would soon come to light.

Her mobile phone vibrated inside her handbag. It was her mother. She had totally forgotten to call her parents with any updates.

'Hello, Mum.'

'Alexis, I was worried to death! You sent me that text message from the airport confirming you had arrived safely, and since then, nothing. How are you? Are you managing to eat properly? Do you want us to fly over to see you?'

'No, Mum. Everything's OK, I'm fine.'

'Are you outside? I can hear traffic.'

'I'm in the West End, about to have lunch with a friend.' Alexis cursed silently. But she'd already said too much.

'A friend? Who?'

'A friend from Sweden who's passing through London.'

'What's his name? Where do you know him from?'

'He's a friend of Linnéa's. His name is Stellan.'

'Stella? Like the beer?'

'Stellan, Mother, with an "n" at the end. It's a Swedish name.'

'I know that. You don't have to explain it to me.'

There was a lengthy silence on the other end of the line – usually a bad sign.

'Mum?'

'I knew it, I knew it … I knew it was going to happen.'

'What, Mum?'

'That you'd move so far away from us. As if it weren't enough to have an ocean stretching between us! Now, you're about to travel thousands of kilometres further! And into the far north, too!'

'Mum, what the hell are you talking about?'

'You tell me you're about to have lunch with "a friend". I know what that means. Quite evidently, with your talent for adapting to new situations, as your dad puts it, you're the one who's likely to move there and not him come here! It's hard enough to bring up kids with no parents around, Alexis, and I know what I'm talking about…'

'Mother, please; stop worrying so much. Believe me, I'm not about to go to live in "the far north". Look, I have to go, I'm almost there. Kiss Dad for me.'

Alexis sighed deeply as she hung up. The scenario hadn't changed a single bit since her teenage years. As soon as she mentioned the name of any new man, her mother automatically planned her life for the next twenty years. Or, at any rate, she managed to enumerate every conceivable problem that could occur over the course of twenty long and chaotic years.

When she'd been eighteen, Alexis had enjoyed some memorable outbursts, chiding her mother for her 'delirium'. Doors had been slammed, words spoken too fast and the reconciliations had proven painful. Now all she could do was avoid the arguments and pacify her mother. She knew she would think back to these ridiculous exchanges with affection once her mother was no longer around. As she neared forty, she had become calmer.

Alexis crossed Grosvenor Square and turned left on South Audley Street.

Her last meeting with Stellan had been at the 'family dinner', as Lena Bergström had referred to the occasion. An evening that had proven as unexpected as it had been pleasant. She had greatly enjoyed the lightness of the several hours spent with the Bergström-Eklunds. She had learned that the Kommissionar and his wife had two sons, aged twenty and twenty-two, both studying overseas – the eldest in London and the youngest in Madrid. They'd asked Alexis many questions about her work. She'd quickly shattered the myth of the dreamy writer waiting for inspiration to arrive like a bolt from the blue, then frenetically creating for hours on end and even through the night, to get as much done as possible before the muse escaped. Alexis' daily routine, contrary to popular belief, had little in common with the wonderful Carrie Bradshaw's: she did not write in bed, wearing just a nightie, elegantly puffing on a cigarette, fitting her work between shopping expeditions or lengthy two-hour telephone conversations. Absolutely not. Not that Alexis would have minded such a lifestyle.

Alexis walked into the 34 restaurant to see Stellan sitting at the back, talking on his phone.

He hung up and rose to greet her, embracing her, Nordic-style. She enjoyed the intimacy of the contact and parted from him with reluctance.

They sat down, boringly discussing the grey London weather, while they waited to get onto more interesting topics.

As they sipped their cream of pumpkin soup they talked about the project that had brought Stellan to London. One of their Stockholm clients had offered them a renovation project in Knightsbridge. Their first overseas job.

'Isn't it awkward to be working with your older sister?' Alexis asked with a sly smile, as she bit into the tasty wagyu beef fillet.

'We get on remarkably well and Lena is wonderfully patient. She knows how to handle me when I get irritable.'

'How long have you been partners in the firm?'

'As a matter of fact, we took over our father's business. He and his partner did everything together: masonry, plumbing, electricity. Lena became an architect and, to my father's delight, she took over the reins of the family business. I followed some twenty years later.'

'And what is your role in it?'

'I'm the boss!' he joked, tapping his chest expansively. 'I find the projects, plan the work, look after all the different craftsmen involved.'

'But how can you switch from being a policeman to becoming a property developer?'

There was a hint of sadness in Stellan's eyes.

Alexis cursed herself. The few seconds Stellan remained silent went on forever.

'I think the more truthful explanation is that I never managed to get over the death of my police partner.'

'I'm sorry, Stellan. Don't feel obliged to tell me about it.'

He sighed softly, his whole body betraying his inner pain.

'Don't apologise; it's been some time, now. I should be able to talk about it without sinking into despondency.'

He leaned back in his chair and took a mouthful of water, his gaze distant, as if he were trying to gather his errant thoughts.

'My partner, his wife and his two daughters were killed in front of me.'

Alexis was taken aback by the honesty of the information.

'After that, it was difficult to keep on working.' Stellan paused again. 'Linnéa had often witnessed me help out my father on small jobs during the summer, doing the accounts, meeting up with clients. She was the one who suggested I join the family business. I briefly went back to being a cop, assisting my father and sister over the weekend and during vacations. A year and half later, I resigned from the force.'

A buzz sounded over the end of his sentence. As if sunk inside a bad dream, it took them a moment to realise it was Alexis' phone. She was about to silence it when she noticed the call was from Emily.

The conversation lasted ten seconds, at most.

She hung up, excused herself to Stellan and left 34 like a thief in the dark, abandoning him to his pain.

But she had no choice.

He is all over the press, the telly, the radio. Front-page headlines in three of the daily papers. They haven't yet given him a name, but he's out there. The subject of a million conversations.

His body is coursing with excitement. He has never envisaged sharing his work with the rest of the world in this manner. Why? Because the Other condemned him to ignorance. He condemned him to perceive only a particular side of reality. And to see just one side of his personality: the one that appeared in the mirror.

Had he known ... had he known the joy all this publicity would give him, the attention he would attract, he would have freed himself, thrown off the yoke earlier. Which would have made his pleasure even more intense.

The idea occurred to him the other evening, when he came across Alexis Castells on Hampstead Heath. Never before has he experienced such a state of exaltation. Never.

It made him wonder why he had been so intent on hiding what he was accomplishing. On the contrary, he should be showing it off! Reveal it, don't conceal it! He has at last come to understand that his little prince and his crown of thorns had no need for a grave.

The only problem was that the Other is going to be furious. Because, as far as the Other is concerned, it is all a private matter. The Other feels no need to show off what he has accomplished. Nor share it with the world. He takes his satisfaction from the hunt and the transformation.

Killing is just a fastidious act that allows him to proceed to the final phase. For the Other, killing is just a means.

Whereas for him, it's a means to an end.

Falkenberg
April 1945

ERICH PULLED TOGETHER the flaps of the coat the Red Cross had given him. Spring here was the same as winter: a frozen kiss. Nature was barely awakening from its long sleep; trees naked; fields covered in eternal snow.

It was exceptionally cold this year, the waitress in the coffee house where he'd enjoyed breakfast had tried to reassure him. He would soon find out whether she was an incurable optimist or not, he reckoned, as he munched on the cinnamon pastry.

When he reached the beach, Erich immediately forgot the vagaries of the weather forecast. It was so damned beautiful, this beach – even more so than the one his parents had once taken him to when he had still been a child. It had an unexpected, savage form of beauty – curving rocks dotted the shore like the bloated stomachs of sleeping giants.

He'd ventured onto the sand in his oversized shoes, laces circling his ankles. He had then sat down and listened to the sound of the surf, like the romantic he no longer was. The monotony of the constant ebb and flow had triggered his anxiety. He'd risen and walked over to the lighthouse he'd noticed further north, on the coast. Later, he would visit the family-run guesthouse the waitress had mentioned to him. He planned to stay there a while. Then he would find a job and would finally be able to live alone, in his own house.

He blinked. The sound of the machine guns still echoed in his ears.

The madness had begun on the 7th of April, when two hundred SS had attempted to lead fourteen thousand unwilling prisoners from the blocks that Hermann Pister, the K-Z Kommandant of Buchenwald, had wanted to evacuate to prevent the inmates falling into the hands of the enemy. Everyone knew what being 'evacuated' meant: certain death – on the road, in the convoys; asphyxiation, thirst, exhaustion; or being battered into oblivion by the soldiers. The inmates had hidden, provoking the ire of the SS, who had still managed to corral almost six thousand men. On the 8th of April, Josias zu Waldeck und Pyrmont himself, the Waffen-SS General, had arrived at the camp to take over from the now disgraced KZ-Kommandant. Ten thousand inmates had been led away. It was just a question of dealing properly with the remaining twenty thousand survivors.

Then, on the 11th, a Wednesday, everything had changed.

The resistance had managed to hide a quantity of weapons in the coal cellar of Block 50, behind a false wall – a veritable arsenal. Erich had only learned about this later, listening to two German survivors speaking to each other about it. All he knew was that a few hundred prisoners armed to the teeth had taken possession of the command post and the Nazi quarters. The SS had fled in panic, genuinely taken by surprise by the attack, dropping their machine guns to escape more speedily. Out of breath and trembling, Hans had arrived at Block 46 to inform them of the situation, before disappearing himself with no sort of explanation. Large explosions could be heard in the distance.

After that, everything happened so fast, Erich found it difficult to recall the sequence of events. That was how he explained things to the American soldier who had liberated him. All Erich knew was that Doktor Fleischer was dead, his skull shattered by repeated blows from a shovel.

'Did you kill him?' the soldier had asked.

'No,' Erich quickly responded. 'It was another inmate who assaulted him.'

Why the hell hadn't he thought of that first? An inmate killing a Nazi – it was obvious, after all!

Erich had got himself on one of the International Red Cross lorries leaving for the Ravensbruck camp. They were going there to pick up the surviving female prisoners and drive them to a staging post in Switzerland first. Erich had swapped his striped, torn and malodorous uniform for warm clothing, socks and shoes. He had then joined the convoy of female prisoners from Ravensbruck leaving for Sweden.

Sweden would never be his homeland, but he would make it his country.

Erich stopped at the lighthouse and began walking back again, gazing tiredly at the sand and dirt mingling under his feet. He had abandoned Doktor Horst Fleischer, left him lying in a pool of blood. Like a dog.

He let out a savage roar, which was swallowed by the wind. He'd acted like a coward. He should have stayed. Had the courage to stand by his beliefs. Maybe if someone had seen their research, they would have listened to him. Doktor Fleischer should have died a hero, not a victim. The laboratory could have been his stepping stone to glory, not his grave.

His right hand began to tremble. He opened it, palm to the sun in an effort to loosen his muscles. This had been happening a lot since he had left the camp. It was a craving as imperious as thirst. As if his whole being had turned dry. He was missing the research work. He was missing Block 46. He missed the smell of formaldehyde. Missed letting his scalpel glide over supple skin, offering each child a share of eternity, as Doktor Fleischer used to put it.

Erich stopped. Wind whipped against his back, his legs, his face, as if trying to punish him for his stray thoughts. He began to cry.

He was weeping for the man who had entered Buchenwald and had never left.

He wept for the man he had become.

EMILY'S GAZE SWEPT OVER the snow-covered forest. Huddled against each other, the trees reached so high into the sky, their crowns seemed to caress the clouds. Strangled by the canopy, the light barely reached the undergrowth, the dimness making this morning's expedition even bleaker.

The previous afternoon, after returning from Katie Mansfield's flat, Pearce had had a call from Bergström: the body of a young boy had been found in Ljungskile Forest, some one hundred and sixty kilometres north of Falkenberg. His eyes had been enucleated, his trachea sectioned and the letter Y had been carved into his left arm. The profiler and her boss had immediately caught a flight to Gothenburg.

Just an hour before, Bergström had brought them to the scene of the crime. Tomas Nilsson's body had been taken away, but the undergrowth was bound to hold clues about what had had happened.

The Kommissionar had made a list of all the sexual delinquents in the Swedish police records. As soon as the examiner could supply an approximate time of death for little Tomas, they would be able to check the alibis of all those at large. It shouldn't take long, as it wasn't a huge list.

Emily noticed that Alexis was standing back, behind the plastic tape surrounding the crime scene. Frowning, her eyes almost closed, she was attentively taking in the area.

Ever since their first encounter, three years earlier, Emily had been conscious of the inner devils against which the writer was struggling. Their presence was palpable even today, if not more so. In Alexis' case, time had not healed; she was still a captive of the mourning process: she hadn't even reached the anger stage.

Emily had thought that travelling here and following the investigation could well prove a form of therapy for the writer. Whatever Alexis' involvement, hunting down the serial killer who had stolen her friend from her might help heal her wounds. She would know that justice had been served. So, relying on her own intuition and not bothering to obtain Pearce's approval, Emily had proposed that the young woman should accompany them on their journey to Sweden.

The Chief Superintendent had flown into a predictable rage at Heathrow Airport. How could a professional like Emily take such risks and go against procedure? The profiler had quietly listened to Pearce's loud arguments until he calmed down to the point where he had resigned himself to the situation and she knew she was finally absolved.

Pearce gave her a quizzical look, then nodded to Bergström. They had seen all there was to see at the crime scene and were now ready to journey back.

—◆◆◆◆◆—

Just over an hour later, they were greeted at the Falkenberg police station by a nervy Olofsson, who guided them towards the conference room where coffee and *kanelbullar* awaited the visitors.

Bergström joined them a few minutes later, carrying a set of photographs of the victim, which he proceeded to pin up on the board set up by the window.

Even though violence had been a part of his everyday life for over twenty years, Pearce still wasn't able to stomach these kind of pictures. It made him completely lose his appetite. Olofsson, on the other hand, didn't have the same problem: he'd just managed to swallow two of the cinnamon buns, each in a single mouthful.

Bergström turned to his guests and gazed briefly at Emily and Pearce. 'However sad it might be for little Tomas and his family, I suppose that Tomas's murder does advance the investigation, doesn't it?'

'Yes,' Emily said, nodding her head. 'With four similar victim profiles – all male children between six and eight, all from single-parent or dysfunctional families – we can be certain of one thing: Linnéa's murder doesn't fit in; it must have been an accident. Maybe she surprised the killer … or killers—'

'You think there are two of them?' Olofsson interrupted, rocking back and forth on his chair, holding his cup.

Emily continued, not even looking back at him. 'She might have come across the killer or killers by accident, and they eliminated her to protect their identity. She was mutilated in a similar way to the other victims, because these mutilations are their signature, or trademark – they're the way they obtain a specific form of satisfaction from the act of killing.'

Alexis closed her eyes for a brief moment, in an attempt to digest the sheer bleakness of what she had just heard and the awful images it evoked.

'You think, then, that Linnéa might have known her attacker or attackers?' Bergström asked, serving a new round of coffee.

'That's what I'm beginning to think. What with Tomas's murder, we now know that our man or men have two sets of hunting grounds: the north and north-west of London and the west coast of Sweden. Just like the killer, Linnéa moved around the same two geographical zones, so this can't just be a coincidence. I'd say the man she crossed paths with here was a person she knew from London and wasn't expecting to see in Sweden. Maybe a friend or a colleague; or perhaps a neighbour or a tradesman she might have recognised.'

Emily paused, staring at the board and its constellation of photos.

'Returning to your question, Kristian,' she began again, turning towards Olofsson, 'I don't know if we're faced with a man operating alone or a pair of men. Serial killers operating across borders are terribly rare, but they do exist. Much more frequent, though, are tandems consisting of a dominating personality and a dominated one. In the case of a duo, we should make a note of the territorial distribution: one killer in Sweden, the other in London. However, I haven't noted any significant differences between the wounds inflicted on the three London victims and those suffered by Tomas Nilsson. Even the Y is the same size, although its orientation is slightly different on each body. If we opt for the solo theory, however, we have to imagine the huge amount of organisation and major resources required to be able to kill in two separate territories divided by thousands of kilometres.'

Bergström rubbed his forehead with the tip of his fingers. 'In your opinion, then, how should we be interpreting the letters? Might they represent their gender?'

'That would be the obvious explanation, seeing that an X was carved into Linnéa's arm. But I'm seriously bothered by the way the direction of the Y differs with each child…'

'Maybe he's just keen to carve his letter in the arm of each victim and isn't bothered about the specific position?' Olofsson suggested, biting into another brioche.

'I doubt it,' Emily declared. 'We're faced by one or two particularly meticulous personalities. Nothing happens by accident. The mutilations are evidence of fantasies, as distinct as words. A language we have to endeavour to interpret. However, there's another hypothesis we still haven't considered…'

Alexis leaned forward on the edge of her chair, her elbows settling on the table.

'Do you mean that the X on Linnéa's arm might be a Y, with a stroke across it, indicating that Linnéa was not part of the plan?'

'Exactly.'

Olofsson hissed with admiration, while Bergström gently bit his lower lips to stop himself from speaking out loudly. Good God, the guy was getting on his nerves!

'This is all very well, but what do we specifically know about this guy, or his sidekick, if he actually has one? What might his motives be?' the inspector asked.

Out of the corner of his eye, Pearce was observing the Kommissionar. The poor guy was about to explode.

Seemingly unaware of the tension, Emily was about to respond when the Chief Superintendent indicated with a peremptory wave of his hand that he would do so instead.

'Serial killers don't have motives, Olofsson. Their needs are purely psychological. They kill because they have a craving to do so and don't even know why. The problem with sociopaths is that you cannot decrypt their behaviour the way you can with normal people. Everything is askew, distorted; it's all filtered through the lens of fantasy. They are usually manipulative, narcissistic and egocentric individuals. But for now, what Emily is certain of is that our man is between thirty-five and forty-five years old, that he is athletic, organised, meticulous, cultured and not pressed for time. That's as far as the London killer is concerned, if we are, in fact faced with a pair of separate killers. Emily will, of course, expand this profile, but those are the elements that remain uncontested for now.'

'So what the fuck do we do? We can't just jail every forty-year-old man who is athletic, organised, meticulous, cultured and holding a passport, surely?'

Bergström could feel a seed of anger rising up his throat again. Why had he been given such an unholy fool to work with?

'You might as well cuff me right now, then!' the inspector laughed, holding out his wrists to Pearce and winking at Alexis.

Pearce smiled back. 'Don't tempt me, Olofsson.'

BERGSTRÖM'S SECRETARY HANDED HIM a tray graced by a large *smörgåstårta* – a sandwich cake made from layers of tasty bread and various fillings – and placed it in the centre of the table. He served Alexis, Emily and Pearce generous portions, and they all began sampling the appetising Swedish dish.

A pleasant silence now hung over the conference room. There was no creaking of chairs, interruptions or overloud chewing: the Kommissionar had dismissed Olofsson and dispatched him elsewhere to complete some enquiries. The three Londoners might well have been somewhat phlegmatic but, as far as Bergström was concerned, the uncouth inspector had exhausted all his reserves of patience. If he'd had to remain in the same room as Olofsson a minute longer, he would have ended up assaulting him. He wasn't proud of the fact, but the inspector seemed to have a special talent for lighting his fuse.

In Gothenburg, from where he'd been summarily exiled a year earlier, Olofsson had made an enemy of half the local station after standing as a witness against one of his fellow cops. Having been beaten up for this, he'd had to bid farewell to the big city and was transferred to Bergström, who had little choice in the matter. The Kommissionar had initially thought he was inheriting a victim; he soon realised that was anything but the case.

As soon as the meeting with the London officers reached an end, Bergström had sent the detective out to question Tomas Nilsson's friends and family, to find out if the child had mentioned meeting anyone new recently. Bergström knew, however, that in London, Pearce had hit a wall on this front: no newcomers had appeared in the lives of the young victims in the months prior to their deaths.

The French woman, Castells, who had taken care, he noticed, to sit with her back to the board, rose, smiling at Bergström, picked up her empty plate and then his, walked past him and served everyone more coffee. She had been taking notes on her iPad while clearly enjoying the *smörgåstårta*, just lifting her head on occasion as if hearing voices.

The two visitors, on the other hand, had barely eaten their lunch. For folk who enjoyed lamb with mint, and chips with cheese and ketchup, Bergström found them rather picky. He could forgive Pearce, who had spent all ten minutes of the lunch on the phone, and was still talking; but the Canadian had looked at the sandwiches with evident disgust before becoming absorbed in checking her notebook.

The Kommissionar glanced at the Chief Superintendent out of the corner of his eye. He admired the professionalism, sense of calm and humble attitude of the chisel-featured, broad-shouldered man.

Pearce hung up and rubbed his temples.

'I've just been given some information concerning Anselme's alibi. He stayed at the Upper House hotel in Gothenburg and the function took place at the Ljus club. How do you wish to proceed, Lennart?'

'I'll deal with it,' Emily intervened.

The DCS threw a deadly look at the profiler.

We all have our burdens: to each an Olofsson, Bergström mused.

'No problem,' the Kommissionar smiled. 'I have to go to Gothenburg anyway, for little Tomas's autopsy. Do you want to come with me, Jack? I'll drop you off at the airport on my way back to Falkenberg, if you want.'

'That would be perfect. I've also been provided with the final details of the alibis of all of Miss Blix's close friends. Nothing worthwhile, there, I fear.'

Alexis kept silent, but the news was particularly welcome. The mere thought that one of her friends might have been responsible for the awful crimes had been weighing heavily on her for days.

Bergström's secretary moved silently through the room, pushing a cart laden with dusty files.

As she had done in London, and hoping that this time it would prove more fruitful, Emily wanted to check every available file on the disappearances of children over the past ten years, with a particular emphasis on small boys living with a single parent or from dysfunctional families. She was hoping to find some pattern amongst the disappearances that could help narrow her profile; that would tighten the net around the unknown killer or killers. She hoped to read through the transcripts of the interviews with the various families and suspects, and to peruse the police and psychological reports. It was an enormous amount of work to wade through.

Bergström picked up the first bundle and set it down on the table. 'Emily, what gives you the idea that it all began here?' he asked, dividing all the files as if he was dealing playing cards.

She knew her answer was unlikely to be warmly greeted, but she had no other to provide.

'Just my intuition.'

Olofsbo, Falkenberg
Monday, 20 January 2014, 16.00

EMILY AND ALEXIS had left the police station a few minutes after Bergström and Pearce, who had gone to meet the Gothenburg coroner. The Chief Superintendent was returning to London that evening. This was not the only case he was having to work on.

Back empty-handed following his interviews with Tomas Nilsson's friends, Olofsson had silently begun to leaf through the missing-children files. He much preferred spending hours with his nose in dusty forms than having to return to Gothenburg and risk coming across any of his old colleagues at the morgue.

Before leaving for Gothenburg with Alexis to check on Anselme's statement, Emily wanted to interview Linnéa's neighbours again. She was convinced they would have more to say than what she had read in Olofsson's report.

Emily parked the car near the turning into a short tree-lined track leading to the shoreside hamlet, and the two women began walking down the narrow, bumpy path, from which the snow had been hastily swept. At the end of the path, by the sea, three yellow wooden houses stood in a straight line. Thirty metres to the right, nearest to the pebble beach, was Stellan's. Two hundred yards further on was Linnéa's.

They rang at the door of the first house. According to Olofsson's report, it was owned by Anders Lager, an electrician.

A tall, imposing man wrapped up in a green woollen jacket opened the door.

'Good afternoon, Mr Lager. My name is Emily Roy and this is Alexis Castells. We're investigating the murder of Linnéa Blix, working alongside the Falkenberg police. Could you give us a few minutes?'

'Do I have any choice?' the man replied in loud, broken English, looking down at them from his full height. Anders Lager seemed to be one of those people who prefer barking to speaking.

'Of course you have a choice, sir.'

'If you say so…' His mouth twisted as if his lips had been caught on a fish hook. Anders Lager could only be in his late forties, Alexis thought, but acted like a grumpy geriatric.

He stepped back a little to protect his bare feet from the glacial breeze pushing its way past the half-open door, still reluctant to invite the two women in. Alexis could see a laptop standing on a pale wooden sideboard, next to a picture frame displaying a set of images of two men on a beach: Lager and his father, probably, considering how alike they looked.

'Could you tell us something about your neighbour, sir?' asked Emily.

'I've already told that Olofsson guy I didn't know Miss Blix!'

'We'd just like to know if…'

'But I'm telling you, I didn't know her!'

Emily took a step forward. She looked so determined Lager moved back an inch or so.

'Surely you have an opinion, no?'

'Even if I had, why should it be your business?'

'Your opinion, as well as those of all of the people who actually were in contact with Miss Blix, helps me put a picture together of her, a more realistic one than the one drawn by her family and friends.'

'So go and ring the Ahlgrens' door, if you're in search of a realistic picture. They'll have a lot to say about Blix.'

And, with that, he closed the door in their faces.

Emily wondered why he was referring to 'them'. Olofsson had only interviewed a Lotta Ahlgren. Who had he missed? There was no point in asking Lager, he wouldn't open the door again.

They left Lager's house, where they were clearly unwelcome, and wandered down the path leading to Lotta Ahlgren's, which was a stone's throw away from Stellan's. They rang several times, but in vain.

Making their way back, they knocked at the door of Linus and Barbro Byquist, a couple of retired teachers. A small three or four-year-old little girl opened the door. She wore an Indian headdress over her long blonde hair.

'*Mormor!*' she shouted out, '*det är inte mamma!*'

'*Jag kommer, jag kommer älskling.*'

A smiling-faced, brown-haired woman came rushing to the door, wiping her hands on a towel.

Emily introduced herself, explaining the reason for their visit. Barbro Byquist invited them in. She had a strong German accent but spoke perfect English.

The three women sat down in the cosy living room, its wide windows looking out on the snowy fields outside.

With the help of her granddaughter, the hostess laid out brioche and coffee on the small table. Alexis tried one and realised her mother was for once quite wrong: it was soft and delicious, the texture of the sweet bread perfect.

'You can speak freely, Estelle does not understand English. My other granddaughter, on the other hand, is bilingual. Her father is English, like you. If only you could hear her speak! A true little Brit!' said Barbro, with unfeigned pride.

She filled three cups with coffee and one with cold milk, and sat herself down, facing her guests.

'I just can't believe what happened to Linnéa, it's just horrible. Discovered as she was, just so close to us ... It stops me from sleeping at night.'

'You knew her well?' asked Emily.

Barbro's head shook gently from left to right.

'Not really, no. But I knew she was a childhood friend of Stellan Eklund's – the owner of the house at the bottom of the path. You know, the ex-policeman?'

Emily and Alexis nodded in turn.

'A good-looking man, for sure. Makes you wonder why he's still a bachelor. You just never know…'

Alexis felt her cheeks redden, not quite understanding why. She took another bite of brioche, hoping Emily hadn't noticed her discomposure.

'Anna was also very friendly with Linnéa.'

'Anna?'

'Anna Gunnarson, Lotta Ahlgren's sister.'

'Ah, of course,' Emily lied, hoping not to interrupt Barbro.

'Lotta's very much something of an old maid, if you know what I mean. But Anna was married. She left her husband some six months ago and has been living with Lotta since, waiting for the divorce to be finalised, according to what they've told me.'

'Anna works in Falkenberg?'

'Oh yes, she runs the flower store – that large shop on Nygatan, by the bank.'

Emily nodded a couple of times. 'And did Mr Lager know Linnéa well?' she said.

Barbro laughed and was echoed by the crystalline tone of her granddaughter. 'Anders is not someone who makes friends. But he's not a bad sort: his bark is worse than his bite. And he's a first-class electrician: he rewired our whole house four years ago. Not had a single problem since.'

'You told Detective Olofsson that you hadn't spoken to Linnéa since she returned…'

'No … Her house was all lit up, but our paths didn't cross. My daughter saw her, though. I didn't inform the detective as she hadn't told me yet. She only mentioned it when she dropped Estelle off, the day before yesterday. She said she caught sight of Linnéa a few days before she was found … It was in the morning, Linnéa seemed to be on her way back from a walk on the beach. She said that she was off to Gothenburg that same evening, to have dinner with a friend who was passing through.'

Upper House Hotel, Gothenburg
Monday, 20 January 2014, 18.30

EMILY FOLLOWED THE INSTRUCTIONS given by the satnav, moved over to the right side of the road and turned off the motorway. Deciphering traffic signs in this country would always be beyond her, she thought, at least until she learned Swedish.

A few minutes later, they were parking on Mässans Gata, just below the Gothia Towers.

Emily walked across the Upper House hotel's hall and reached the white lacquered counter where she introduced herself to the receptionist. The curvy blonde shed her fixed whiter-than-white smile, fingering the pearls in her necklace as if they were mere beads. She scanned the hall with a worried look on her face, then discreetly spoke into her phone. She barely had time to hang up when a tall, thin woman in her fifties, wearing an elegant silk-and-wool suit, materialised out of nowhere in front of the profiler.

Kerstin Jensen, the hotel's manager, led the two investigators to her office while Emily explained the reason for their presence, carefully mentioning the search warrant that the public prosecutor had authorised.

'We require access to your records to check if a certain Richard Anselme was here and assess what he might have been up to. Likewise for Linnéa Blix.'

Kerstin Jensen froze for a brief moment and nervously dragged the tip of her fingers through her hair. Then she regained her composure and put her glasses on.

'Well … Linnéa Blix has never stayed with us – or, at any rate, not under her own name…' she said softly, her lips curling and her fingers running across his keyboard. 'We do have a Mr Richard Anselme, arrival on the 2nd of January. He stayed in the Grand Executive Suite. I have the specific times he entered his room during his stay. I'll print a copy out for you. I can't let you know when he left the room, though; our magnetic passes are only used to open the doors to the rooms.'

Kerstin Jensen printed the document and handed it over to Emily.

'Do you have closed-circuit TV in the hotel?' she asked.

'Only in the reception area and in the lifts. We retain the recordings for a month, and then they are destroyed. Which particular day are you interested in?'

Emily consulted the document Kerstin had given her, then passed it over to Alexis.

'January the 5th, a few minutes before 2.12 in the morning, and just before 8.59.'

While Kerstin picked up the phone and saw to Emily's request, Alexis studied the jeweller's movements. The function he said he'd attended with Linnéa had taken place on Saturday the 4th of January. That night, Anselme, or whoever was in possession of his magnetic key card, had gone into the room at 2.12. According to his credit-card records, he'd checked out on Sunday morning at 8.59.

Kerstin hung up, turned the computer screen towards the two young women and the recording began playing.

At 2.07, they recognised Anselme crossing the reception hall, holding a tall brunette by the hand. Another man walked into the shot, rushing by. The two men greeted each other effusively, after which they all took the lift together. Kerstin opened a new window on her screen and the trio appeared in a low-angle shot in the lift. The couple were kissing, mouths locked tightly together while the jeweller looked on.

Emily and Alexis had seen enough to guess how the rest of Anselme's evening had developed.

Kerstin, who appeared in no way shocked by the turn of events, opened a third window on the computer screen. It showed Anselme coming out of the lift at 8.48 the following day, without the couple he had been with earlier, rolling a small suitcase behind him. So it appeared he had genuinely spent the night at the Upper House Hotel; he had been telling the truth.

Emily and Alexis thanked Kerstin Jensen and made their way to the Ljus nightclub, where Richard Anselme claimed to have spent the Saturday evening.

━━━━

The club was on Avenyn, in the heart of Gothenburg, behind heavy, red, double steel doors. It wouldn't be open for another hour.

Jon Kasten, the manager, a man in his thirties with slick-backed hair and a healthy tan, greeted them at the bar.

With its walls covered in a gallery of old, dull mirrors, its wooden oak panels and array of low tables flanked by brown leather armchairs, Ljus could have been mistaken for a London gentlemen's club.

'A gentlemen's club in the country of gender equality? Never,' he joked in reaction to Alexis' remark.

'We're hoping to check on the whereabouts of two specific people who might have been here on the 4th of January,' Emily explained, sitting on a tall stool. 'Do you have cameras by the entrance? Or surveillance staff?'

Jon shook his head.

'Neither. We have a bouncer…' He stopped talking and briefly frowned. 'Did you say January the 4th?'

Emily silently nodded.

'Yes…' he said, consulting his mobile phone. 'The fourth; that was our *Nyckeln* evening. The Gimme Group hire our premises once a month for a rather … particular evening.'

'Tell us more…'

Jon blushed behind his tan. 'They organise their own version of a

Falkenberg
February 1948

ERICH GULPED HIS COFFEE down while he enjoyed his *havregryns-gröt* – oat porridge laced with apple compote.

He had missed the sausage and mortadella of German-style breakfasts for a few months, but now he had grown accustomed to Swedish porridge, which he had to admit was more hearty. Often, when his list of patients was too long and he didn't have enough time for lunch, he would add a couple of slices of polar bread over which he had spread butter and topped it with cheese.

He slipped on his woollen coat, his cap and his gloves, and walked out into the snow. Before setting off down the road, he gazed for a moment, marvelling at the carpet of white powder unfurling all the way to the sea, and ignoring the bitter wind that burned his lungs and raged against the quivering branches of the trees.

It turned out that the girl who had served him his first Swedish coffee had been right, after all. Since he had arrived, the winters had been severe but spring always came around, radiant and punctual.

He'd surprised himself by adapting so well. He could now master the language perfectly when speaking, and his written skills were improving daily. And it appeared the Swedes and the Germans shared a form of rigour, which made the organisation of his daily life a cinch.

Erich parked his car outside the clinic, picked up his satchel and got out, to be greeted by snowflakes, floating around like a swarm of butterflies.

'*Hej*, Erich.'

Pernilla's pink tongue was brushing seductively against her strawberry-coloured lips.

'*Hej*, Pernilla. So, what do we have in store for today?'

'There are two patients waiting, according to Janne. The first is an eighty-five-year-old man and the second…' Her long blonde hair swept across her rosy-cheeked face as she shook her head. 'Oh, the second one … it's not a pretty sight, Erich. Not pretty at all…'

Erich walked through a series of doors and entered the room that was reserved for him. He took his coat, cap and gloves off, opened his satchel, slipped his white coat on, and turned towards his two patients for the day.

His eyes opened wide with surprise when he noticed the ghost-like shape spread out on the right-hand bed. He wet his dry lips and swallowed a couple of times. His pulse quickened. He put his hand forward, but then pulled it back and closed his eyes. He would begin with the old man.

BEGIN-WITH-THE-OLD-MAN.

Concentrate at every stage. Slowly, but surely.

He wiped the fresh sweat from his forehead with the back of his hand and turned towards the left-hand bed. The file indicated a death by pulmonary embolism at 2.00 that same morning. Erich pulled the sheet away from the body and folded it at the foot of the bed. He slowly manoeuvred the dead man's limbs to test the cadaverous rigour. He then made an incision in the neck, at artery level, and inserted the cannula through which he would inject the formaldehyde. He then began to massage the ears with the tips of his fingers to facilitate the flow of the chemical through the inert body. He closed his eyes while he kneaded the cartilage. The skin was still supple but the lobes were large and swollen. He continued, handling the shrivelled skin of the face, then moved on to the hands, concentrating on each individual digit. He completed his massage, palpating the gnarled palms of the dead man's body. There was no need to waste time on the other parts of the body as it would be dressed for the vigil.

Erich knew that it would take a long time to have his medical diploma transcribed and authorised. But it was obligatory if he wanted to complete his surgical studies. In the meantime, he'd had to find work. He knew all too well that, without his diploma duly certified, he couldn't apply for any of the positions that were of genuine interest to him. When he had come across the advertisement from the funeral parlour, he'd initially dismissed the idea as something of an insult. A stupid idea. Then, after reflection, he'd found it interesting. Stimulating. Almost exciting.

He'd met the owner, had explained his situation and proposed he should be paid slightly less while he was still being trained. While the medical aspects of the embalming process presented no difficulties, he was quite ignorant of the aesthetic side of the task. But, after a few weeks, the owner had soon allowed him to work alone on the dead bodies.

His first patient had been a forty-six-year-old woman who had died falling from a horse. He could still recall the experience: it had been both terrifying and wonderful. With no one overseeing him, his memory had carried him straight back to Buchenwald. Block 46. Doktor Fleischer. His whole body had buzzed with the same excitement that had animated him back then. He had remembered the coldness of the children's bodies under his hands. Bodies rid of their envelope of flesh.

Erich had dutifully forgotten. He had forgotten about regulating his diploma. The resumption of his studies. He had accepted that his task was no longer to keep people alive. He would rather help them to die.

Erich stepped round the bed in which the old man lay and approached the other one.

He read the file. The patient was six years old. For six, he wasn't very large. And somewhat skinny. His thoracic cage bulged as if it was attempting to flee the body, which, with every passing second, was losing what was left of its humanity. He slid the sheet off the naked body and observed it in silence. Then he allowed himself

ALEXIS LAZILY CLIMBED OUT of bed following seven hours of restless sleep. Unsettling dreams she was unwilling to interpret had followed one after another in a continuous stream, peregrinations that had left a bad taste in her mouth. It was not surprising: the revelations about Linnéa's sex life had disturbed her. It was not for her to judge her friend's tastes, but she was annoyed that Linnéa had never confided in her. Did she give the impression of being a prude? Intolerant? Or both? On the other hand, why should Linnéa have opened up to her? Her sex life was her own business. But with Anselme; really? And participating in a sordid 'padlock' evening, to boot? Alexis shook her head. Matters seemed to be moving too fast.

She took her mobile phone from the night table. There was a message from Alba, inviting her to dinner. Alexis had left London in such haste that she hadn't had time to warn anyone. She'd only, out of courtesy, informed Stellan about her return to Sweden. She felt she owed him at least that, after fleeing halfway through their lunch, just as they'd reached the confession stage. Had a man acted that way with her, his face would have quickly served as a dartboard!

Another message reached her, just as she was moving across the room. It was Emily, suggesting she should join her at 9.00 to visit those neighbours of Linnéa's they hadn't been able to interview the previous day. Alexis replied with a quick 'OK' and went to take her shower.

Deep within herself, she felt a strong need to pursue the investigation. She wanted to be present when they caught, judged and locked up whoever it was that had once again spread death and horror across her path. She had to be there and Emily's presence made this possible. Who would have suspected that the profiler would have proven so cooperative? Alexis was well aware how difficult it must have been for Emily to impose her decision on her colleagues: the way DCS Pearce had greeted them at the airport had been far from welcoming.

Alexis truly didn't wish to know what motivated the profiler to be so accommodating. By now she knew there was no point asking why this particular door had opened; sometimes opportunities presented themselves, then closed just as quickly, of their own accord. She just accepted the fact.

She checked the time. She had a few minutes left to blow away the cobwebs of the difficult night before her meeting with Stellan. She applied a touch of concealer around her eyes and then some mascara. She felt she had no need for blusher: in Sweden the cold weather could be relied on to make you rosy-cheeked.

Wrapped in her padded coat and wearing a pair of *après-ski* boots, she ventured out into the icy air, so much steadier than on her first occasion here.

An appetising smell of cinnamon lingered in the busy tea room. Alexis found the only empty table, by the window, and didn't have to wait long for Stellan to arrive. She ordered a coffee and a saffron brioche; Stellan opted for a prawn sandwich and a latte. Alexis grimaced at the idea of eating seafood for breakfast.

Stellan noticed her expression and burst out laughing. 'You don't know *Kalles Kaviar*? The Swedish version of taramasalata? My sister smothers her bread with it every single morning. Lennart even dips it in his coffee!'

'Thanks, but I'll pass,' Alexis said, grimacing even more. 'The smell of fish when you're straight out of bed is not my cup of tea. I'll stick to your saffron or cinnamon brioches. I've also heard about your *surströmming* – a fish with a pestilential odour, left to macerate in soda…'

'…proclaims a French woman, who takes nationalistic pride in her array of odorous cheeses,' Stellan remarked, with a mocking smile.

'Cheeses are different,' insisted Alexis, biting into her brioche. 'You're going to make me regret defending your food to my own disbelieving mother.'

'I notice you say "food", not "gastronomy".'

'As you said, I am French,' she replied, with a wink.

Stellan raised his arm to catch the attention of the waitress and ordered some more hot drinks. When he spoke in Swedish, his voice had a different tone altogether. It was deeper, smooth as velvet.

'So how come you're tagging along with Scotland Yard?' he continued. 'Are you writing a book about Emily Roy?'

'No … but that would actually be a great idea,' said Alexis. 'Lennart has told you about the latest murder?'

'An old colleague has been a touch indiscreet. Have you known Emily long?'

'For a few years. I met her when I was researching one of my books, actually.'

'Lennart told me she was trained at Quantico and used to be with the Canadian police force. She boasts a hell of a CV, it seems.'

'Yes, she has quite a reputation. Why are you so interested in her?'

The waitress brought over their drinks. Stellan took a few sips of his before he answered.

'She contacted my old boss in Gothenburg, to find out more about the death of my partner and his family. Add to that her interest in Linnéa's possible lover…' He paused and looked anxiously into his cup.

'Were you Linnéa's lover?' Alexis couldn't prevent the words rushing out, as if her lips had caught fire.

He smiled. It was a tired and sad expression.

'No, Alexis, I was never Linnéa's lover.'

Olofsbo, Falkenberg
Tuesday, 21 January 2014, 08.45

EMILY WAS DRIVING SILENTLY, eyes fixed on the asphalt. On the radio, the sound of a cello and a piano playing a jazz duo made her feel rather sluggish. The grey weather outside matched her mood: a barrage of clouds held the sun captive and made the early morning look more like dusk.

It took ten minutes to reach Lotta Ahlgren and Anna Gunnarson's. Ten minutes during which Alexis experienced some peace of mind, without any further dark thoughts invading her consciousness. Just ten minutes. But she couldn't be too demanding, could she?

Anna Gunnarson, an opulent, short-haired blonde with a face full of freckles, invited them into the living room.

'I'm sorry, Lotta had to leave early today. She's had to stand in for a sick colleague. She said she'll call you to make another appointment.'

Emily smiled back at her hostess, who set down a plate of plain biscuits on the table and began to serve them coffee. With her loose jeans, woollen sweater and halting gestures, she looked like anything but a traditional housewife, Alexis noted.

'You speak very good English,' Emily said, to encourage her.

'Our mother is American.'

'Have you been living with your sister long?' the profiler continued, slowly sipping her coffee.

'Almost seven months, now.'

'Did you know Linnéa Blix before you moved here?'

'Oh yes, for over ten years. What a terrible thing to happen. Shocking.'

'As I was explaining to your sister over the phone,' Emily continued, 'we're trying to create a timetable of Linnéa's movements throughout the first weekend of January. We were hoping you could be of help.'

'The weekend she died, you mean...' Anna Gunnarson whispered, eyes fixed on the bottom of her cup.

'Yes. Saturday the 4th and Sunday the 5th of January.'

Anna straightened up and pulled a mobile phone from her jeans pocket.

'Let me see ... the 4th and 5th of January ... No, I didn't come across Linnéa.'

'Do you remember if the lights were on at her place?'

'I just can't remember.'

'According to Barbro Byquist's daughter, Linnéa was planning to spend Saturday evening in Gothenburg with a friend who was passing through. Did she ever mention this?'

Anna frowned then silently shook her head.

'Is there anything you can think of she might have mentioned in passing, and that could be of use in our investigation?'

'I just can't think of anything, no. I'm sorry.'

Emily's mobile phone rang and she stepped over to the opposite side of the room to take the call.

Pensive, Anna drank a mouthful of coffee. She seemed to have forgotten Alexis' presence and was peering down at a corner of the coffee table, her hand moving slowly across her chair's armrest, as if she were trying to caress its ribbed, velvety fabric. Her wrinkled eyes suddenly grew in size, but Emily interrupted whatever had just occurred to her by rushing back across the living room.

'I'm sorry, Anna, but we have to leave. Thank you for your time. Your sister has my details. Please don't hesitate to contact me if you remember anything relevant.'

⋙

A quarter of an hour later, Emily and Alexis were sitting down next to Bergström in the police station's conference room. Richard Anselme was about to be interviewed once more by the Metropolitan Police in London, and Pearce had suggested Emily should observe the interview via a video link.

Inspector Andrew Durham appeared on the screen. He waved to them and explained how the interview would be conducted: there would be no picture in London, so Anselme would be unaware of them watching. However, Durham would be able to hear their comments through an earpiece he was wearing.

Durham left the room and returned a few moments later accompanied by Anselme, whose handmade John Lobb shoes echoed across the concrete floor. He took off his marine-blue coat and smoothed out the creases in his grey suit jacket, looking around at his surroundings with obvious disdain.

'Mr Anselme,' Durham began, 'we believe you haven't been telling us the truth about the nature of your relationship with Linnéa Blix.'

'Really?' the jeweller replied, with a touch of contempt in his voice.

'The *Nyckeln* evenings organised at the Ljus club in Gothenburg are rather … particular … wouldn't you say?'

'So?'

'So, it would have been advisable to let the police know you were hitting the sack with the victim the night of her death.'

'I would quite agree with you, if it were true.'

Durham remained silent.

Anselme shifted in the chair, folding then unfolding his legs. He was becoming impatient.

After three uncooperatively silent minutes he finally spoke. 'I was not "hitting the sack" with Linnéa,' he said abruptly. 'But I certainly enjoyed her company.' The superiority in his smile had now faded and his voice was flat.

'You weren't sleeping with her, but went together to a "padlock" evening?'

'Yes.'

'Was that something the two of you did regularly?'

'No, it was the first time.'

'What time did you see her last?'

'I've already told your colleague that I have no idea. We split up long before I finally came across the key that fitted my own padlock; that's all I remember. I went off to take a look at the other guests; she was standing by the bar, alone, when I left her. Her play partner hadn't found her yet.'

Alexis was startled.

'Her "play partner"?' Durham repeated, equally surprised.

'Yes, someone had planned to meet up with Linnéa at the club.'

Alexis felt a knot tighten in her throat.

BERGSTRÖM WAS BUSY in the kitchen, his mobile phone wedged between his shoulder and his ear.

There were two ways to find out who Linnéa was planning to meet at the 'padlock' evening, but neither seemed to be leading anywhere.

Before leaving for Sweden, Linnéa had informed Anselme she would be coming with someone that evening. The jeweller had then asked her to warn his secretary, Paula, so she could get in touch with the organisers: Linnéa's friend would have to be put on the list to be allowed access to the club. However, there was no way to get in touch with Paula; she'd just got married and was away on her honeymoon.

The other way was to get the name from the Gimme Group, which had organised the event, but they had redirected the Kommissionar to their lawyer, which was slowing matters down considerably.

Towards the end of the afternoon, while they were still wading through the seemingly endless amount of files covering the many child disappearances, the Kommissionar had suggested to Emily, Alexis and Olofsson that they should keep on working at his place, in front of a nice warm fire. Emily had seemed uncomfortable with the idea, but Alexis had accepted on their behalf.

Olofsson, though, had declined the invitation in order to attend the scene of a suspicious-looking suicide. On his way out, clearly confident that Alexis was unable to understand a word of Swedish, he'd mentioned to Bergström how sorry he was not to be able to spend more time with the 'hot French girl'. Bergström found his attitude repellent.

The Kommissionar hung up and turned back towards Emily and Alexis, who were leafing through the investigation files in the living room.

'Bad news: none of the sexual delinquents on file could have killed the little Nilsson boy; they all have solid alibis. And, as for the Gimme Group, the organiser of the *Nyckeln* evenings won't be able to forward the list of participants until tomorrow morning.'

While Alexis carried on sorting through the piles of pages and the photographs, Bergström brought in some *janssons frestelse* – a gratin of potatoes, sprats and fresh cream.

Having completed her own trawl through the files, Emily felt bereft and looked around her. Thinking he understood now at least a little about how Emily functioned, Bergström thought he'd set out something tempting and see if she had an appetite for talking.

'My phone rang just as I was about to ask you what asphyxiation might possibly reveal about our killer,' he said, generously filling his guests' plates.

Just like a feline spotting her prey and getting ready for the chase, Emily's eyes narrowed. 'Many, many things. Asphyxiation is a form of torture. The killer takes pleasure from watching his victim slowly die. Killing a child is relatively easy for a grown adult: all he has to do is strangle him or beat him over the head. Our killer, on the other hand, has opted for a slower and crueller execution method: he first inflicts a strong blow to the back of the head to immobilise the victim, make the kidnapping easier, then drags him back home. As the autopsy has confirmed, this is not a mortal blow. His prey now powerless, he fits the head inside a plastic bag, which he secures around the neck with some adhesive tape, then binds the victim to prevent him from struggling when he awakes. He then sits down and waits. He waits for his prey to regain consciousness so he can witness the suffocation at first hand – the spectacle he craves.

'What makes you think that he watches them die?' Alexis asked. She hadn't touched her food yet.

'The enucleations and the slitting of the throat.'

Emily drank a mouthful of water and continued, her whole body in a state of agitation. 'Once his prey is dead, he pulls the plastic bag away from the face. This is when he is no doubt assaulted by shame: the prey turns into a child again, and thus a victim. His sense of humanity briefly returns and he becomes aware of the sheer horror of what he has done. All of a sudden he is haunted by the spectacle he has witnessed: the child's horrified features, his cries of panic and agony. So, to bring it all to an end, in order not to see these eyes swollen with fear and pain, not to hear the weak voice strained by suffering and terror, he pulls out the eyes and the trachea. The victim is instantaneously depersonalised, turned into mere flesh. He has simply become prey again, and the killer can continue in peace.'

A heavy silence followed Emily's explanation.

Alexis broke it. 'So you believe the actual killing is the apogee of his actions?'

'I'm unsure what satisfies him most. But one thing is certain: his sense of all-pervasive power, and therefore his arousal, reach a paroxysm when he dominates his prey fully. The actual killing is one of those moments. But our own perspective on his killings also provides him with much in the way of satisfaction. The fact that he abandoned Logan Mansfield's body without burying it means he is deriving pleasure from the knowledge he is being hunted down, studied by the police, being discussed in the media. These are all elements from which he derives sexual enjoyment and creates new fantasies. The only thing that bothers me in my profile is the victimology. This killer attacks high-risk targets: children, who he wishes to dominate both physically and psychologically. But he's choosing children already in some form of peril, who are more vulnerable than the average child, which means he wants to minimise his risk of failure, of getting caught. This demonstrates some form of opportunism, even cowardice, and doesn't quite feel right to me.'

It was incredible the way death could make the girl so talkative, the Kommissionar pondered, sipping from his glass of Campo Viejo.

'So the killer must have the use of a large, isolated location where he can mutilate the body at leisure?' he queried, his arm tracing a circle in the air above him with the now empty glass.

'No, not necessarily. A small room would suffice, as long he has access to water. Maybe he's even gone as far as soundproofing it.'

The silence hanging between them lasted a few seconds, as they processed Emily's explanations.

Bergström began to clear the table and brewed more coffee. He filled five cups, and set two of them on a tray.

'I'll just take some coffee to Lena and Stellan. I'll be back shortly.'

Alexis, who was about to begin working her way through the files again, looked up at him quickly. 'Stellan and Lena are here?'

'They're upstairs, in Lena's study. They're working on the London renovation project. They didn't come down to say hello because they didn't wish to disturb us. Come up, if you like; I'm sure they'll be glad to see you.'

Emily didn't lift her eyes from the new file she had begun studying. Having received no reaction from her, after a couple of moments Bergström and Alexis left the room.

Located up under the roof, where the attic must once have been, the study ran along the whole length of the house. Lena had placed her work desk facing a circular window, the copper frame of which was reminiscent of a porthole. Despite the darkness of the night, Alexis could distinguish the sea, like a wilderness of speckles, shimmering under the moonlight.

Lena was sitting at her desk and Stellan was standing next to her, both glancing down at a computer screen. They turned round together to greet their visitors and share a Nordic-style embrace with Alexis. Now accustomed to the habit, the young woman acted as if she'd been doing this all her life.

'You've finished your work?' Lena asked, rolling her shoulders to ease the tension in her body.

'Nowhere near it. We just came up to bring you coffee.' Bergström handed them the tray.

'And the profiler?'

'She's busy profiling. I don't think she even noticed us coming up to see you.'

'Would it bother you if I went downstairs for a few minutes? I'd love to see what your Canadian Sherlock looks like.'

'She's as eccentric as she is antisocial; but quite attractive,' said Bergström smiling widely.

His wife affected to ignore his teasing and the three of them walked downstairs.

In the kitchen, the folders were piled up high on the table and Emily's backpack had disappeared.

The Kommissionar gave Alexis a quizzical look. She shook her head.

They'd left the door to the cage open and the feline had escaped – gone out hunting once again.

Falkenberg
July 1970

AGNETA'S HEAVY BREASTS SWUNG to the rhythm of her riding him. Her breathing quickened. She leaned, one hand on Erich's torso and bucked, head thrown back, her long hair caressing her lover's midriff. Her trembling thighs tightened and she cried out with pleasure. A few seconds later, she dropped down onto the bed across from him and stared at the ceiling, gasping for breath, her body still vibrating in the wake of her orgasm.

Erich pulled up his pants and trousers. She hadn't even given him time to properly undress.

'No, no, no, no, no…' she murmured, sliding back towards him, her eyes predatory. 'You knew what you were getting into, seducing a younger woman. Time to show your worth, now…'

She unzipped the trousers, pushed the pants aside and again began to stimulate his penis.

The girl was a surprising package. She approached sex with no reservations whatsoever and with such transparent honesty that it made the whole experience exceptionally pleasant. A sign of the times, maybe. Agneta must form part of these squadrons of liberated women who used their vaginas as if they were phalluses. While it was somewhat tiring, as he was twice her age and had lost some of his vigour, their relationship was both easy and practical: she had no need for reassurance or expressions of love, which saved him risky lies and calculated flattery. What a change it was from all the other women he had slept with previously. They had all been so damned demanding and needy when it came to affection!

She stretched like a cat, not that it interrupted her endeavours.

He enjoyed Agneta's body. The suppleness and elasticity of her milky skin. The way her flesh had retained the firmness of childhood. Her breasts were too large, but he could live with that. He just avoided concentrating on them when their swinging made them look like udders when they fucked.

All of a sudden, his whole body tightened. Erich closed his eyes and his sperm rushed out, straight into the mouth of his mistress. Again, he pulled up his trousers, in order to distract her from the idea of yet another bout, but she cuddled up to him and almost immediately fell asleep. He remained motionless, savouring the clarity of the moment and the way his ejaculation had briefly heightened the vibrancy of all his senses.

They had known each other for several months and now met a few times a week. Always at his place. One day, Agneta had arrived unannounced and Erich had made it clear this should never happen again. Since that particular episode, she always called him on the phone before coming to visit.

Two years before, following the death of her parents, Agneta had inherited the family house, which she had sold for a small fortune. She had since brought her studies to a temporary halt and was, in her own words, 'searching for herself'. When they had met, she was about to leave on a trip around the world. But she had decided to postpone her departure and instead take life day by day. And, for now, her life was all about making love, as she had once teasingly whispered to him, theatrically biting her lower lip; it was an expression she had probably heard in some movie.

Escaping Agneta's embrace, Erich slipped on a sweater and walked down to his workshop. He would soon have to enlarge the space: he needed more room.

Before setting to work, he lingered over his collection, observing the sixteen bodies with a critical gaze, allowing his fingers to slide over their soft curves. The muscles had perfect definition. He had managed to impart just the right colour – like meat, a perfect equilibrium between flesh and fat. Doktor Fleischer would have been proud of him. The eyes were still an uphill struggle, but he was confident he would eventually succeed.

He put on his overalls and the protective cap, covered his shoes, dug his fingers into the gloves and set to work. He felt happy.

The only negative element in the whole affair was that he had to content himself with whatever happened to cross his path. Unlike in Buchenwald, where Doktor Fleischer could select whatever pleased him, even children, he had little actual choice in the matter.

He had begun his collection the day he had been brought a six-year-old child, dead from leukaemia. What was his name? A French first name … Not that it mattered. That particular day, Wednesday the 4th of February 1948, two bodies were waiting to be transferred to the Gothenburg medical university to be used for autopsy practice by the students. A twenty-six-year old woman and a sixty-nine-year-old man. No one had claimed their bodies and they had been stored in the cold vaults for some time. Oh yes … Antoine, the boy was called Antoine. In order to smuggle out the girl's body, he'd had to conceal it inside the child's mortuary bag, which was scheduled to be forwarded to the undertaker. He had delivered the little one to them but taken the girl's body back to his place.

To initiate her transformation, he had begun by severing her breasts. Febrile, hard with excitement, he'd had to interrupt the operation several times for fear of making a mistake.

Back then, his work environment had been somewhat improvised: he'd used his bath tub and equipment he brought home from work. For a working surface, he'd had to be content with the wooden table from the kitchen, which he'd covered with towels. Since then he'd had the workshop tiled, installed adequate lighting and, of course, had acquired a proper dissection table.

Erich consulted the wall clock. It was time for breakfast. Walking upstairs, he could smell the fresh coffee. Agneta must be waiting for him in the kitchen. He had forbidden her from ever entering the workshop. He didn't like to be disturbed when he was working.

She was wearing one of his shirts and a pair of his socks. Why did women have this ridiculous habit of wearing the man's clothes after leaving their bed? What made them so much more comfortable than their own clothing?

Agneta smiled at him tenderly. 'You got up early. Do you have a lot of work?'

He nodded in reply and sipped from his cup of coffee, still standing up. He was in no mood for small talk. It was time for her to leave so he could enjoy a peaceful Sunday.

She sat down, crossing her legs and placing her hands on the table. Then she looked up to him with a joyful, serene glint in her eyes.

'I'm pregnant.'

The young woman's mouth stretches open, revealing a row of suspiciously white teeth. He smiles back. Visibly satisfied, she continues her monologue, her voice loud and squeaky. The way she is dressed offers no clues as to the contours of her breasts, waist or legs. Below the circular collar of her black dress, she wears a string of pearls, the metaphorical chastity belt of the bourgeoise. It's only when she tilts her head to allow her hair to fall freely that her theatrical pose shatters. There she is, sexually on parade, her long curls sliding across her chest and shoulders like the hands of an eager lover.

Two hours later, her dress has been pulled up to her waist and her knickers are dancing around her ankles as she is gasping with pleasure inside the bar's spacious toilets. He comes, his face buried inside the cascade of brown curls, thinking back to the silk-like softness of Tomas Nilsson's hair.

EMILY UNBUTTONED HER ANORAK, slipped a hand into her inside pocket and took hold of the small black box. She opened it, gazed at its contents for a moment then put it back where she had found it and began her run, listening all the while to the discreet churn of the waves and the squashy sound of her trainers tramping into the snow-covered sand. The torch she was holding lit the beach with every step she took.

The serial killer spoke to her with every act he committed, but she still couldn't interpret his language properly, and the portrait she was forming of him was still maddeningly incomplete. Frustration was eating away at her. The only way to fight it was to find open space, nature. She had to regain her focus. Be disciplined. She had to bring her thoughts on track; like the straight beam of her torch, they had to concentrate on the case and the case alone, not get sidetracked. Which is why, the previous evening, she had fled Bergström's house, where there were too many distractions, too much frivolity.

Back at the hotel, she had come across an interview with Pearce on the BBC. He was telling the journalist that the investigation was making progress, and kept on repeating, as if they were new revelations, the few facts that were already known to the media. No one had yet made a connection between the murders in Sweden of Linnéa and Tomas Nilsson, and those of the small boys in London. Hopefully this would continue.

The glacial cold slammed against her face. Emily quickened her pace until her lungs felt as if they were on fire. The pain coursed through her body, making the whole exercise unbearable. She concentrated on her breathing, which was loud and regular, as she inhaled the heady odour of iodine and expelled cloudlets of warm air through her mouth and nose. Another few minutes and all the questions she was struggling with would loosen their grip on her. They would begin to float freely across her mind, waiting for her to hopefully arrange them into some form of order.

—◆◆◆◆—

At eight o'clock on the dot, after showering at the hotel, she pushed open the door to the police station. She came across Bergström in the corridor, holding a mug in his hands.

'*Hej*, Emily. The files are in the conference room. And coffee,' he added, beaming broadly at her before moving back to his own office.

The profiler was grateful that he hadn't remarked on her behaviour the previous evening. She installed herself in the conference room and set to work.

She was on her second cup of coffee when Bergström rushed into the room, a triumphant look in his eyes.

'I've just received the list of the "padlock" evening's participants. You'll never guess who was there with Linnéa!'

BERGSTRÖM, EMILY, ALEXIS and Olofsson stood on one side of the one-way mirror looking into the interview room. With a nod of the head, the Kommissionar indicated to Emily that she should go in.

Olofsson looked towards his superior, his jaw drooping and his eyes wide open in protest, looking more like a silly clown than a policeman.

Bergström concealed his ire, gritting his teeth. '*För helvete*, Olofsson! You've been in the force twenty years and I still have to explain things to you? Don't you understand it's better for this particular interview to be conducted by a woman? Which you don't happen to be, last time I looked. Or am I wrong?'

Olofsson lowered his eyes and made himself smaller, like a dog reprimanded by his owner.

In the interview room, Anna Gunnarson gazed at Emily, looking particularly anxious. The profiler sat down facing her, setting a small black bag on the table.

'You don't mind if we speak in English, Anna, do you? Or would you prefer to talk to a Swede?'

'No, it'll be fine.'

'You were with Linnéa on the eve of her death.'

Anna closed her eyes briefly.

'I presume,' Emily continued, 'that you didn't inform the police of the fact because you had no wish to end up in the headlines. Which would have presented something of a problem when you own a shop right in the centre of town.'

Avoiding Emily's gaze, Anna did not answer.

Emily opened the bag she had placed on the table and took two pairs of trousers, two T-shirts and a pullover from it. Alexis recognised them as clothes they had found in the wardrobe in Linnéa's room.

'These are yours, aren't they?'

Anna nodded slowly.

'Were you Linnéa's lover?'

'No, no, not at all!' Anna cried out.

Emily leaned forward and crossed her hands on the table. 'So, explain some things to me, Anna. Explain to me why we found your clothes in Linnéa's wardrobe, and not in the drawers in the guest room. Explain your presence at the Ljus club "padlock" evening to me. I know you were both there together.'

'OK, OK…' Anna whispered, rubbing her forehead with the tip of her fingers.

She exhaled a heavy sigh before continuing.

'When I separated from my husband, Linnéa suggested I come and stay at her place while she was away. I only went there occasionally, when I wanted a bit of privacy. Linnéa slept in the small room; she enjoyed the view of the lighthouse. Her room didn't have a proper wardrobe, so she left her stuff in the room I used. As to the "padlock" evening…' A feeble laugh escaped her lips. 'Her friend, Richard Anselme, was passing through Gothenburg. He'd invited Linnéa out to celebrate the launch of his new collection. I'd had a quite difficult week, so she suggested I come along to the party to cheer myself up.'

'All three of you went to the Ljus club together?'

'No, I was already in Gothenburg. I joined her at the club.'

'At what time?'

'Ten p.m.; I was at dinner before that.'

'So Linnéa had already been there for some time before you joined her?'

'I don't know.'

'She was with Richard Anselme?'

'No. I never met Richard Anselme,' Anna answered quickly, her eyes lowered. 'When I found Linnéa, she was at the bar and it took us a whole half-hour to puzzle out what the evening was all about.'

Emily frowned.

'You hadn't realised the kind if party you were both at?'

'No, not at all. Richard had just told Linnéa that it was to be a rather exclusive evening.'

'How did Linnéa react when she realised?'

A smile dawned across Anna's sad face. 'It made her laugh.'

'She wasn't angry at Richard Anselme?'

'No, not at all. She found the situation rather funny.'

'Did you stay there for the rest of the evening?'

'Yes. We just parked ourselves at the bar and watched the crowd.' Anna's face darkened. 'Then we went outside to smoke. Well, I was the one who wanted to smoke; Linnéa just tagged along. That's when I recognised the husband of a friend of mine entering the club. I called out to him, and while the bastard was begging me not to say anything to his wife, I lost sight of Linnéa. I never did...' Anna's jaw was trembling. Silent tears ran down her cheeks. 'I went back down into the club again. I thought she'd gone back in and might be waiting for me downstairs ... but she wasn't at the bar and I couldn't find her anywhere.'

'Didn't you try to call her?'

'Mobile phones didn't work downstairs in the club, so I waited for ten minutes, thinking she might be with her friend Richard, then I walked out again and called her, but all I got was her answerphone. I wasn't particularly surprised not to reach her, though; she rarely used her mobile when she was in Sweden. It was part of "detoxifying" herself, as she put it,' Anna added, miming invisible inverted commas. 'I'm not even sure she had it with her.' Anna swallowed hard. 'So, after that, I just got hold of my coat and left.'

'For Falkenberg?'

Anna nodded. 'I went straight to Linnéa's, but she wasn't home.

So I stayed with Lotta, my sister. I did try to reach Linnéa several times, but I never got past her answerphone.'

On the other side of the one-way mirror, tears were clouding Alexis' vision.

Emily briefly touched Anna's arm with her hand. 'Anna, I would like you to retrace, as precisely as you can manage, those final few minutes you spent with Linnéa.'

The gap between Anna's eyes tightened. 'But … I've just told you what happened.'

'There is a strong possibility that your mind has stored information about the evening that you are subconsciously ignoring. And there could be something there that could give us a clue as to Linnéa's killer. That's why I want to try and retrieve that information. Would you be willing for us to revisit, and re-examine that part of the evening together?'

Her face sombre, Anna agreed.

'Thank you, Anna. Make yourself as comfortable as you can in the chair. Let your hands drop, palms upwards, against the top of your thighs, and relax your shoulders.'

Anna did as she was instructed. Her body lost its stiffness and now gave the appearance of a disarticulated puppet.

'Perfect. Now, close your eyes. Breathe through your nose, deeply, slowly, then exhale again through your mouth. That's it, perfect. Breathe again. Exhale. Once again. There we are.'

Emily's words slowed; her voice now a whisper.

'Let's return to the moment when you decided you needed to smoke. The club is below ground; you walk up the stairs…'

'Yes…'

'Where is Linnéa?'

'She's behind me.'

'What colour are the steps?'

'They're wooden. The wood is painted black.'

'And the walls?'

'The walls are dark red, covered with a damask material.'

'Are the stairs busy?'

'Hmm … two or three people walking down.'

'Can you see their faces?'

'No … I just feel them pass me … The only light comes from the spotlights to the sides of the steps. I have to keep an eye on my feet to avoid stumbling.'

'Do the stairs smell of anything in particular?'

'The inside of the club smells of melted wax. But there's another smell – a sugary fragrance. It's from a woman walking down the stairs.'

'You reach the lobby. What do you do?'

'We pick up our coats before we go outside.'

'What is Linnéa saying to you?'

'I … I don't know … I can see her smile as she slips her coat on.'

'Describe her coat to me, the way she's done her hair.'

'Her hair is loose. She's wearing it down … And her coat … I'm not sure any more…'

In the next room, Olofsson turned to Alexis and Bergström. 'What is the profiler hoping to achieve? That the flower seller might remember how many pieces of damned chewing gum were stuck to the pavement?'

Alexis answered before Bergström even had the opportunity to open his mouth. 'It's a cognitive interview, Kristian. Emily is trying to unlock Anna's memories. It's a technique that often works very well with eye witnesses.'

Annoyed at being lectured, the detective crossed his arms across his broad chest and widened the angle between his legs in a vain attempt to assert his masculinity, his eyes still fixed on the one-way mirror.

Anna was rubbing her forehead. All of a sudden, she raised her eyebrows and opened her eyes wide. 'The coat; Linnéa's coat was blue … a sort of electric blue.'

'Very good, Anna … So Linnéa slips on her electric-blue coat. She smiles at you. What makes her smile?'

Anna closed her eyes again and sighed deeply. 'I … I don't know … I can't hear what she's saying…'

'Do you pick up your own coat?'

'Yes, I take my own coat. Linnéa already has hers and she's standing by the wall waiting for me.'

'Is anybody else in the lobby with the two of you?'

'It's crowded ... I do remember seeing a man holding an umbrella on his way out.'

'What does he look like?'

'Quite short, blond...'

'Why do you notice him in particular?'

'For a brief moment, I thought ... it was my ex-husband...'

'But it isn't him...?'

'No, it isn't him.'

'So, what do you do now?'

'We go outside ... Linnéa first...'

'Is it cold?'

'Very ... As we walk out, Linnéa yelps, complains about how harsh Swedish winters are.'

'What are you doing now?'

'I'm lighting a cigarette while Linnéa speaks ... She's talking about the renovations at her house in Falkenberg ... She's telling me about the flooring...'

'Where exactly are you standing?'

'On the right, outside the club's door. On the pavement.'

'Is it busy?'

'There are ... twenty or so people around us...'

'Is the street well lit?'

'Yes, it is, there are street lights.'

'You're busy smoking...'

'Yes...'

'Where is Linnéa?'

'Facing me.'

'Where is she standing in relation to the road and the club's door?'

'We're looking sideways at the club. It's on her left. She's facing north on Avenyn.'

'Is the street busy?'

'Some passers-by…'

'What is Linnéa doing?'

'She's rubbing her hands together – she's not wearing gloves. She's talking to me … I'm not sure about what exactly. I've just noticed Per – Per Patriksson, my friend's husband. He's with a young woman who can't even be twenty … He fathered three children; his wife is busy back home taking care of them, while he's off playing with girls the age of his own eldest daughter…'

Anna opened her eyes again.

'Do you want a glass of water, Anna?'

She shook her head from side to side, passed her tongue over her dry lips and closed her eyes again.

Emily waited a minute or so for Anna's breath to slow down and for her to relax again.

'So Per is standing behind Linnéa…' the profiler continued.

'Yes…'

'You step towards him…'

Anna nodded once more.

'Does Linnéa come with you?'

'No … I'm just so shocked to have surprised Per here that I move away from her without saying a word.'

'Does she call out to you? Say something?'

'I … I don't know…'

'What are you saying to Per?'

'I ask him where Marlene, his wife, is. He stares back at me and begs me not to say anything, that it was all a mistake to have come to this party, and that he is about to leave, anyway.'

'How do you respond?'

'I tell him to stop bullshitting me. He pleads that it's difficult for a man to recognise the woman he has married once she's become the mother of his children. The young girl with him tries to interrupt him, then pulls him by the arm towards the entrance to the club.'

'You can see the club's entrance clearly?'

'Yes, behind Per.'

'So you have your back to the road?'

'Yes…'

'Describe to me what you can see behind Per.'

'I … the bouncer … He's opening the door … People are walking in…'

'What's happening now?'

"Per goes off. He leaves the girl just standing there.'

'What does the girl say?'

'She shouts an insult after him and walks into the club.'

'What direction does Per take?'

'Towards the bottom of Avenyn, on the right. He crosses the road.'

'Do you watch him all the way?'

'Yes…'

'What can you see on the right? On the pavement by the club?'

'On my right there's a group of people busy talking…'

'What do you see?'

'Couples…'

'They're all in pairs?'

'I'm not sure … it's all a blur … no, I don't think so. Definitely the two standing a bit further away … the woman – or is it the man? – raising an arm … The woman, I think. Yes, the woman is moving her arm through the air.'

'Can you distinguish their faces?'

'The woman has her back to me, partly concealing the man. I can only see his black outfit … and his hood.'

'Does the woman have short hair? Long hair?'

'Short … blonde…'

'Are they close to any of the street lights?'

'They're partly in the light…'

'What colours do you see?'

'Black … blue, too.'

'Blue.'

'Yes, it's the coat of the woman waving her arms…'

Anna stopped and instantly opened her eyes, as if waking from a nightmare. She had just come to realise what she had witnessed. The blonde woman didn't have short hair: it was buried inside the folds of her coat. And she was wearing a blue coat. Electric blue.

Anna had actually seen Linnéa and her killer.

Falkenberg
February 1971

ERICH PULLED THE BODY out of the tub, thinking how much life would change now that he would soon have a partner of his own. He positioned the diminutive, flayed little being on the drying table, and gave it a long, critical look. The result was almost perfect. He could move on to the final stage. He smiled. A smile that lit up his whole soul. That was exactly what he had needed. This specific type of flesh. Young. Lesion-free.

It had all come together thanks to Agneta. He had come to understand this the very day she had announced she was pregnant. He'd immediately turned on his heels. She'd run after him in tears, but he was much faster than she was. He had walked all the way to the beach, wondering how he had failed to read the girl so badly. Had failed to understand her language. How he could have allowed himself to be driven down a road that was just not suited to him. He'd sat down in the sand, his eyes fixed on the shining crests of the waves as they basked in the sun. He'd watched them caress the shore then ebb back towards the horizon, crashing against the rocks. Something Doktor Fleischer once said came to mind: only children are granted access to eternity. Only children. And then he had swiftly realised the profound meaning of this coming birth. His initial reaction had been too hurried. This child would not be a burden – it would be the arrow in his bow. This was the child who would allow him access to posterity. To eternity.

He'd gone hunting that very evening. Seeking a choice prey.

Tracking, selecting, killing. He could no longer wait for fate to drop a body in his path. He no longer had to adapt whatever came his way. He had to select carefully, so that he could carry forward a perfect, immaculate heritage. He had a responsibility to both his successor and himself.

Upstairs, the telephone was ringing, but Erich couldn't hear it.

꘎꘎꘎꘎

'Your husband isn't answering, Agneta. I'm sorry.' The midwife's voice reached her through the fog.

Agneta was trying hard to summon the strength to overcome the latest contraction. She barely had time enough to catch her breath before the unsettling feeling that she was both dying and alive swept through her again, and the pain returned, like an unstoppable wave. It rose for just a second, but crested immediately, furiously, lashing her stomach, her back and reaching down to her thighs. Agneta gripped the edges of the bed hard – her fingers freezing, freezing, freezing – in a bid to prevent herself drowning in the pain.

Her delivery paralleled her pregnancy: a long, lonely journey. She had reckoned that, as a man, Erich was finding it hard to find a connection with the new sort of woman she had unwittingly become. Her sexual appetite had remained the same. She hadn't put on that much weight either; but the new curviness of her body didn't seem to be to Erich's taste. He rejected her advances and systematically begged her to get dressed again. She should behave like a responsible human being and think of the baby's health, he would repeatedly tell her. Her body had become a temple.

As soon as the baby had begun to move inside her, he had spoken to it in German, morning to night. Agneta couldn't understand a word of what he was saying, but she could clearly see and feel how much Erich already loved their child. But not her any longer, it seemed. During the course of those endless months, he had never demonstrated any true care for her. He had overseen what she was eating, regularly checked her pulse, and analysed her urine, but, apart from that, he just ignored her. Totally. Her body was not a temple, but a vessel. The vessel that carried and would deliver his child.

'Push, Agneta, push…'

There was no need to tell her what to do, her whole body was screaming at her to push. And every movement in that direction felt like a short-lived deliverance. She heard herself bellow out. Breathed in short bursts when she was instructed to stop pushing. Then bellowed again. Another shattering stab of pain cut through her, followed by a strange sensation of freedom, then tears, or rather whining.

'Look, Agneta, this is your son.'

She noticed a reddish bundle being carried through the air, its limbs folded back like a frog's. It was placed against her chest. The small, hungry mouth closed on her nipple, the tiny fists settling on either side of her breast, as if marking its territory. Exhausted, Agneta closed her eyes, gently holding this beautiful little thing against her, body to body.

⟐

She returned to Erich's house four days later, after leaving the maternity ward. The anger brewing inside her had faded. She had come to terms with it. She hadn't been able to get in touch with him, but she knew him well: when he was working in his laboratory – and God only knew the amount of time he spent there – he didn't hear the phone ring. Maybe it was also her own fault that he had not come seeking her: she had all too often threatened to move away with the child.

She was waiting for Erich in the kitchen, holding her hungry little frog to her breast.

'I thought you had left. With my child.'

Erich's voice made her jump. She turned round. Instantly, Agneta realised what attracted her so much in this man. She shook her head, a smile stretching her plump lips.

'This is our son, Erich. His name is Adam.'

Erich approached their child and placed his large hand on the bald skull.

'He's big and fat.'

'Fifty-five centimetres and four kilos nine hundred grams. Yes, a very big baby.'

She didn't say a word of what she had done to take revenge for his absence. It could wait. And, anyway, it wasn't that important. In his way, he would forgive her in the long run.

And this child would mend their relationship, she was absolutely certain of it.

ASSISTED BY BERGSTRÖM AND ALEXIS, Emily unloaded the first batch of folders from the cart and placed them in the middle of the table. Olofsson reluctantly rose from his chair to help them.

'We'll organise this a different way,' Emily explained, her voice neutral. 'We will thoroughly examine all the disappearance files, but this time around, we will go back fifty years.'

Olofsson kept silent, even though he was dying to open his mouth. Bergström seemed to be in a foul mood, almost hostile towards him, and he didn't even know why. He thought it best to make himself invisible. Despite all the ungodly hours he'd been working since the beginning of this particular case, generally, life in Falkenberg was something of a doddle, and he had no wish for it to change. Besides, he was getting sick and tired of this female profiler. A pretty face, granted, but below it she was flat as a bread board. A curveless body, all straight angles. On top of which, Madame was happy to lead them a merry dance, lording it amongst the hills of old, dusty files, while the investigation made little progress. Why did no one realise that her methods were just a lot of hot air? She'd interviewed the flower seller for over two hours, and why? All to learn that Linnéa wore a blue coat and blow-dried her hair before going out! If these were Scotland Yard's best, then ... Supposedly, they now knew where Blix had met her killer. Big deal. But Anna Gunnarson was unable to identify him, so what was the point of it all? Was he the only one to realise this was all useless bullshit: Bergström and the sexy one took everything that Madame-my-left-frontal-lobe-is-larger-than-both-my-tits said as gospel.

He felt compelled to speak out. He had to. Of course, he'd deliver it with his customary elegance and charm, as he always did. Yeah, that's it.

'Why fifty years – why be so precise, Emily?' he asked with a broad smile.

'I was coming to that, Kristian. I'm increasingly convinced we are facing a duo in which the dominant/dominated dynamic is at work. But I don't believe that they divide the tasks on a territorial basis. On the contrary, they hunt and kill together. That's why the wounds are all alike, as it's always the same man who is responsible for them. If the *dominated* one must be between thirty and forty-five years old, as I am led to believe, his *dominant*, on the other hand, is likely to be at least twenty years older. The dominated one is an educated man, hard to impress or manipulate and he's the one who is now in the ascendancy. So, the dominant must be between fifty-five and sixty-five years old, maybe even older, albeit in good health. It's very likely he's been active for some time. We should look out for his signature amongst just one particular type of victim: boys between six and eight. If we assume he is no older than sixty-five and that his interest in children began around the age of twenty, we must therefore focus our investigations all the way back to 1969. Forty-five years ago.'

Thank you so much, but I can *count*, Olofsson rebelled silently.

He asked a further question. 'And what did you learn from the cognitive interview?'

Bergström threw a dubious glance at his detective, wondering what he was leading up to.

'The cognitive interview showed me that Linnéa knew the killer – well enough to recognise him under his hood and coat at night.'

Olofsson rocked his chair back and forth with feigned nonchalance. 'Didn't Anna say the street was well lit?'

'Yes. But the light from lamp-posts is angled and creates shadows across a face if you're wearing a hood or a hat.'

'What difference does it make?' Olofsson's tone was becoming increasingly impatient.

'I'd previously established that our main suspect might have been a friend, a colleague, a neighbour or a tradesman she often came into contact with and would have been able to recognise. But, thanks to the information provided by Anna Gunnarson, we know she recognised the person in an instant, despite the partial light. We can therefore assume she knew the person well.'

Alexis could feel cold sweat on the back of her neck.

'In addition, the cognitive interview taught me that the next victim, in all likelihood, lives in the centre of Gothenburg.'

Olofsson repressed his frustration, grinding his teeth loudly.

'So, as I was saying, we must now operate differently,' Emily continued. 'We must comb through the disappearance files and note down for each one the gender, the age, the colour of the eyes and hair of the child; whether he came from a single-parent or nuclear family, and whether this was a dysfunctional family; the date of his disappearance; the approximate hour, if that information is available; the last place the child was seen; and the address where the missing child lived.'

'So we don't look out any longer for the investigation logs, the psychological evaluations or the interviews?' Alexis enquired.

'No, not for the time being. All we require are the items of information I've listed. I'll take care of the actual analysis.'

Emily moved out of the room for a few minutes to make a phone call.

When she returned, Alexis, Bergström and Olofsson were busy filling in the gaps in the forms Emily had prepared earlier, attentive and focused, like students at an exam.

ALEXIS HAD GIVEN UP wading through the files in order to accompany Anna Gunnarson to Linnéa's. Anna wanted to pick up her belongings, which Alexis had sorted out and labelled as part of her inventory, believing they had belonged to Linnéa.

Anna entered the house first. She placed her feet carefully, casting a worried eye on her surroundings, as if she was discovering the place for the very first time. Alexis followed her, observing her gestures. She watched her open the drawers, the wardrobes, the cardboard boxes, retrieving insignificant objects in silence, her movements tentative, hesitant.

Having gathered her stuff, Anna walked as if sleepwalking towards the kitchen and sat down at the table, her body burdened by sadness.

'Is that it? You have everything?' asked Alexis, sitting down next to her.

Anna slowly nodded her head, her fingers skimming across the few breadcrumbs still littering the tabletop.

'I think I have everything, yes. Thank you.'

All of a sudden, her shoulders began to shudder. She sniffed, trying hard to contain the tears welling up inside her eyes.

Alexis placed one hand on the woman's shoulder and, with her other hand, stroked her hair with almost maternal tenderness. Anna didn't blink, seeming to welcome the physical closeness and the strange form of intimacy that mourning allowed them to share.

'I saw Linnéa only the day before yesterday,' she whispered, her voice broken with sobs.

Alexis got nearer to her.

'I was in the street, walking towards the store and I saw her, waiting for me. She looked so sad. So sad…' Anna wiped her nose with the back of her hand. 'I didn't even tell Lotta. She spends most of her time worrying about me. I don't want to make things even worse.'

'When my partner died, a few years ago,' Alexis confessed, 'I saw him once, three weeks following his death. He was sitting on the bed in our room and was smiling at me. The same, open smile he always gave me when I woke up in the morning and my eyes were still only half open. Such a commonplace everyday gesture. Silly, really. For a few seconds, he had returned. He'd come back to me.'

The words had flown from her mouth before she'd even been able to think. They'd floated from Alexis to Anna, freed by the sadness, liberated. Her mourning for her partner had been like an inner quest and she had finally succeeded in finding some peace.

She took Anna's hands in hers and the two women shared a few minutes of comforting silence as they watched the black sea outside, whitewashed by the moonlight.

After Anna left, Alexis was about to call for a taxi when a mad thought rushed through her brain. She slipped on her coat, shivering at the thought of the glacial gusts of wind awaiting her outside, then went out of the house to confront the polar night.

Two minutes later, she had arrived at Stellan's.

The two recessed bulbs situated on each side of the front door switched on automatically and bathed her in naked light. She suddenly wondered what the hell she was doing here, at night, begging for the company of a man she barely knew. What the fuck was she doing here? She should have returned to the hotel. Asked Emily what she could do to help. Or consulted her notes again. Done something constructive. For the sake of Linnéa. Not for herself.

Stellan opened the door. His surprise was quickly replaced by a worried look. 'Is everything OK?'

Alexis nodded, her cheeks red, more from embarrassment than because of the cold.

'Come in, you must be freezing.'

She stepped across the threshold, her brain in overdrive, hunting for a justification for her visit.

'You were at Linnéa's?'

'Yes. With Anna Gunnarson.'

He frowned.

'Anna … Gunnarson?'

'Your neighbour Lotta Ahlgren's sister.'

'Oh yes, yes, Lotta. But why her sister? Did she know Linnéa?'

'They were friends.'

'Really?'

'Yes, Anna had been staying at Linnéa's for some time.'

'Linnéa told me she sometimes let a woman friend stay, but I was under the impression it was someone from London; I'm not quite sure why.'

Alexis took her coat and shoes off with unnecessary slowness, hoping to stretch time enough to come up with some brilliant excuse for her visit. But all she could think of was the feeling of being naked. Taking your shoes off indoors was a very hygienic, Swedish custom, but it somehow lacked glamour.

She followed Stellan into the living room.

'Do you want something to drink?'

She nodded, avoiding his eyes.

Stellan placed a couple of glasses on the table and sat down on the sofa next to her.

Alexis granted herself a few extra seconds while she tasted the wine. A Bordeaux. Heady. But full of flavour. She could feel Stellan staring at her.

'You're no stranger to … all this …' he said.

The wine swirled inside her glass. She knew Stellan was not refer-ring to the drink they were sharing.

'You mean investigations into serial killers, or mourning?'

'The two go hand in hand, don't they?'

A wave of desire ran through Alexis, a totally inappropriate response to Stellan's question. It felt as if it was about to consume her.

'The two indeed go together.'

She felt dirty; soiled by the strength of her desire, her lascivious thoughts. She had no right to think of herself again, no right to banish her pain. Not yet. This was not the time to say farewell to her partner, replace him. She had the right to go to bed with any old person when her hormones were raging, but never with someone serious.

Stellan's eyes swept across the table. He was waiting for her to say more, explain herself, share her thoughts, but Alexis had no impulse to confide in him about her particular hell. It was a burden she had to carry all the time, and it was heavy enough as it was, without talking about it.

He nodded, his eyes still fixed on the table, and Alexis wondered if she had somehow spoken out loud. He set down his glass and turned towards her. *He's about to get personal too*, she thought, lassitude sweeping over her, the tiredness that came of continual bouts of therapy and meetings with broken men.

She was about to beg him not to say a word when Stellan leaned towards her, his gaze questioning. There was a feverish look in his eyes, as they swept across her body. Surprise froze Alexis immediately, then disappeared in a stroke at the very moment Stellan's lips pressed against hers. She melted and caught fire at the same time, as if he were directing the sun to move across her cold body. Her final thoughts crumbled and her mind went blank.

Stellan's mouth travelled from one lip to the other, then reached the cradle of her neck. Out of breath, he waited a little, then put his tongue between her lips. Desire electrified Alexis and a wave of heat reached her lower stomach. Gasping, she fell onto the sofa, eyes closed, limbs heavy, a near-drunken feeling taking hold of her.

She heard the rough fabric of Stellan's jeans rub against her, the click of his belt buckle falling on the floor tiles and the hushed sound of his trousers sliding down his legs. He pulled her knickers down and shivered as he caressed her wet sex. She opened her thighs and pulled him towards her. The heat and weight of his chest against hers put her instantly and completely at ease, a sensation she hadn't experienced for as long as she could remember.

She only opened her eyes again when the orgasm radiated through her lower body. Her eyes met Stellan's. He had a satisfied, serene look, touched with tenderness, and it made her shiver with joy.

Cornwall, England
July 1982

AGNETA STOLE A KISS from her son. Adam was always excited when he was about to leave for Sweden. He was never happier than when spending time with his father.

As long as she could remember, Erich had unconditionally governed her son's heart. On the orders of King Ebner, because maternal milk was best for the child, Agneta had breastfed Adam until he was sixteen months old and endured the painful bites of his small, voracious teeth. She alone had been the one to rise at night to calm her son down, to change his nappies, sing him lullabies, look after him. But Adam had eyes only for his father. The way he looked at him ... eyes so full of love and admiration, as if Erich was perfection personified. There were times when she felt she was not even part of the same universe as Adam; she had become invisible, whatever efforts she went to, to make his childhood happy, healthy and balanced. 'A mother's role is thankless,' her own mother had always said, when she had been an unruly teenager. 'You'll understand that when you become one yourself,' she would say again and again. Of course, mother.

If only her parents were still around ... Ever since the day Erich had abandoned her after she had informed him of her pregnancy, she had missed them even more. Agneta had revisited her memories and regrets – all the occasions when she had unwittingly hurt them because of her capricious nature. Had she known how little precious time with them she had left, she would have acted differently. They had died much too early. She had still been only nineteen and so immature. She hadn't been 'complete', as her father put it. Her parents would have seen what she hadn't in Erich and warned her.

Nothing had worked out the way she had hoped. Erich catered to their needs, and Adam and she were never left hungry. Apart from that he had been a despicable life companion.

When she had first known him, he was already locking himself inside his laboratory all weekend. Following Adam's birth, though, he spent all his free time there, apart from the daily, sacred hour when he would take a walk with his son. She was never allowed to accompany them. She herself no longer had any place in Erich's life. She had merely become his son's nanny.

Never, not on a single occasion since her pregnancy, had he touched her. Not even a fleeting caress or a chaste kiss. Erich had installed himself in the small bedroom and Adam had slept with her until she had left for England, four years ago, now. Not that Erich was abstinent. She had smelled the sex of other women rising from him. The bastard didn't even take care to shower after returning from his extracurricular fucks.

She had tried to elicit a reaction from him, to provoke him. First, she had opted for the silent approach, slipping into his bed at night. Without even casting a glance at her naked body, he had ordered her back to her room to sleep. The memory of that humiliation still lingered, how Erich had trampled on her self-esteem. Next she had tried tears, but with no more success. On her last attempt, she had stood facing him, holding a knife in her hand, threatening to mutilate herself if he didn't treat her better, like any decent man. He had stared coldly at her and his indifference had wounded her more than the cuts she had wanted to inflict on herself. Never had she felt so insignificant and scorned. Everything she had been proud of – her body, her erotic appeal – had been shattered into a thousand pieces by Erich Ebner.

How she had come to regret having spent all the proceeds from the sale of her family home! Her parents had put a block on her inheritance until she had reached the age of thirty, so she had been unable to leave Erich and start a new life elsewhere. There had been no other choice than to stay put.

Two miserable years had gone by. On the verge of despair, she'd finally contacted her aunt who lived in England. The old cow had no wish to get involved, believing Agneta was just being melodramatic and trying to get hold of the money early. Agneta had had to wait until the egocentric bitch had finally realised the gravity of the situation and agreed to lend her some money, in advance of the inheritance.

So Agneta had escaped to England with her son. Because Adam was *her* son. At the maternity ward, in order to take revenge on Erich, she had declared his father as unknown, and had given him her name alone. Legally, Erich had no connection or rights to him. He wasn't even aware of the aunt's existence. So he would be unable to contact or find them.

Life in Cornwall would have been perfect had not Adam proved inconsolable. He couldn't bear being away from his father. Four months after their arrival, Agneta had obeyed her aunt and agreed to get in touch with Erich. As soon as he had been reunited with him, Adam began to live fully again.

These days, he spent half of his school holidays in Falkenberg. Agneta was forced to accept that father and son had managed to establish a solid and harmonious relationship; to the extent that she could make Adam obey her, simply by threatening to cancel his Swedish holidays or to inform Erich of his misdeeds. This was how she had succeeded in putting a stop to the child's worrying pyromania. The double threat had worked wonders.

Adam turned round and blew his mother a kiss. Agneta's features were so sad, he blew her another across the open palm of his hand, his lips twisted as if he were miserable. But it was just a pretence ... Because he was, at long last, about to see Father! He didn't want to say, but he would have much preferred to be living with him. Time in Sweden went by too fast, whereas, when he was with his mother, every second lasted an eternity … until the next holiday came around…

Father had explained how he should adapt to the situation. In Sweden he should act like a Swede, and in England like an Englishman. As to German, he had to master it to honour his ancestors and their culture. Father gave him lessons – things he had to learn by heart and study once he returned to Mother's. And when he came back to Falkenberg, he was questioned on the subject. On this occasion, Adam was to recite a particular poem. He said nothing of all this to Mum. Neither had he told her that, when he was in Falkenberg, he used Father's name. It was much easier that way.

He was in a great hurry to go fishing for crabs. Small Swedish kids threw them back into the water soon after they caught them, but Father had explained that was the wrong way to proceed. A crab, once captured, had to be sacrificed. So, they would bring them back to the house. Father had shown him how to break their legs, just like Adam did with the wings of flies. Then it had been his turn. Father had handed over one of the crabs, the smallest one, but Adam had felt guilty because he had blinked briefly as the pincer had broken between his fingers. He hadn't done it on purpose, it was just that the cracking noise had surprised and disgusted him. Father had told him that, if he wanted to become an excellent surgeon, he could not close his eyes, even if the sight, the noise or the odour of something took him by surprise or disturbed him. His own body must constantly be alive to sensations.

So Adam had practised, surreptitiously of course. But where he lived with Mum, there weren't any crabs, so he had used cats – the kittens the gardener was planning to drown. He'd hidden them in the old hen house and practised there.

Now, he never closed his eyes. Father would be so proud of him.

Father had promised that, during the course of the next holidays, they would step things up. He wasn't sure what he meant, but it nonetheless excited him and it could only be wonderful, because they would be doing it together.

And the next holidays began today.

Grand Hotel, Falkenberg
Wednesday, 22 January 2014, 19.00

EMILY PLACED THE FOLDER on the bed.

It had been a productive afternoon: Alexis, Bergström and Olofsson had sifted through a veritable mountain of information. It was now a matter of analysis, which would take her most of the night. The Kommissionar had also contacted the Gothenburg Rikskriminalpolisen to check whether, over the course of the past sixty years, any victims had been found with their eyes pulled out or without their trachea. His colleagues had not reported any trachea instances, and the eye gougings had usually been tied to crimes of passion or cases of gang warfare.

Emily unlocked her safe and pulled out the envelope containing the photographs of the London crime scenes. She sat down on the bed, crosslegged, and placed her notepad next to her.

Before browsing through the new information, she wanted to reconnect with the case, to the narrative being subconsciously written by the serial killer. To do that properly, she had to examine all the snapshots of the crime scenes again, one by one, as if she were seeing them for the very first time. Because she had mentally recorded every single detail of the images, they had become a familiar landscape she could gaze at without truly looking. Now she had to come off automatic pilot and force herself to study things afresh.

Once she had completed her examination of the final photograph, Emily re-read the questions she had listed in her notebook. During the course of the hour that followed, she forced herself to criticise every conclusion she had previously reached.

'Victims washed clean. Of what? Why?'

The killer cleaned his victims. Yes, he was eliminating all traces of himself, but maybe that was only coincidental. Emily was more inclined to interpret this washing as a mark of remorse, of respect: the killer was taking care of his victims, making them presentable. These ablutions were as necessary as the enucleation. Was it perhaps a purification ritual? As children symbolised innocence, he did not wish to dirty them through his actions. And neither they, nor Linnéa had been sexually interfered with.

'Why the Y carved into the left arm?'

Emily noted down what the left arm evoked for her. *Vena Amoris*, she wrote, almost as a reflex. An old Egyptian belief according to which a vein directly connected the left hand's ring-finger to the heart. OK, but then why carve the Y into the arm, and not the hand?

Inside her handbag, her mobile phone buzzed.

She picked it up and was greeted by the nasal voice of Arthur Hannah, an old colleague from the Canadian police. She'd left him a message earlier in the day, asking him to take a look at the case.

Art was in charge of the geographical profiling department at the famous Mounted Police Force. Since she had been working at the Yard, Emily had sought his help several times. Using complicated mathematical formulae, Arthur was always capable of locating the domicile or place of work of the criminals he was hunting down. He was also an unconditional fan of Bruce Springsteen.

'Hey, Art.'

'Fuck me, Em, your guy is some nasty piece of shit. Another fat bastard who orders his daily Starbucks every morning, like all of us, and kisses his wife every night while no one knows he's locked the neighbour's son in his basement for the past ten days. And people think he's worth a trial and all that fuss? People are crazy. If they only saw what we witness every single day, they'd burn them alive in a public square, I'm telling you.'

Emily frowned silently and listened to him puff on his cigarette.

'I don't know why, Em, but your case, it somehow makes me

think of "What a Wonderful World". When Thiele and Weiss wrote that song, they must have hoovered up so much coke it was coming out of their arseholes. What's "wonderful" about all this, eh? Anyway, I'm happy for you; you seem to be having a lot of fun at the Yard. Classy, business trips to Viking land, eh?'

'Did you manage to go through all of it?' the profiler asked, trying to get him back on track.

'Yep, and it's ruined my plans. I was hoping for a quiet day at the office! I was about to sit down, listen to a 1981 bootleg and watch the Live in Dublin DVD, but, instead of spending time with my mate Bruce, I had to start devising a set of equations to pinpoint some congenital idiot whose childhood was traumatic enough to make him gouge out eyes and tracheas as if they were weeds. I really believe people should think a bit longer before they shit kids out. If they come out so twisted, it would have been better to use some form of protection.'

'What have you found?'

'I'm sorry, Em, but my mathematical model just can't tell me anything about the guy in question. Your story is a proper mess: London, Sweden, four kids, the woman. A real clusterfuck. There's nothing I can do with all those separate elements. I agree with you in thinking there might be two of them, but it just makes matters even more complicated...'

Art's voice sounded guilty. There was nothing worse for him than to have to concede defeat to a criminal.

'Did the inscriptions lead you anywhere, by the way?' he asked. 'Guys who pull eyes out and cut tracheas are already twisted, but intellectual knife tattoos – it's a bit much.'

'You mean the letters carved into the arms?' Emily asked, not quite understanding what might be intellectual about them.

'Yep.'

'I'm not sure why they are angled differently. But for now, the only plausible explanation I found about the X and Y was that he was marking them according to their gender.'

Art roared with laughter on the other end of the line. 'Fuck, Em, I just realised I'm going senile … If my wife were here, she'd take the piss and blame Bruce for making me gaga … Can you believe I didn't realise it was a Y?'

'Really? What did you think it was?'

Emily listened to Arthur Hannah's explanation and then hung up, aghast.

Her colleague had just thrown a whole different light on the investigation.

Falkenberg
July 1982

ADAM WOKE UP, STARTLED. He pushed the sheet away. His pyjamas were soaked. He slipped a hand under his body. The bed was wet.

His fists tightened with rage. His mother had placed the pads in his luggage, but he had disposed of them before arriving in Sweden. Had Father come across them, Adam wouldn't have been able to look him in the face, or, at any rate, contemplate that half-smile that never left his features and demonstrated how proud he was of his son. Last time, he had told him that a boy of his age should not wet himself. It should be sufficient to order one's body to stop. 'Assert your will,' he had told Adam.

Father was a hero. He was a survivor of World War Two. He'd told Adam the story of the long months spent in Buchenwald concentration camp. He'd also mentioned Doktor Fleischer. Adam had asked him whether there might be a street in Germany named after him, as he was a hero. Father had explained this was not the case; that real success was not to have a name on a plaque, but to be able to succeed fully with the projects you undertook. So Adam had tried in vain to follow the precept of 'asserting his will'. Every night, before falling asleep, he whispered to his body. Ordering it to obey, not to betray him, to banish the shame. But it didn't work and once again he had woken bathed in urine.

He got up, pulled the sheets off the bed, folded them and placed them under the mattress. As soon as Father was away, he would wash and dry them. He undressed, slipped on a new pair of pyjamas and opened his cupboard to pull out some spare bedding. He searched around, stood on a stool to look through the top shelf, but couldn't find any more sheets. He would have to spend the rest of the night with just the bed cover, but when Father came to wake him the following morning, he would instantly realise that Adam had succumbed again. There was nothing for it, Adam would have to make a silent visit to the laundry room to pick up new sheets.

Returning to his room, Adam noticed a light on downstairs – in the laboratory. Their routine was to sleep between nine at night and seven in the morning. This was the same for both himself and Father. He knew he'd heard Father close his door on the other side of the corridor, after wishing him a good night earlier. Maybe he'd forgotten to switch off the light? Or maybe there was an intruder…? Adam was not allowed to go down to Father's lab, but if someone had broken in, he had a duty to confront him, didn't he?

His pulse quickening, Adam looked around him. He saw nothing he could use against the thief. But he had to be courageous. He had to protect Father. After all, he had inherited his character; he, too, should be a hero.

His heart beating in overdrive, he slowly opened the door to the cellar, praying to himself it wouldn't creak. 'Assert your will. Assert your will,' he repeated to himself, hoping this might assist his quivering legs to move forward.

Holding himself against the wall he crept down the cellar stairs, cautiously watching where he stepped. A strong smell of disinfectant reached his nose, making him blink.

Arriving in the cellar's main space, he found himself facing a row of metal shelves. He stared at the shelving. Surprised, he tentatively extended a hand forward. His fingers came into contact with shining skin, not unlike the meat that hung in a butcher's window.

Fascinated, and completely forgetting the danger he had been prepared to face, Adam stepped towards the centre of the room. A completely naked boy lay stretched across a metal table.

He was about to touch the boy when he noticed Father. He froze. But it wasn't anger he saw in his father's eyes; it was surprise.

Father gestured slightly with his head, seeming to invite Adam to continue exploring his surroundings. Adam walked around the body and placed his left hand on the child's wrist; it was as cold as the table on which it rested. Remaining calm, with his other hand he snapped the forefinger backwards until it cracked loudly.

He then looked up to his father, who was staring intensely at him. 'See, Father, I no longer have to close my eyes.'

Falkenberg Police Station
Thursday, 23 January 2014, 07.00

ALEXIS CAME RUSHING THROUGH the swing doors of the conference room, out of breath and dishevelled. Emily didn't even look up
at her.

Thirty minutes earlier Alexis had received a text message from the
profiler asking her to get to the police station as soon as possible.
She'd quickly slipped the same clothes she had worn the day before
over her body, still warm from the caresses of the previous night.
Stellan had accompanied her to the door, and, following a final kiss
she could still taste on her mouth, she'd run to her appointment.

The profiler pulled a batch of thick cardboard folders from her
rucksack. A mess of tracing-paper sheets escaped and floated down
to the floor like dead leaves. Emily picked them up and set them
down on the table, her face inscrutable. Her gestures were slow and
deliberate, with the precision of a Japanese ritual. It was clear that she
had also dressed in a hurry: her untidy chignon had slipped down to
the nape of her neck, her boots were unlaced and her features looked
as crumpled as her sweater.

Bergström and Olofsson were next to arrive, followed by the
Kommissionar's secretary, whose name Alexis still didn't know. The
secretary set a tray with four cups and a tall thermos on the table and
left silently, as she always did.

Emily looked up and acknowledged her audience, checking if
everyone was present. Alexis handed her a cup.

'I've found something,' Emily began, drinking a large mouthful of coffee. 'I've run through all the data we collected yesterday and isolated a definite pattern. There is a regularity in the disappearances. From 1970 to 2013, a small boy disappeared every nine months or so on the west coast of Sweden. The children were all between the ages of six and ten, brown-haired and originating from orphanages or dysfunctional families. Over time, the pattern becomes even more precise: two orphans, then a child from a problem family, and so on and so on. In most cases, the police concluded that the kids had run away or been killed by someone close to them. None was ever found again. Not a single one.'

'Why so, in your opinion?'

Alexis and Bergström turned towards Olofsson. There was nothing ironic, unctuous or accusatory in his question. For once, the detective even seemed to be sincere.

'Because, between 1970 and 2013, the bodies have been buried or kept in one or more private cemeteries. But, in 2013, something must have happened: a disturbing element, which caused the killers to change their *modus operandi*. They began killing in London, disposing of the bodies with less application. Now, they abandon their victims in plain view.'

'"A disturbing element"?'

Olofsson's calm and courteous demeanour persisted. Bergström was beginning to wonder why the detective had not shown signs of similar humility earlier.

'A stimulus, or perhaps stimuli – maybe the end of a relationship; the death of a loved one; a birth or the loss of a job – that might have created a stressful situation that led to crime, or forced a drastic change to the modus operandi established during the course of the previous killings.'

Alexis intervened, rubbing her temple with the tips of her fingers. 'So, according to you, there haven't been signs of similar precision since 2013…' She was trying to order her thoughts as she spoke, her eyes fixed on the cup of coffee. 'Maybe the way the duo functions has been affected? Possibly the dominant one is ill, bedridden, maybe even dead? And, as a result, the dominated one is no longer under his influence. He has taken the opportunity to rebel.'

Emily nodded. Bergström stood up and served some more coffee.

Alexis continued. 'Could it be that the dominant one, as you refer to him, began his work around 1970, long before all this…'

'Exactly…'

'…and found and trained his partner to kill alongside him?'

'Hunting and killing together. Hunting down the prey is a crucial factor. Pleasure is triggered once the victim is identified: they follow him, study his habits so as to identify the ideal moment for the kidnapping.'

'What sort of relationship did you have in mind – a father and a son?'

'Yes, a sort of father-son relationship, but not necessarily an actual father and son. We could be looking at more distantly related members of the same family or group – say, an uncle, a cousin or someone close to them.'

'And do you think they had already been on a killing spree in London but no one was aware of it?'

'No. Their initial collaboration began here in Sweden. We can be certain of that. From the outset, their crimes were committed in Sweden and only in Sweden. In 2013, the new, disturbing element comes into play and changes the nature of their relationship, their synergy. The dominated personality adapts: his situation prevents him from coming to and killing in Sweden. So he commits crimes in London, instead. He cannot fully escape his craving for the act of killing. He badly needs his rituals: the hunt, the act of killing, the mutilations, the disposal of the body.'

'So, how do we proceed now?' asked Bergström.

Emily leaned against the table, her arms folded, her gaze determined, like a lioness about to assault her prey.

'There's something else. I called an old colleague back in Canada, Arthur Hannah. He's a geographical profiler. I only got in touch with him yesterday, as his methodology seldom works unless there are five or more victims. He wasn't able to determine the domicile or physical locations of our killers, but he offered me a fascinating interpretation of some of the clues we've managed to gather so far. He put his finger on something specific. Something I should have noticed myself.'

Emily picked up a felt-tip pen and traced a capital Y on the board, and then another one, smaller this time.

'The capital Y that has been carved into the arms of the victims' – she indicated the first one with her finger – 'resembles the diminutive of the letter gamma.' She pointed to the smaller y.

The profiler turned the board round. She had pinned four close-up photographs of the actual letters carved into the arms of the dead children.

'Let's refer to these letters as gamma. Each has a different orientation, depending on the body. It's a substantial variation; comparing the first and the third bodies the mark is situated at completely opposite angles.'

Emily's forefinger brushed against the first photograph then moved over the second one as she continued her explanation.

'Following the shoulder-to-hand axis, the gamma is pointing north-east on Andrew Meadowbanks, south-east on Cole Halliwell, south-west on Logan Mansfield and north-west on Tomas Nilsson.'

'Shit … What can it mean?' asked a nonplussed Olofsson.

Bergström and Alexis, as much at sea as the detective, looked at the inscriptions, still with no understanding of where Emily was leading them.

Emily drew four minuscule gammas, each one oriented according to the coordinates she had just spelled out.

'We have the end-points of a cross. And knowing that a capital gamma is shaped this way…' She drew an upside down capital L, its base now topping the letter. Then, on her previous sketch, she replaced the four tiny gammas with a further four upside down Ls.

Alexis rose from her chair in one single movement, holding her hand to her mouth. Bergström swore loudly in Swedish.

'What we have now is a swastika, ring a bell?' said Emily

'And the Nazis wore their armbands on their left arm,' Alexis said, her voice blank.

'Exactly,' Emily concluded.

BERGSTRÖM AND OLOFSSON were overseeing the investigations, barking out orders to the various police personnel, who were either busy on phones or sitting at their computers. Their superiors' demand: find people linked to the Nazis or World War Two who might be living or own property in the region.

'It isn't so easy…' a policewoman complained to one of her colleagues. 'Do you think Nazi sympathisers wear an armband to advertise themselves, like carrying a designer handbag?'

'Focus on the dates,' said the other officer, chewing on his gum.

'What dates?'

'The dates we've been told to concentrate on. Key moments in the lives of the suspects, if I understand it correctly.'

'Can you make it a bit clearer? My son spilled his orange juice inside the car, this morning. I had to go back home, change his clothes and then the bloody dog had diarrhoea and pooped all over the place. I had to miss most of the briefing.'

'Another good reason I'm still single,' her colleague commented, with a grim smile. 'The profiler referred to "stress factors". For example, divorces, births, loss of a close relative, of a job, or even the actual death of a suspect. Those sorts of things.'

'Well, I have no doubt dying can be stressful.'

Her colleague raised his eyes to the ceiling.

'So what are the dates we have to look out for?'

'1970 and 2013.'

'So why did the English woman choose those years?'

'She's Canadian. The disappearances began in 1970, but bodies have only begun to surface since 2013. And you'd better hurry up, as neither Bergström nor Olofsson are in good moods.'

'Speak of the devil…'

Olofsson appeared behind the two officers, carefully balancing four steaming cups of coffee in his hands, walking towards the conference room.

'There's something I don't understand…' he said, entering the room and setting the cups down on the table.

Alexis passed the coffees around, as the detective watched her.

'…I just don't get why our culprit makes things so difficult for himself. It would have been so much easier to just carve a swastika on the arms of the victims, surely?'

Emily wrapped her fingers around the hot mug. 'Our man is cultured and it might be that the resemblance between the capital Y and the small gamma amuses him – at any rate, that's if we're dealing with the dominated party.'

'Hold on, I'm lost…' Olofsson said, ruffling his hair.

'Something in 2013 disturbed the life of the dominant one and/or the dominated party, profoundly affecting their relationship, their habits, the way they function. At first, the dominated half of the duo feels lost, then he slowly begins to enjoy this new form of liberty. He becomes creative, although obviously remains prey to his fantasies.'

'He still hasn't the guts,' Olofsson commented.

Emily formed a weak smile. 'He's still not bold enough to listen fully to his own fantasies, so he keeps a distance, so to speak: he slightly changes the ritual his Pygmalion – the dominant half – has taught him. It's a bit like lying by omission; it's a minor transgression, but it gives him huge joy.'

'You mean that, before 2013, the dominant half wasn't carving Ys, or small gammas, into his victims?'

'Indeed. Either he carved the full swastika or – it's my leading theory, right now – just a single branch.'

'Why a single branch?'

Concerned, Bergström turned towards the detective. He must have something particular in mind to be so openly attentive and fawning.

'The dominant personality considers each killing, and therefore each victim, as an integral part of a work of art, a painting if you wish, that he's gradually creating with every new death. A piece of work dedicated to the glory of Nazi ideology. Just as there are four branches in a swastika, he requires four victims to complete his painting. But, let's just return to the dominated half. I don't think he's allowing himself to deviate too far from the established modus operandi. So he retains the branch of the swastika dear to his Pygmalion, but changes it slightly as part of a cultured inside joke: a small gamma resembling a capital Y, a letter which also represents the sex of his victims.'

'The bastard must have been laughing his head off when he carved the X into Linnéa, then…' Olofsson looked around the room to see how the others had reacted to his remark. He regretted it immediately when he came across Alexis' pale features.

'Excuse me, Kommissionar. I've found something of interest…' A young woman stood at the door. No one had heard her enter. 'I've found a name that appears to fit with the details you've given us. I'm not quite sure if it's the person we're looking for, but I thought it would be worth raising it with you…'

'So, don't keep us waiting, Jacobsson,' Olofsson roared.

The young woman blushed deeply, and struggled to say anything else for a brief moment. Bergström forgot to chide Olofsson for his blustering attitude. He also wanted to hear the name.

'I've found an Erich Ebner, a German living in Sweden since 1947. Born 1920 and died in 2013.' She paused dramatically.

'Did he have a son in 1970?' Alexis barged in.

'No, I found no link to 1970. But there is a problem…' She paused again and Olofsson sighed impatiently.

'…He was a deportee. He was locked up in Buchenwald concentration camp. So I was asking myself … why would a deportee carve a swastika, seeing it's a symbol of his oppressors?'

Emily turned to Jacobsson. 'Have you heard of Stockholm syndrome?'

The young woman nodded.

'Maybe this Buchenwald prisoner was under the authority of a particularly cruel SS officer. He might have become so traumatised that he developed an emotional indifference to the horror around him, and even began to feel a sort of affection for his jailer: an affection that might have made him appropriate his feelings, thoughts, beliefs.'

Bergström's face shuddered with disgust. 'Really, Emily? Do you believe a prisoner who went through hell on earth, a hell that repeated itself day after day, could ever feel empathy for his torturer?'

'You have to consider this contaminating affection like an illness, Lennart. Like a cancer. Surviving inside a concentration camp was an unbelievable feat. People talk about the sheer barbarity of the Nazi camps, but only the survivors can truly understand the horror that lies behind those words. In order to survive, these prisoners had to submit themselves, body and soul, to unthinkable tortures. Emotional indifference to what surrounded them could be construed as a form of self-protection.'

'You make it sound as if this might well be our man. What if he's not?' Alexis interrupted them.

A strained silence fell on the room.

'What was his occupation, by the way?' Olofsson enquired.

Jacobsson passed her tongue over her lips to wet them before answering. 'Embalmer.'

'An embalmer, is that a joke?' the detective asked with a total lack of irony.

'His address?' Bergström said. He spoke more curtly than he would have wished. The nervous young recruit was almost on the edge of tears.

'Here, in Falkenberg.'

'The exact address, Jacobsson, please.'

She handed a piece of paper she held between her quivering fingers over to Bergström.

Bergström's mouth opened wide and closed even faster. He knew the address well. And he knew the person who now lived in Erich Ebner's house.

Falkenberg
July 1987

A SHIVER RAN DOWN Adam's spine. The hunt had proven exhilarating. His muscles still resonated from the sheer excitement.

Father had insisted he sleep for an hour and a half towards the end of the afternoon, so he would stay alert through until morning. They had waited for the night to get pitch black before setting off, a little after eleven.

For the first time, he had been the one to get the van ready. Father had placed him in charge of this part of the operation. Adam had then systematically checked the fuel and oil levels, the tyres and the tools they would require to manage Oskar's extraction.

They'd been watching him for nine months now. According to the correspondence they'd found when sorting through the rubbish bins, Oskar was now with his second host family, and it was evident things were not working out. The mother laboured night and day at the hospital; the oldest brother, fourteen years old, often went off on escapades and, when his wife was on duty, the father copied the son and went off gallivanting on his own as soon as the child had gone to bed. A perfect situation.

Work and application ensured you live a life of abundance and excellence. So why opt for mediocrity? This was a question that Adam always asked as he followed the victims selected by Father. All these folk – shortsighted and lazy – lived like pigs, wallowing in small lives totally devoid of true pleasure. At the end of the day, with Father's help, Oskar and the others would be spared their insignificant existence and all its attendant vulgarity. Its uselessness.

To get hold of Oskar had been child's play. The kid was downright stupid. He had no sense of danger. He had opened the door to Adam, had followed him and climbed of his own free will into the van. He had only begun to struggle when Adam had fastened the bag around his neck. Adam had held him firmly in place, watching as the bag stuck to the face, his eyes opened wide and the plastic was sucked into his mouth with every successive breath, until his head dropped against his chest.

Father had then driven them back home.

'Adam, pass the disinfectant and the wipes.'

Not only had Oskar peed all over himself but he'd also defecated. So, naturally, they'd had to clean him. Shit was all over the place, and it was necessary to hose the dissection table down. Adam hated that part of the process, but Father dealt with it, his face impassive, as if he had immunised himself against the smell.

Once Oskar and the table had been properly cleaned, Father cut open the bag that Adam had tightened around the boy's neck and shaved his hair. He used clippers then completed the job with a blade. Adam would wipe the shining scalp while Father held the scalpel to draw the branch on Oskar's left arm.

When, five years earlier, Father had taken him into his confidence and he'd joined the project, he had been adamant: Adam should master a complete knowledge of anatomy; he had to observe and note every stage of the process in minute detail. This had required extreme concentration. He even had to memorise the exact dosages. Fear of forgetting, making a mistake and disappointing Father had disturbed his sleep for several months.

'Adam!'

Father was handing him the scalpel. Adam looked down at Oskar's arm; it was still untouched. Disconcerted, he seized the blade in one hand, taking hold of the cold arm in his other hand and began his work. Father would be proud. He'd been practising for some time now, in secret, on hares. Penetrating the flesh to the correct depth, and then drawing the perfectly straight and perpendicular pairs of lines was not as easy as it appeared.

It was only last year that he had dared ask Father about the significance of the half section of the capital T he usually drew.

'It's not half a T, Adam; it's a branch of the *Hakenkreuz*. People call it a swastika. But *Hakenkreuz* is its correct name, as it's formed by four capital gammas.'

'But why do you draw a swastika, Father? I was under the impression you had fought against the Nazis?' The words had escaped his mouth before he could hold them back.

'In memory of Doktor Fleischer,' Father had calmly stated, without getting angry.

There. He had completed his gamma. It was perfect.

With his shaven scalp, his paler-than-pale skin and his scarred arm, Oskar no longer even resembled Oskar.

Father allowed himself a modest smile. Adam straightened himself with pride.

'Clean everything up, while I go and make breakfast.'

It was the first time Father had left him alone with one of their victims. But Adam knew he had earned it.

He placed the scalpel on the glittering tray.

When he turned round, Oskar was fixing him with wide-open, crazy eyes. Staring at him with the same look of panic he had displayed when Adam had put the plastic bag over his head. The child began to scream. The strident cry pierced Adam's eardrums.

'Shut up! Shut up! Close those fucking eyes! I don't want to see them. Shut up, I said!'

He took Oskar by the throat and tightened his grip as hard as he could manage. But Oskar was not listening. He was still screaming like a pig having his throat cut.

Adam didn't want Father to have to return and think he was not up to the task. He had to do something; something to keep Oskar quiet, for him to look away. It was vital the kid obeyed him.

Adam took hold of the scalpel again and held it against Oskar's chin. He dug into the flesh and slashed vertically across the skin until he had reached the sternal notch. He then sectioned the trachea and set it down on the dissection table.

Sweating abundantly, he wiped his forehead with his sleeve and listened. All he could hear was his halting breath. The cries had faded.

Now it was just a matter of keeping those damned eyes closed.

Skrea Beach, Falkenberg
Thursday, 23 January 2014, 11.00

EMILY PARKED IN FRONT of the imposing yellow-wood villa, finding space between a Porsche Cayenne and a Jaguar coupe. Three police vehicles and two SKL vans also occupied the vast private esplanade.

She walked to the back of the house and met up with Bergström and Olofsson in front of the old garage. Karl Svensson, Linnéa's ex-husband, stood back, next to a serious-faced blonde who was shrieking into her phone. A nervous twitch animated Svensson's lower lip and chin. Arms crossed over his chest, he stood with his back to the barn.

'As you can see, we're waiting,' Bergström explained to Emily, his voice on edge.

'That blonde bitch is beginning to get on my nerves,' Olofsson spat out. 'She's already been on the phone with the prosecutor for half an hour, complaining non-stop. What the hell does she think – that the more she screams, the more likely the prosecutor will be to say, "It's OK, if you insist, I'll cancel the search warrant and Karl Svensson will no longer be a suspect"?'

Bergström reckoned Olofsson was saying aloud what everyone else was thinking. He would also have liked to be able to shout like the lawyer and complain like Olofsson. It must be nice to be capable of venting your anger – to scream until you're out of breath!

He was under so much pressure. The prosecutor was calling him every single hour to check what point the investigation had reached.

234 JOHANA GUSTAWSSON

Linnéa's ex-husband was a celebrity. If the search proved fruitless, the Kommissionar would find himself in hot water. Svensson's lawyer might possibly take them to court and he could lose his job.

But still, he couldn't help himself thinking of little Tomas Nilsson. He could picture the naked body in its envelope of frost, the black eyes unnaturally large and empty, his neck slit open like a zipper on an old pullover. Despite the severity of his wounds, Bergström had felt like taking the child in his arms, kissing his forehead, warming him up, reassuring him. He'd thought of his own sons. When they'd been Tomas's age, they'd always strongly resisted taking baths. He and Lena always had to run after the two little monkeys as they dashed away naked, as fast as the wind, seeking improbable hiding places scattered around the house. His sons … if anyone had laid a hand on his sons … There was a question that was running through his mind to the point of giving him a migraine; it was simple, almost desperately trivial: how could anyone do this to a child?

He looked over at Emily. She was listening to Olofsson's rant, impassive, serene. A form of quiet strength radiated from her that he wished he could share.

'Where's Alexis gone?' Olofsson asked him, his voice a little calmer.

'To the municipal library. She's checking up on Ebner.'

Alexis' presence at the search of Svensson's house would have been a procedural mistake, so Emily had suggested she investigate Erich Ebner separately.

The lawyer hung up and nervously stepped towards them, her client on her heels.

'You can go ahead,' she conceded curtly.

'Mr Svensson, if you could accompany me to the police station,' Olofsson grinned.

'You won't find anything in my workshop!'

Bergström approached him and stood face to face. 'Thank you for letting us know where to begin the search, Mr Svensson.'

Falkenberg Municipal Library
Thursday, 23 January 2014, 13.00

ALEXIS RUBBED HER EYES with the tip of her fingers. She had been browsing through the articles on the microfilm reader screen for two hours already, and her eyes were tiring. Erich Ebner's name didn't appear in any of the library's databases. So she had had to consult all the local papers since the 11th of April 1945, the date of the liberation of the Buchenwald camp. As she couldn't understand Swedish, all she did was look out for Erich Ebner's name. If she were to come across a mention, she would have it printed out and take it to the station. She had seventy years of newspapers to wade through and still had a long way to go.

Thanks to the *personnummer* – the national identification number given to each citizen of Sweden – the police had access to some basic facts about Erich Ebner in their archives. He had been born in Munich, Germany, in 1920, had been naturalised Swedish and no longer possessed a German passport. He had practised as an embalmer with a funeral parlour from 1947 to 1993. In 1955, he had bought the house he had been renting in Falkenberg since 1947. In 1995, Jakob Svensson, Karl's father, had purchased the property from Ebner on the annuity system while he was still alive. On the 5th of October 2013, Erich Ebner's body had been found in his bed by firefighters called to a blaze nearby. The coroner had established it was a natural death, and was in no way suspicious, as he had been ninety-three. Everything pointed to Ebner having no immediate family, and no friends or neighbours that might have noticed his absence.

However, the *personnummer* system having only been introduced
in Sweden in 1947, it was not possible to establish the precise date
Ebner arrived in the country. Bergström assumed that the deported
prisoner had settled in Falkenberg in 1947, the date of his first
declared employment, but Alexis was less certain. And as she was
unwilling to leave matters to chance, she had decided to widen the
scope of her investigation by an extra two years.

Checking her phone for messages, she swallowed a mouthful of
water.

Before leaving for the library, she had contacted the Buchenwald Memorial Foundation in Weimar, Germany. She had left her
number on their answerphone, explaining it was an urgent request,
and she had been waiting since for them to call her back.

Alexis changed the reel and began browsing again, wondering all
the while why Ebner had decided to settle in a small coastal town in
Sweden. She could understand why he had chosen to flee Germany,
since his country, overtaken by the Nazis, had betrayed him. There
was no doubt Ebner would have resented his homeland, but this
wasn't enough of a reason to opt for Sweden. He must have had a
link of some sort to the Halland region and the area around Falkenberg. Maybe he had family there, friends who lived in the area in
the 1940s?

Alexis cast another glance at her phone. No sign of news from
the Foundation. However, Stellan had sent her a short but explicit
message: 'Tonight?'

Sweet memories of the previous night bloomed in her mind like
sudden flowers. She shook her head to disperse them before they
faded, choked by her fears and anguish, like weeds she was unable to
rid herself of. She wanted to see him again. Have Stellan make love to
her, surrender to his embraces. Her mind empty, her body receptive.
Her heart ... her heart was irrelevant. All she wanted was to go on
this journey again, revisit those feelings he had released.

Alexis texted 'Yes' in response and, after a few seconds of reflection, added a couple of exclamation marks.

She was about to set her phone down when the screen lit up again. She walked out into the corridor to take the call. Hilda Thorne, from the Buchenwald Memorial Foundation, was calling her back.

Alexis explained that she was seeking the Foundation's assistance to track down the family of an erstwhile Buchenwald inmate named Erich Ebner, who had died in Sweden a few months earlier. She was enquiring informally rather than officially, hoping Mrs Thorne would be amenable.

'Let me check on the name and see what I get. It will only take a few seconds.'

An impatient Alexis bit her lips.

'OK…' Hilda said after a moment, 'Erich Ebner … German, born in Munich in 1920. Interned in Buchenwald on the 17th of July 1944. Communist, political prisoner. Medical student. He worked in the quarry, the gas ovens and the medical experiment block. It appears he never joined any of the ex-prisoners' associations.'

'Have you got a photograph?'

'No.'

'Any information about his parents?'

'No. And, before you ask me to check for other Ebners, we do have a mass of them. If his parents had been interned in Buchen-wald, it would be indicated on his identity record. That's all I have in my records.'

'Do you know who else might have been working at the gas ovens or in the experiment block at the same time as him? I reckon it's not worth asking about the quarry, as the list would prove too long…'

'We don't hold that sort of information.'

'Were there any Swedes in Buchenwald during the same period as Erich Ebner?'

'No.'

Hilda was sympathetic, thought Alexis, but you had to extract every item of information as if by force.

'Can you give me a minute, please, Hilda?'

Alexis closed her eyes and concentrated. She had to connect all the known facts, search for links. What elements dominated Ebner's profile? German. Political inmate. Who'd made a new life for himself in Scandinavia. In Sweden.

An idea suddenly came to her.

Sweden and Norway were the two Nordic countries that had the most in common, culturally speaking. The two languages were so similar that Swedes and Norwegians understood each other with ease.

During the course of World War Two, the two countries had followed different paths: Sweden had opted for neutrality, whereas Norway, pressured into capitulating by Nazi Germany in 1940, had chosen the path of resistance, with Johan Nygaardsvold setting up a government in exile in London.

'Were there any Norwegians incarcerated in Buchenwald?' Alexis chanced her hand.

'Norwegian students, yes. Three hundred and fifty, if my memory is correct, arriving in January 1944.'

Ebner had been deported to Buchenwald in July 1944.

'Might there have been any medical students amongst them?'

'Yes.'

'So they might have been assigned to the medical experiment block, yes?'

'Let me check ... Yes, you're right: the experiment block, the infirmary and the pathology block.'

Alexis felt electrified. Erich Ebner must surely have crossed paths with at least one of them.

'Would it be possible to obtain a list of these Norwegian students and their current contact details, and if they've since died, the details of their families?'

'I can indeed forward the list of the contacts we have, but I can only provide you with the e-mail addresses, not the telephone numbers.'

'That would be perfect. Can you indicate which of them were medical students, please?'

'Of course.'

'I'm sorry to be putting such pressure on you, but do you think you could manage to do it today?'

'It's no problem: the lists are already available, you should be getting them in a few minutes.'

'Hilda, I'm being terribly demanding, but is there also a chance you could contact all of this group of ex-prisoners and ask if any of them knew Erich Ebner? I could provide you with some copy. Maybe some of the survivors might have mentioned his name to their children … As we're probably looking at tens of thousands of people, you could do it faster than me…'

'I could send a group e-mail and leave a note on our website.'

'Oh, Hilda, thank you so much. That would be fantastic.'

Alexis hung up and typed out the e-mail to be forwarded to all the erstwhile Norwegian students and their families. Then she would resume her trawl through the newspaper archives.

The wider she cast her nets, the more likely she was to catch some fish.

BERGSTRÖM SCANNED THE BARN with a look of satisfaction dawning on his face. A throng of white suits were busy poring over Svensson's workshop. The heavy silence was occasionally interrupted by the hushed passage of the protective shoe covers they were wearing or the hollow clink of the forensic team's metal cases. A curious sort of mood reigned: somewhere between excitement and disgust, impatience and apprehension.

When the Kommissionar, Olofsson, Emily and the forensics team had walked into the barn and switched on the light, the whole group had frozen where they stood.

'Fuck…' Olofsson had shouted. But even he had been lost for words that could describe the brutality of the scene revealed by the crude, sharp lighting.

Facing them stood a cube made of red, soot-stained bricks, three metres high and two metres in length, its square edges reinforced with steel cleats. At its centre was a half-moon-shaped hole, fifty centimetres in height and seventy across, with a set of double metal doors, left open.

'Am I crazy, or doesn't this resemble a gas oven?' one of the scene-of-crime guys asked.

A concert of sighs and throats being cleared was the only response. There was much to examine around the oven itself. Two metres to its right stood a tub a metre in diameter, next to a trestle table over which a series of surgical instruments were laid out, along with a pair of long blacksmith's tongs. Close by, hanging on the wall, two overalls and two pairs of gloves full of holes could be seen.

Bergström gave the go-ahead for his troops to fan out and begin the search, and everyone set to work with the sad memories of little Tomas Nilsson fresh in their minds.

The Kommissionar approached one of the technicians, who happened to be leaning over the large, empty tub.

'Can you tell what was inside?'

'Hydrofluoric acid. Very corrosive.'

Bergström thought of all the boys who had disappeared since 1970 whose bodies had never been found.

'Enough to dispose of a child's body?'

'If you add nitric acid and put a lid on the tub, it would do the job, yes.'

'Can you confirm if it ever housed nitric acid?'

'I'll check and let you know.'

The Kommissionar's eyes sought Emily out and caught sight of her just as she was walking back into the workshop. He hadn't even noticed she had gone out.

'Is there a problem, Emily?'

'The house is vast, isolated. This barn alone must be around a hundred square metres. But the garden is rocky and almost non-existent. I can't see how he could have disposed of the bodies, unless…'

'Dissolved them in a vat of acid?'

She looked back at him in surprise. 'No. The bodies of the children must be under the house or the barn. We'll have to scan the floor.'

'Björn!' the Kommissionar hailed a colleague over.

A technician who had been examining the contents of Svensson's trestle table turned towards them.

'Do you have a scanner anywhere in your van that could analyse what's under the floor?' the Kommissionar asked.

Björn Holm, who headed the forensics team, slid off the mask protecting his mouth, freeing his thick grey moustache. 'The SKL van isn't Mary Poppins' handbag, Lennart. The radar was left back at headquarters. Do you need it right now?'

Bergström nodded.

Björn sighed heavily.

'OK … I'll have it brought over. It'll be here in an hour and a half.'

※※※

Two hours later, Holm had completed the subterranean scan of the barn's floor and nothing had been found. He set the geological radar aside and looked at Bergström and Emily, his face showing signs of exhaustion.

'Are you really sure this must be the place, Lennart?'

Bergström nodded silently.

'So, now we go over the house, do we?'

Bergström nodded again.

Followed by Bergström and Emily, Björn quickly crossed the few metres separating the barn from the main house, trying to get out of the glacial outside air as quickly as possible.

'Where do we begin?' he asked, having switched the radar on again.

'The kitchen,' Emily ordered.

Björn followed her instructions unquestioningly. Dragging the radar equipment behind him, like a dog on a leash, and his eyes fixed on the control screen, he began his inspection of the room. He systematically combed through the American-style kitchen then moved on to the store room.

'Lennart!'

Bergström squeezed himself into the narrow store room, with Emily right on his heels.

'You've got something?'

'I think so, yes: there appears to be a cellar or something of the sort beneath the whole length of the kitchen. The trapdoor seems to be right under my feet.'

'Didn't you realise that before you set your feet down on it?'

Björn ignored the irritable tone of the Kommissionar's remark and pointed at the ground. 'Take a look. A thick parquet floor. And, below it, a concrete layer ten millimetres thick, I think. And before you ask me, I'm with forensics, not a mason. So, I have no pneumatic drill or crowbar with me.'

'There's no way you could pass for a mason, Björn, if you think using a pneumatic drill or a crowbar to pull out parquet flooring and a centimetre of concrete would work,' the Kommissionar responded, smiling broadly. 'Go and play with your brushes and magic powders, and I'll go and get my own simple drill from my house.' He gently slapped the back of the SKL chief and grinned.

Björn nodded, a half-smile peering through his thick moustache.

———————

Bergström refused to let anyone else use his drill and took charge of the digging process. It took him twenty minutes to pull out the wooden parquet and break through the layer of concrete.

Once he'd managed to open the trapdoor, the light below came on automatically, revealing a set of stairs covered by a thin film of dust. Bergström went down first, Emily, Olofsson and Björn following him, all clad in white suits, their shoes covered, their hair tucked under plastic caps and wearing latex gloves.

They reached a room about four metres by three, with a ceiling height of approximately 220 centimetres, its floor and walls covered with white tiles. A large table and a stainless-steel cart stood at its centre. To the right were a steel tub and a further two carts. At the back, facing the entrance, someone had filed away a dozen cardboard boxes on a set of metal shelves fixed to the wall. To the left was a door.

'It feels like an abandoned morgue,' Olofsson commented, his voice a whisper, as if speaking to himself.

Emily advanced towards the door and cautiously began to turn its handle.

Again, motion sensors had been installed and a light automatically came on, illuminating the room. It was much larger than the previous one, extending under the whole house. Shelving ran from floor to ceiling, almost geometrically aligned, precise, meticulous.

Emily took a few steps into the room and froze instantly. Her heart was beating so hard she was unable to hear the cries of fear and horror emanating from her colleagues.

As far as their eyes could see, rows of children's bodies were laid out along the metal shelves. Skinless bodies, their muscles exposed to the air. A film of thin muscle fibres barely covering their bones.

And, all of a sudden, she heard them. All the children. Their screams. Dark and savage. A chorus of lamentations streaked with pain and despair.

She placed her hand on that of the child lying closest to her; it was a thin, icy little hand, and it felt like a signal to cry, cry along with all the others until the pain that weighed on her so much stopped, until it just evaporated. She could now tell the children that she could hear all of them, that they were no longer alone.

KARL SVENSSON PEERED at the dirty wall as if searching for a window. From time to time, he adjusted the collar of his checked shirt, then returned to his contemplation of the wall.

When Bergström entered the interview room, Svensson looked up at him with disdain.

Anger ran through the Kommissionar's body like poison, slowing his breath and tightening his muscles. Bergström was angry at himself. He loathed his lack of professionalism, of proactivity, of flair for his work. He had been keeping an eye on the sculptor for some time, but had never been able to catch him in the act. The young girls had always pretended they'd met Svensson while hitch-hiking or had just been modelling for him, and none of the parents had been willing to lodge an official complaint. If only he'd done his job properly, Bergström thought, insisted, persevered, they might not have reached this stage.

Olofsson had gone to check on Karl's comings and goings at the time of Tomas Nilsson's disappearance as well as those of the London children.

Emily had remained in the cellar with Björn. She hadn't responded when the Kommissionar had suggested she join him for Svensson's interview. Instead she sat on a stool, her face just a few inches away from the cheeks of one of the cadavers, as if she were whispering into his ear.

Bergström sat down facing Svensson and placed a thick cardboard folder in front of him.

'When did you move into your villa, Karl?' Bergström's voice was calm, but underneath the table his fingers were quivering uncontrollably.

'Mid-November, last year.'

'Why did you decide to leave Stockholm?'

'As I seemed to be coming to Falkenberg almost every weekend to see friends, I warmed to the idea of settling here. And I also needed a larger space to create in, to work in.'

'There's no "space" like that in Stockholm?'

'Stockholm will never be on the west coast.'

'Why not Båstad? Your mother comes from there and you spent most of your summers there when you were a child, didn't you?'

'My father hails from Falkenberg, and my grandparents lived just yards from Skrea Beach.'

'Why did your father acquire this particular house?'

'I don't know. He's the one you should ask.'

'You have no idea? You were twenty-four in 1995 when he bought it; surely you remember something?'

'I was living in London then.'

'And you no longer visited Sweden?'

Svensson sighed with annoyance. 'The house had direct access to the beach. There weren't many places that offered you that sort of view in Falkenberg at the time. And the fields surrounding us are also part of the property.'

'The previous owner sold it to your father in instalments, for a derisory sum and continued to live there. Do you know why? Did they know each other?'

'I don't know.'

Bergström's fingers tapped out a rhythmic pattern on the card-board folder. Svensson watched as the fingers moved, and wetted his lips.

'You moved into the house in November. That was just after the death of the previous owner?'

'No. I had some renovation work done, it took six weeks.'

'What sort of work?'

'A paint job, a new kitchen, a new bathroom.'

'And new flooring?'

Svensson swallowed audibly. 'Yes.'

'And the cellar?'

'What cellar?'

'The cellar under the house.'

'There is no cellar.'

Bergström looked at Svensson with undisguised anger. 'Did you know a certain Erich Ebner?'

'He was the previous owner of my house.'

'Correct. And do you know what else you have in common?' Bergström opened the cardboard folder, took a few photos and laid them out on the table, facing Svensson. 'You like children.'

On the edge of panic, Svensson glanced at the photos of naked young girls. Sweat was pearling down his forehead and temples.

'They're models. For my sculptures. And they're not children. They're all older than fifteen.'

Bergström looked back at him, a note of doubt spreading across his face.

'I'm not so certain, Karl … As I was saying, you share your love of children with Erich Ebner.'

Bergström placed another four photos on the table; bodies recovered from the cellar.

Svensson jumped out of his chair. His back right up against the wall, he pointed at one of the photos with an unsteady finger.

'Fuck, what is that? What is it?' He was shrieking, saliva flying out of his mouth.

'One of the flayed kids we have found in your cellar, Karl.'

'But I have no damned cellar! There is no cellar in my house!'

'And the tools you keep in your workshop, Karl?'

'No, no, no, no, no…' His hands held together in prayer, his chest thrust forward and his eyes wide open, Svensson seemed to be begging for his life. 'Listen to me, Kommissionar…'

'And the oven, Karl? The tens of litres of hydrofluoric acid? The surgical instruments?'

'Listen … listen to me…' Svensson opened his mouth wide as if gasping for air. 'They're my work instruments. I use all those to sculpt the glass. The tub, the hydrofluoric acid, the oven in which I shape the glass… everything! The asbestos gloves … and what you say are surgical instruments – they're dental tools from the 1940s: that's how I cut the glass, with metal heads, knives too…'

He sat down again, placed his hands flat on the top of the table. He moved them nervously several times, widening the space between his fingers then bringing the digits together again, as if he were trying to draw a specific figure.

'It's all for my sculptures, Kommissionar,' he continued, his voice unsteady, each word accompanied by a downward movement of his head. 'It's for my sculptures. I would never, absolutely never harm a child. Never. But where … where did you find these…'

'In your cellar, Karl, as I said before.'

Svensson brought his hands to his face and began to sob, his whole body shaking from side to side. 'But what cellar? I don't understand; I just don't understand…'

Bergström leaned against the back of his chair.

'Do you know what also bothers me, Karl? It's the fact that the young woman who had given you an alibi for the night of Linnéa Blix's disappearance – well, she's now changed her mind.'

OLOFSSON BLINKED as he shook his head. The memories of the flayed children stuck to the back of his eyes like a piece of paper caught between the wipers and the windshield of a car, bothering you throughout your whole, endless journey.

At first, coming across all the bodies of children, he had suspected a bad joke. With their opaque eyes and visible muscles, they could have been made out of plastic. They hadn't decomposed and no rotting smell emanated from them.

This awful sicko had torn their skin away and treated them with some sort of solution. And he had then filed them away on the shelves like random pieces of meat, a label attached to each ankle indicating their provenance. Yes, that was just what they were – slabs of meat labelled according to origin.

Olofsson had felt like running away. But the three other cops he was with had more guts: he'd had to demonstrate he was as tough as them. Bergström had immediately contacted the prosecutor and the coroner, while Björn had called in the rest of his team. As for the Canadian woman, she had approached the cadavers so closely he had almost felt sick.

He had to confess, though, the bitch didn't appear to be fazed in the slightest. He would never admit to it, but he had been rather impressed by her cognitive interview with Anna Gunnarson the day before. He would never have thought that just chatting about clothes and hairstyles would help her put a finger on elements crucial to the investigation. And all that stuff about the swastika had proven to be the cherry on the cake. There was no doubt she was extremely savvy.

As a clever man, he'd swallowed his pride and made himself insignificant. If he could get himself on the profiler's good side, he could learn a lot. Maybe then people would respect him a bit more.

A window opened up on his screen: he had just received an e-mail. Hopefully it would be good news.

Bergström had asked him to interview the owners of the two other properties in Svensson's hamlet. Maybe they had known Erich Ebner? Or had they possibly seen Ebner and Svensson together? Olofsson had traced all the owners back to 1947, when Ebner had moved in, but only Lars Rhode and Markus Stormare, the current owners, were still alive.

Lars Rhode, eighty-five, had bought his house in 1989. He had rented it out to summer visitors every year, and had never actually lived in it himself. He couldn't recall any specific complaints or remarks made by his tenants about any neighbours and nothing about Ebner. Unfortunately, he hadn't retained any detailed records about his past tenants.

Markus Stormare, whose e-mail he'd just received, suggested they speak on the phone that evening.

The detective immediately dialled his number. When Stormare answered, he quickly recognised the Skåne accent, its r's pronounced the French way, flat.

'My father was from around there. He bought the house in 1975,' Stormare explained. 'My parents were thinking of moving here when they retired. They had spent their whole life in Skåne and wanted a change of landscape. But my father fell ill and we had to rent out the house while we waited for him to get better. I never had the heart to sell it or live in it myself.'

'Did you keep a record of your tenants?'

'I must have some e-mails and phone numbers for the past ten years, I think, but not for earlier. They were only summer rentals.'

'Do you recall if, amongst them, there might have been a family that came several times?'

'Yes – a Danish couple with two little girls, the Knudsens. They rented the house for ten summers in a row, towards the end of the 1970s. Martha and Marius Knudsen. I remember them well, because they stopped coming all of a sudden after a nasty argument with one of the neighbours.'

Olofsson froze. 'Do you know which particular neighbour?'

'No, not at all, but I'm sure the Knudsens will have a better recollection.'

AS SOON AS SHE HAD WALKED through the door of the conference room, Emily began her off-the-cuff lecture, interrupting the conversation between Bergström, Olofsson and Alexis, and spitting out the brutal details of what she had discovered.

They had found sixty-two bodies in Svensson's cellar. A label fixed to the ankle of each indicated a place – in all likelihood where the kidnapping had occurred and/or the child's home – as well as a year, undoubtedly that of the child's death. If the dates were to be trusted, the killer, Erich Ebner, had begun his killing spree in 1948.

Emily paused. Not so much to cushion the blow for her audience, who listened aghast to her information, but to get a grip on her own emotions.

The process of thinking through and building a psychological profile was such an intimate thing. Normally, she journeyed through every individual stage alone; she would never think about sharing the speculations that inevitably accompanied her road into the mind of the killer and then towards the killer himself. But, today, sharing her thoughts in this manner gave her an unexpected feeling of catharsis: she was letting go of an immense weight, or rather the people in front of her were helping her to do so. This served to clear and energise her mind.

'1970, as we had initially believed, happens to be a key date in the creation of Ebner's criminal personality,' Emily continued, taking her coat off. 'That year, a brutal and radical change in his victimology appears: according to the coroner's early conclusions, most of the victims prior to 1970 were adults – men and women. Thereafter, we have only found male children. The years on the labels correspond to all the disappearances we had found evidence of.'

Olofsson's chair, on which he was rocking, ground to a halt. 'Adults? I thought he was only interested in boys between six and ten?'

'Something crucial must have happened in Erich Ebner's life in 1970. The most likely hypothesis is the birth of a son, as Alexis had suggested, or news of a pregnancy. But, according to the Swedish records, Ebner never had a child. This is something we have to investigate further.'

'Could 1970 be when he first met his partner in crime?'

'I don't think so. His associate must be at least twenty years younger than him, I'd say, and I doubt that our dominated party is now in his sixties. I remain convinced of the validity of my existing profile and believe the man must be between thirty-five and forty-five.'

'If Ebner had been killing since 1948, we should be confronted with more than sixty-two bodies, shouldn't we?' Alexis asked.

'Between 1948 and 1970, Ebner would kill every fifteen to eighteen months, and not every nine months, as he appears to have done since 1970. However, even bearing in mind this lengthy cooling-off period, yes, we are still missing bodies. Some of the children kidnapped since 1970 were not found in the cellar. About twenty, if our calculations are correct.'

Olofsson stopped loudly munching on the potato crisps he had been eating. 'So where are they, then? What if someone else kidnapped them? How can we be certain it was him?'

'The nine-month cycle is too precise to allow any doubt. It would be too much of a coincidence.'

'And the swastika?'

A growing migraine was laying siege to Bergström's head. He sighed before wearily answering. 'As Emily had foreseen, a branch of the symbol, was carved into the left arm of every single victim found in the cellar.'

'So how did the crazy bastard manage to halt the decomposition of the bodies?'

Bergström cleared his throat. 'The coroner believes Ebner practised polymeric impregnation, meaning that he replaced all the organic liquids in the body with silicone to help preserve the bodies of his victims. It's a very lengthy process, which might explain the nine months between murders. Notwithstanding the significant symbolism – it matches the length of a pregnancy; although I don't think that's what Ebner had in mind.'

Emily opened a bottle of water that had been left on the table and took a long sip from it.

'There is another significant date where Ebner is concerned: 1987,' she continued, as if the conversation between the Kommissionar and the detective had not even taken place. 'From 1987 onwards, the enucleation and excision of the trachea become systematic.'

'Could this be where his associate comes into play?' Alexis suggested.

'Exactly. Enucleation and the excision of the trachea are important changes in the ritual. A subject who has been killing for forty years does not modify his procedure out of nowhere or change his modus operandi overnight. So, the emergence on the scene of an associate could well explain these post-mortem mutilations. Ebner commits his first solo crimes in 1948; in 1970, something happens that leads to a change in the type of victim. He is joined by and trains a partner, who begins to obey his own personal fantasies in 1987, when the enucleations and excisions of the trachea appear. Ebner dies in 2013. His associate is now emancipated and eliminates from the modus operandi all the elements that displease him, i.e., the transformation that had been at the heart of the ritual for his Pygmalion.'

Emily helped herself to coffee and continued, as if speaking to herself.

'So we are left with Erich Ebner as the dominant half, for whom killing is just a means – the grim act necessary to accomplish his medical or artistic experiment, whichever way he sees it. A man who disliked any form of publicity and succeeded in remaining anonymous for over sixty years despite his killing spree. Then, onto the scene emerges a dominated party, who perpetuates the crimes alone following Ebner's death. His hunting pattern, during which he observes and tracks his victims until he knows all there is to know about them, as well as his dual hunting territory, in London and Sweden, inform us of the fact he is particularly meticulous, patient and organised. He's also intelligent and cultured, as we've learned from our analysis of his little game with the resemblance between the Y and the letter gamma.'

'Doesn't sound at all like he's the junior partner, this guy,' Olofsson commented, still rocking on the two back feet of his chair.

'He was only the dominated half when it came to the relationship with his Pygmalion. In his social and professional existence, he's a man with an unhealthy desire to control those who surround him and impose his authority. That's how he compensates for all the frustration he subconsciously experiences for having been held back and directed earlier. He must have lived under the yoke of his mentor since 1987, at least – the date when the enucleation and excision of the trachea processes come into play – and had to submit to someone else's twisted fantasies. Since the death of his partner, though, he has flowered, become his own man, and is now free to explore his own fantasies. He continues the work of his Pygmalion, because he is conditioned to do so, but he gradually begins to modify the previously established rules of the game: he kills in London, no longer transforms the victims, replaces the capital gamma with a lower case gamma, buries his victims, kills a woman, then, led by his no doubt narcissistic personality, begins to leave the bodies above ground so he can admire them at leisure. Each new transgression is experienced as a victory and an act of liberation. Little by little, he is moving out of the shadow of his mentor. He gets used to this new leading role and begins to forget the rigour and care his erstwhile partner had taught him: every new deviation from the norm is a mistake that sets us on his trail.'

Olofsson rose, sweeping away the dust of crumbs hanging from his pullover. 'So, what about Svensson, is he our second guy, part of our terrible duo, or not? Svensson could have become friendly with Ebner, as he lived close to his grandparents' home, and maybe he was the one who convinced his father to purchase the house so he would have no need to move the whole, morbid collection of bodies away. Once Ebner had died, he sealed off the underground section, as he's not into the whole Doctor Frankenstein scene, but he didn't want to get rid of all the souvenirs of the good old days with Ebner. We also have to bear in mind that he's Linnéa Blix's ex-husband.'

Alexis observed Emily. She was gazing at the cork board, miles away from the conversation, lost in her own thoughts, her mind wandering on some inscrutable journey. Maybe she too was thinking of the families of the sixty-two victims found in Ebner's cellar. How the trauma of their disappearance, transmitted from generation to generation, must weigh on their family history like a lead curtain. They were finally about to get some answers, albeit atrocious and barbaric.

BERGSTRÖM HUNG UP THE PHONE and turned towards Emily.

'Björn has just confirmed they found no fingerprints in Svensson's cellar. Which means that, while he was dissecting and handling stuff, he must have been wearing gloves. As to DNA traces, with the amount of bodies to be checked, it's going to take a hell of a long time before we can start any comparison.'

Emily leaned her elbows on the table, laced her fingers together and pressed her lips against her hands. It was no surprise to her that the cellar was devoid of fingerprints: Erich Ebner had managed to kill over sixty-five years without raising suspicion, which was a testimony to the care he had taken.

At that moment, Olofsson rushed breathlessly into the conference room. He stood himself in front of his colleagues, legs apart and chest thrust forward, posing like a cowboy.

'Do you want the bad news or … the bad news?'

He stared at Bergström and Emily in turn, a look of disgust curling his lips.

'OK, so I'll begin with the bad news, then. Jacobsson's been through the list of Markus Stormare's tenants – he's the owner of the house next to Svensson's. No one ever mentioned Ebner. Not a single memory of even having seen him, in fact.'

'And the contact Stormare provided? The Danish couple?'

'Martha Knudsen is calling me back around 1 p.m.'

'And what's the other piece of bad news?' Bergström asked, sighing deeply.

Olofsson looked at his notepad.

'I checked on Svensson's alibis for each murder and they're solid. He was in Stockholm when Andy Meadowbanks died; he stayed there the whole week. As for Cole Halliwell's dates, he was seen with his agent and potential buyers in Gothenburg; there was no way he could have travelled to London. And in Logan Mansfield's case, he was at home for three days in a row, accepting deliveries of glass from the same supplier, and the delivery driver remembers him well, as they had something of an argument. He has no alibi when it comes to Tomas Nilsson, but he was in Berlin when the child was kidnapped.'

Bergström rubbed his eyes. 'And Linnéa Blix?'

'Oh, yes! Svensson was busy having fun in bed with his agent's daughter, who's only fifteen. He was at her place when Linnéa disappeared. Which is why he asked his young friend, a great piece of ass by the way, to provide his alibi.'

'The girl's confirmed all this?'

'Confirmed by the girl and the pizza delivery guy Svensson opened the door to. And I was about to forget the third piece of bad news: no trace of blood has been found in Svensson's workshop or on his tools. It appears to be true that he's just messing around with glass in his barn, and nothing else.'

Inside his jeans pocket, Olofsson's phone vibrated.

'It's Martha Knudsen,' the detective said as he took the call. He switched the speaker on and set the phone down on the table. '*Hej,* Martha, this is Detective Olofsson.'

'I hope I'm not calling you too early. I have to go fetch my grandson Anton at the train station. So best have our chat now, because then I have to take him to play on his sledge with our neighbour's children. So, you said you wanted to hear about those summers we spent in Falkenberg, is that it?'

'That's right, Martha.'

'Well, we liked the area so much we decided to settle there when we retired. We're in Varberg, now. And as our youngest daughter lives in Kungsbacka, it's convenient. Our eldest is in Philadelphia...'

'You rented Markus Stormare's house towards the end of the 1970s, is that correct?'

'From 1977 to 1986. Before, we stayed at the camping grounds by the beach, but when my husband got promoted, we were able to afford a rental. And it was such a lovely house, I can tell you! You can't imagine how happy the girls were!'

'Markus Stormare mentioned a disagreement with a neighbour…'

'Oh dear, yes – in 1986, our last summer spent there … What an awful story, so awful…'

'What happened?'

'Linda, my youngest daughter, would follow her older sister everywhere, just like a cute little dog … And, as Linda was twelve years old that year, we let her take her bike to join her sister at the beach, as it was barely five minutes away. One day, it was towards the end of the afternoon, we saw her return in tears … well, more than that, in a state of shock, she was even violently sick over the porch, and then came rushing into our arms. She sobbed frantically the whole evening; there was no way we could console her! I can't tell you how worried I was! It was only the next day she was able to tell us what had happened and then only because my eldest daughter put pressure on her. Linda adored her sister, you understand…'

'So what happened, Martha?' Olofsson was growing impatient, but Martha Knudsen seemed completely unaware of it.

'The son of one of the neighbours – well, I'm not even sure if he was his actual son – had killed a rabbit in front of Linda. First he had broken its legs, one at a time, asking my daughter to listen to the noise it made … I still have goose-pimples just thinking about it. Then he had snapped the animal's neck and burned it in front of her. Awful, just awful.'

Martha Knudsen paused briefly. She inhaled and exhaled loudly, then continued her story.

'My husband was furious. He called the police, but they didn't want to get involved, so we took it on ourselves to pay the neighbour a visit.'

'Was he called Erich Ebner?'

'I don't know what his name was, but he greeted us on the doorstep and assured us that, the boy – I don't know what he was called – would never have done such a thing.'

'The boy who scared your daughter, how old was he?'

'I don't know. We never saw him. Our daughter told us he was tall; that's all we knew.'

'And before this happened, had your daughter been seeing much of him?'

'No, apparently not. We generally did everything together, but our elder daughter had begun to spend some time with a group of youngsters from the area … She was fifteen, you know, so she went to the beach with her friends, boys and girls, and no longer with us, her parents. We were old folk, you understand…'

'Might you have any photographs from that time – pictures this boy might appear in?'

'I only have photos of the four of us, but I'm sure my daughters have kept some photos of the friends they made. Maybe he's in some of them…'

Olofsson wrote down the phone numbers of Martha Knudsen's daughters, thanked his loquacious interlocutor and hung up.

While he left a message on the Knudsen daughters' respective answerphones, Bergström translated the substance of the conversation for Emily.

'A triad,' Emily murmured after listening to the tale.

'What?'

'According to Martha Knudsen, the boy who was staying with Ebner, whether he was his son or not, tortured animals. And I now believe this is the man who discovered Ebner after he died. He took the time to move some of the bodies to his own place, as a souvenir, then sealed the cellar under a layer of concrete, and in all likelihood started a fire close by and called the fire brigade. With respect for his mentor, he arranged for Ebner's body to be discovered while he still resembled the man he had once been. But, doing this, he was careful not to take any risk of being associated with the dead man, and managed to preserve his own anonymity so he could continue his mentor's work in peace. He was used to setting fires, he'd been doing it since he was a child, as well as killing animals. We are confronted by two of the three components of the Macdonald triad: at least two of the three behavioural characteristics signifying the presence of criminal potential in a child long before he has become an adult. The third traditionally sees him wet his bed beyond the normal age and I have no doubt our boy also was prone to that.'

'You think that…'

'…We have found the second half of the killing duo. All we now have to do is identify him.'

Falkenberg
October 2013

ADAM WATCHED FATHER SIP his evening soup. His hand, wrinkled like an old apple, trembled when he filled the spoon. The journey from plate to mouth seemed a perilous one.

Just like a tree bent by the intensity of the wind, Father's body had weakened under the weight of the passing years. Erich Ebner had finally contracted the grey plague. Normality had caught up with him. But even as he suffered from it, he knew it was inevitable. His body was a shipwreck, but his brain remained clear of the water. Since his sixtieth birthday, he had kept his memory sharp through daily exercises and one had to admit his faculties were still tip-top.

That morning, Adam brought up once again a subject matter that Father had been carefully avoiding for six years.

'Father, you must listen to me. It's time to move the workshop to my place.'

Erich placed the spoon on the plate, as if it now weighed too much. 'I've already told you, it's out of the question.'

Adam ran an impatient hand across his forehead. Father just wouldn't listen. Maybe he should ignore him and move the bodies? Were Father to die suddenly, he was the one who would find himself obliged to resolve all the problems. Urgently, at that.

'You know what will happen when you die, Father. This house will no longer be yours, nor mine.'

'I had to sell it. At the time, I had no other choice.'

'I know, Father. I don't blame you for what you did. But, right now, you have a choice. I have a job, I can help you … We have to get organised if we don't want to be forced to act hastily. I can take care of it.'

Erich finished his soup and wiped his withered lips. 'My body might be slowing down, but it doesn't mean I'm ready to meet the Grim Reaper, Adam. I'll know when the time approaches, and only then will we begin to plan matters. Not before. Don't rush me into my grave, son.'

Adam gave an exasperated sigh, then nervously shook his head. 'All I'm asking you to do is to make some arrangements for your exit, as all parents do for their children. You aren't immortal, Father, despite what you think.'

'My departure is fully planned. You won't have to deal with anything, Adam.'

'I'm not referring to your cremation, I'm concerned about your legacy. Everything we've built together. Why are you so obstinate? Why won't you listen to me? Have I not provided you with enough evidence that I can take over your work? Do you think I'm not capable of carrying the torch?'

Erich's gaze moved from his plate to the clock on the wall. He was indicating to his son that he should leave.

Adam rose so sharply his chair toppled over. He left without picking it up from the floor, simmering with anger. He got into his car and slammed the door again and again, until he was overcome by tears of frustration. Once he had managed to calm himself, he realised he was sitting in the passenger seat and he was overcome with rage once again; the tears began flowing once more.

Father no longer hunted at night. He couldn't stay awake long enough. Before, he had never shown signs of tiredness. But, one night, Father had declared Adam should go out alone, from now onwards, to do the recces and the extractions. Adam had agreed, as he always did. Erich Ebner informed and ordered. He never consulted. Which is why Father had never started a new life for himself. Even his wife, who was the most submissive woman Adam had ever known, had abandoned Erich to his fate. At the end of the day, Adam was the only one who had the grit to buckle under and remain with this man.

Adam shifted into the driver's seat and drove off. For the last five years, he had been the one to stay up at night. During the daytime, Father would join him sometimes to check on addresses and plan the operations in minute detail, but, at night, Adam had to manage without him. Carrying out a kidnapping alone had not proven easy. He'd had to double his precautions and become hypervigilant.

Tonight, he was planning to observe Tomas Nilsson, their next victim. This particular broken family didn't seem to adhere to any fixed pattern, which complicated matters somewhat.

＋＋＋＋＋

He returned, starving, to Father's place at 6 a.m. the following morning. Normally he would take a couple of sandwiches along, but his precipitous departure the previous evening had prevented him from doing so.

He took a shower, then walked downstairs to join Father in the workroom. He would wait for lunchtime before raising the subject of the move again. He was confident he would eventually end up convincing him.

Adam slipped into the protective suit, put on the gloves, the shoe covers and the hair net, and stepped into the workroom. His father wasn't there. He quickly glanced in every corner but couldn't find him. He took off his protective clothing and ran up to Father's room on the first floor.

He was still in bed. Adam approached, already guessing his hand would be touching a cold body. He ran his fingers through the thin, white hair and kissed the high, intelligent forehead, the resolute chin and the calloused hands. He asked to be forgiven for their latest row, for his own anger, but he knew that his father had left with his heart full of respect and pride for his son. Their close connection transcended any sort of petty family argument. Even in death, Father would reign over his life.

Adam spent nine hours at his side, at times mourning in silence and at others serenely laying his face against his father's chest; a form of closeness he was sorry he hadn't practised more when he'd been alive. He told Father about the joy he'd experienced living by his side, the honour he had felt, all through his life, to have been Erich Ebner's son. He then kissed him on the cheek and bade him farewell.

He walked down to the kitchen, found the notepad Father kept alongside his journal and gathered his thoughts. He had to come up with some sort of strategy. A new one. Initially, he had planned to store the majority of the bodies at his place. Recreate Father's workshop. But he wanted Father's approval to begin the work … and now he was dead, that bastard Jakob Svensson was waiting like a vulture to get his hands on the house. Every month, he sent his lawyers to check on Father's health. Their last visit had been just three weeks ago.

Adam was due to return to London in less than forty-eight hours and would not be able to go back to Sweden for at least ten days. This meant he had little choice; he would have to act fast. Two days would not suffice to transport all the bodies; another solution had to be found. He knew what Father's advice would have been: whatever you do, do it well. So he would move as many bodies as he could in the time he had to hand, while avoiding taking any unnecessary risks. He would then seal the trapdoor leading to the workshop. Once it was all done, he'd contrive for Father's corpse to be found. There was no way that he was having Svensson's people discovering him lying in bed in a state of advanced putrefaction.

Adam set his pen down.

Yes, the plan was perfect. And grandiose, too. With the army of dead prey locked up forever in the workshop, he would be offering Father a mausoleum, not unlike Emperor Qin Shi Huang's. It would be a wonderful *hommage* to Father. He would die a hero, just as he had lived.

IT HAD BEEN A SHORT NIGHT, but her sleep had run deep. Tiredness had conquered in the struggle with anxiety.

Alexis had been obliged to cancel her dinner with Stellan the evening before, and he'd then had to leave on a business trip that morning.

She was surprised how much she missed him. She barely knew the man, after all. Incredible, she thought, how she was incapable of having the slightest emotion without feeling compelled to analyse it. She must surely learn to function differently: her lifestyle was just becoming too exhausting and mechanical.

Calling on her inner resolve, she banished all the petty overthinking from her mind, the comments and remarks she could almost hear her mother already making, and focused instead on the exquisite sensation that was her craving for Stellan.

She switched her phone onto speaker and listened to her messages, then stepped over to the bathroom. Just as she was dressing, the phone rang.

'Yes, Mother, I'm about to go out, I…'

'Dear God, Alexis, don't tell me you're involved with this terrible story … But of course, you are, aren't you?'

'What are you talking about, Mum?'

'It's on every channel, Alexis! The bodies they've found at the sculptor's place! Linnéa's ex-husband!'

Alexis hunted down the remote and switched on the TV. She

flicked through the channels; the same images were appearing on every network. The whole world was focused on Falkenberg.

Men carried black rubber bags, one after the other, into medical vans. The camera moved along. The scene was being filmed from afar, and the image was indistinct, but it was evident the bags contained bodies.

Alexis imagined Bergström's fury, while her mother chattered endlessly away at the other end of the line.

'...even the sun rises late in Sweden! Couldn't you have gone to a spa resort or Club Med, like all single girls of your age, instead of—'

Losing patience, Alexis hung up abruptly, before she said something she would later regret.

Her phone rang immediately. It was Alba. She was obviously calling for the same reason as her mother.

'Oh, I'm so happy to reach you, Alexis. I was so worried ... Let me put the speaker on; I'm at home, with Paul.'

On the other end of the line, Alexis could hear the coffee machine purring. It was just past seven in the morning in London.

'Are you OK? Don't you think it's time for you to come home now?' Alba's words were indistinct, masked by the sound of chewing; Alexis could imagine the thin slice of buttered bread.

'Don't you think this whole business is getting rather dangerous, Alexis?'

'The whole thing is disgusting,' Paul commented. 'So it's Linnéa's ex-husband who's behind it all?'

Alexis opened her mouth then closed it again. She wasn't willing to answer that sort of question. 'I'm not allowed to say anything, Paul, I'm sorry,' she said at last.

'I know, I know ... But they've arrested him, I hope? Thinking of a monster like that roaming free, it's hardly reassuring...'

'Don't worry her, Paul ... Can't you tell she's in a terrible state? Do you need any help, love, anything we can do? Do you want me to come over? Or Paul?'

'No, no, no, thank you, you're darlings, but everything is fine. I'll soon be back, I promise.'

Alexis put on a pair of tights, thick woollen socks and her corduroy trousers. She was pinning her hair back, as she had no time to brush it properly, when the phone rang for the third time. It was a Swedish number.

'Alexis Castells?'

Alexis cautiously said, 'Yes.'

'Good morning, I'm Charlotte Linkvist. You sent me an e-mail concerning the time my father spent in Buchenwald. His name was Andreas Ulvestad.'

Alexis couldn't recall all the Norwegian students who'd appeared on the list supplied by Hilda Thorne, but she thought it best to pretend she was familiar with the name.

'Yes, I remember,' she said.

'You mentioned that you were hoping to gather information about a prisoner called Erich Ebner.'

'That's correct. He was a German political inmate who immigrated to Sweden after the war.'

'My father often talked about some of his comrades, but Ebner's name doesn't ring a bell. However, after his liberation, he wrote a sort of journal about his deportation to Buchenwald. I came across it after he died, but have never summoned the courage to read it. I thought maybe Ebner might be mentioned in it. I don't wish to part with the notebooks, but I can have them scanned by my assistant and send them to you by e-mail?'

Alexis suddenly found herself energised. 'That would be so good of you, Charlotte. That would be just perfect.'

'Just give me a second.'

Alexis heard the handset at the other end being lowered onto a desk, four equally spaced beeps, a buzzing noise, then a distant conversation.

'If I hang up, I might forget about it, so I'm dealing with it right now. My personal assistant will take care of everything. You should have the material in an hour or so at most.'

Friday, 24 January 2014

He drags a chair towards the TV screen, sits just a few inches away from it, naked, his back straight and his hands holding his knees in a vice-like grip. The cold metal freezes his backside and his balls and spreads goosebumps across his smooth body. He watches the images being shown on every network time and again, his eyes open wide.

It's only taken him three months to destroy sixty years of work. He closes his eyes. Sixty years in three months.

His nails dig into the flesh of his legs.

He knows the Other is furious. The Other is screaming his lungs out from amongst the dead. Vociferously claiming he isn't worthy of his trust. That he should have fought his vanity not wallowed in it.

The Other is right.

He grips his hair and pulls, mouth open wide, cheeks drawn by his loud sobs.

HE-IS-RIGHT. With every word, a clump of hair comes loose.

He rises suddenly and runs to a corner of the room. He cowers there like a child on the naughty step, eyes fixed on his feet, arms alongside his body. He must make penance. Find forgiveness. Expiate his sins.

Almost with a jump, he moves away from the wall. Shakes his head. No, no. It's not entirely his fault. The Other should have listened. He had a plan: transfer the bodies to his place, keep them safe. Keep the collection out of harm's way. If the Other had not been so obstinate, nothing would have happened.

And even if the Other still talks to him all the time, just like a scratched record, death has freed him from all of his obligations. And it's such sweet freedom – much too sweet to abandon now. Oh, the sheer joy of being able to hunt alone, direct events, without having to bother with all the months of careful planning, isolated in the cellar inhaling the formaldehyde and dissecting the kids.

He has now discovered the orgasmic pleasure of sharing. His works are inspected, studied, analysed by experts. Admired, even; he is certain of that.

He squeezes his erect penis in his hand.

He must defend his territory. Chase away the intruders so he can begin hunting again.

He'll start with that nuisance of a profiler. He will cut her breasts off and feast on her nipples. He's heard that nipples taste like squid.

THE ATMOSPHERE in the conference room was gloomy.

Bergström, Olofsson and two officers were silently reading Andreas Ulvestad's diaries. The Norwegian prisoner had written all too eloquently about the daily horror of Buchenwald.

From time to time, one would stifle a cough, or sigh with dismay.

Alexis and Emily set down their belongings, then each sat down facing a desktop computer. Not one person interrupted their reading to look up at them.

Unable to help comb through Ulvestad's diaries, which were written in Norwegian, Emily and Alexis had been to the library to continue the research into Erich Ebner. They'd already pored over hundreds of pages, but had not come across anything of use: his name was not mentioned anywhere.

Alexis checked her e-mails, hoping someone might have picked up her message in a bottle, but all was silent on that front.

She walked over to the small kitchen to make some coffee, thinking about the young man Martha Knudsen had mentioned. She was certain he was Ebner's son. Ebner had been a solitary man, shielding himself from the world and retreating into a haven of peace. The only person he would have granted full access to his world would have been a direct descendant. A descendant fashioned and indoctrinated by him.

'Jag har hittat något!'

There was no need for a translation: the tone of the remark spoke for itself.

She rushed back to the conference room, the packet of coffee still in her hands.

Bergström, Emily and the two officers were gathered around Olofsson, who was brandishing his forefinger above his head, not unlike a school child calling for attention.

'Erich Ebner, surgical student. Ulvestad and his medical student mates would meet up with him on Sunday afternoons, by the latrines, where they wouldn't be disturbed by the SS. Why in hell the latrines?'

'Probably because the SS avoided going there, what with the disgusting smell that came from communal toilets like that,' Alexis explained.

Olofsson gestured his understanding and continued. 'Err ... he says the discussion often took place in English, but most of the time in Norwegian, because Ebner wanted to learn their language...'

'Does Ulvestad say why?' Bergström enquired.

'No ... He writes about Buchenwald before it became a concentration camp, the "opposition between culture and barbarity". He talks about Goethe, Schiller, Liszt and Bach, who all lived in Weimar ... Oh, here he goes on about Ebner again ... Ebner wanted to escape Germany as soon as he could get away from Buchenwald ... He was appalled by what Hitler did to the Germans and Germany ... so had decided to live in Sweden ... Ah! His mother was Swedish...'

'I knew it!' Alexis cried out.

'...Ebner's father was born in Falkenberg, in the state of Brandenburg in Germany. One of the Norwegians had remarked to him that there was a coastal town in Sweden with the same name. Ebner answered it was a sign from fate and that's where he would go to settle. It was right after that that an SS officer, hidden behind the latrines, assaulted him...' A grimace of disgust spread across Olofsson's face. '*Helvete*! Ebner fell face down in the mud and shit ... The officer took hold of him by the arms and pulled him away across the ground like a slab of meat, I quote, "who'd been hunted down". Ulvestad writes that he never saw Ebner again following that day, but heard it said he was now part of the group of guys recruited to work in Block 46, the experiments block…'

Olofsson's phone rang. He picked it up, his eyes not leaving the pages of the journal and handed it over to Bergström.

The Kommissionar listened to the caller, answered in Swedish, then switched the phone's speaker on and set it down on the table.

'It's Linda Steiner,' he said. 'Martha Knudsen's daughter. I've just explained to her that Emily Roy and Alexis Castells, a pair of English-speaking consultants, are working with us on the case, and she's agreed to speak to us in English.'

'I was telling the Kommissionar that I got your colleague's message,' Linda's voice echoed from the phone. 'I've just seen the news about Karl Svensson and the bodies discovered in his house, next to the old Stormare villa…'

She paused so long that Alexis wondered if the connection had been lost.

'…I assume your questions about the summer of 1986 are connected to this affair…'

'Can you tell us about the incident that summer, Linda?' asked Bergström.

Again, it felt like an eternity before she finally answered. Olofsson raised his arms to the sky to show his impatience.

'One night,' Linda said at last, 'without my sister seeing, I followed her after she left the house without permission. I quickly lost her in the dark. But on the beach I saw a good-looking boy, who was taking a midnight swim. I fell in love with him on the spot – you know the way you can when you're only twelve. For the next few days, I spied on him. He lived in the house next door, so I used my telescope to see when he went out, and then found some excuse to leave our place at the same time. At first, I just watched him from a distance; but then, one day, I went out into the open, pretending I was lost. For three whole weeks following that, I would meet up with him every day – without telling my parents, of course. Until that day. It was after…'

Linda paused once again.

She hadn't mentioned the boy's name a single time, Emily noted. What else had Linda given him, aside from her love? Emily wondered.

'...He made me close my eyes,' Linda continued. 'When I opened them again, he was holding a rabbit in his arms. He gave it to me and asked me to stroke it. While I was feeling its fur, he pulled something out of his bag ... I'm not sure how to describe it ... it was like two pieces of wood connected by metal dividers, with a hole set in its centre. He took the rabbit from me and forced its head into the opening. The rabbit began to struggle. I didn't know what was happening or what he was hoping to do. I just watched, not understanding the situation at all. He told me to listen, that he was about to create a symphony, just for me. Then he took hold of one of the animal's legs and then the other and snapped them suddenly, as if he was quite used to doing it.' Linda exhaled, a heavy sigh streaked with sadness. 'Then he opened the trap and twisted the rabbit's neck. And then he burned it. He never stopped smiling the whole time he did all this.'

Another silence. As if the words were still painful enough to halt her breath.

'I was so shocked and fearful that I did not even try and flee. I was scared that he might hurt me, I suppose. I left at the usual time – two hours later. And I promised I would meet him again the next day.'

Alexis thought she would be able to understand it if Linda's whole life had been utterly marked and conditioned by those two hours she had spent with the young torturer.

'Linda, this is Emily Roy speaking. What was the boy's name and how old was he?'

'Adam Ebner. He was fifteen.'

Olofsson thrust his fist in the air, in a sign of victory.

So Ebner had had a son. A son whose surname had not been registered, for whatever reason. But now they had a first name and could delve into the matter further, Alexis thought.

'Did he live with his father?' Emily continued.

'No. He just came over for the holidays. His parents were separated. He lived with his mother.'

'Do you know where he lived when he was with his mother? What
her name was?'

'No, he didn't tell me, sorry.'

'Have you kept any photos of this boy?'

Linda gave a bitter laugh. 'Yes. Don't ask me why.'

ALEXIS' PHONE RANG just as she was putting on her coat to follow Emily to Linda Steiner's home in Kungsbacka. When the caller had explained the reason for contacting her, she had suggested that Emily leave without her and had sat down again, her notepad within easy reach.

Bergström and Olofsson were following the only trail they had: the first name and the birth year of the second member of the murderous tandem. Ebner's son had been fifteen in the summer of 1986, so the whole police station was combing through the Swedish records to find any Adam born in 1970 or 1971.

Alexis had totally forgotten their presence. She was listening to Théodore Langman explain, in his somewhat precious and pedantic French, how much he had been touched by the message from the Foundation.

'You must understand, Ebner saved my life, Madame Castells. This was long before Fleischer had transformed him into such an inhuman monster...'

'Fleischer?'

'Yes, it means the butcher. His name suited him perfectly...'

Alexis was uncomprehending. 'Who was Fleischer, Mr Langman?'

'Oh, I'm sorry ... My son is right ... I always talk about the war as if everyone knew my story ... It was in October 1944. I was six years old at the time. I had just arrived in Buchenwald with twenty other French children or so. After the sanitary inspection, an SS officer led us outside, all still naked. The wind was as cold as ice and one of the kids, who was already in bad health, fainted on the spot. The officer approached him and shot him in the head. Then, he said in French, "You're in luck, one of you has just volunteered. I only have three left to select." Then he had us stand side by side and selected the three smallest in our group, of which I was one. He asked us to take a step forward. He informed us that the purpose of the game was to remain standing, on both legs. If we fell, we would never see our parents again. If we managed to stay upright, he would reward us with a hot meal. He began with the child who was standing at the end of the row. He hit him repeatedly with his truncheon until he was dead. He then moved to the next of us, who was on my left.' His voice broke. He stifled a cough.

'I don't know what was worse, the screams or the sound of the truncheon hitting their bodies…'

Alexis closed her eyes, as if the sound of the brute's weapon resonated inside her mind. She knew that the cruelty of the SS was more than simply a matter of following orders.

'Then it came to my turn. I collapsed on the ground after the second blow, pretending I was dead. The SS officer was exhausted by then, so he stopped hitting me. He shouted out in German and, after a confusion of noises and absolutely terrifying sounds, I was thrown onto a hard, cold surface with the bodies of my three other companions on top of me.

'I was being shaken from left to right for a good ten minutes, the shattered skull of my companion almost choking me. Then I felt as if I was being thrown over someone's shoulder and after that carefully laid out on something like a straw mattress. I don't know how long I was left there to wait, but I forced myself to keep my eyes closed, to control my fear, not to tremble or cry…

'I think I finally became unconscious because some time later I was woken up by a stern male voice. I heard metallic sounds and smelled sickening odours. This went on for a few hours, I would say – or, at any rate, that's how I remember it; it felt endless.

'Finally a set of hands touched my body. This shocked me, and I opened my eyes. Two men were staring at me. It felt as if the Grim Reaper himself had sent along two of his minions. One was tall and thin, wearing a white overall, his face sort of aristocratic, with large blue eyes. This was Horst Fleischer. The other man was naked, his hands dripping with blood: that was Erich Ebner. Fear gripped my guts. But Ebner smiled at me tenderly; he spoke to me in a low voice, in German, and then in English. I didn't know either language when I arrived at the camp, but, believe me, I was forced to learn them fast. Ebner then spoke to Fleischer, begging him. Fleischer was silent. I remember seeing something like amusement in his cold eyes. He was examining Ebner, wallowing in the feeling of superiority my presence had conferred on him: he could have me killed on the spot, you see, just by pointing his thumb towards the ground – like Caesar. Even though I didn't understand what was being said, I knew that my fate was in the balance. Then Fleischer cried out "Hans!" and an SS officer came to the door and clicked his heels. Fleischer gave him a series of orders, and he nodded at the end of each sentence.

'All of a sudden, Fleischer took me in his arms and set me down on my feet. I was petrified. I was expecting to be shot in the head or beaten to death, thinking that my turn had finally come. I remember thinking of my mother right then. My mother. The beauty spot on her neck that I enjoyed caressing with the tip of my forefinger while I sucked my thumb. I was holding my breath, so I wouldn't smell the cloud of rot and human waste that surrounded me, so I wouldn't taste the odour of detergent in the room. I only smelled my mother's orange-blossom perfume.'

Alexis noticed that both Bergström and Olofsson were giving her strange looks. So as not to interrupt Langman's story, she gave them the thumbs up, indicating all was well, a gesture which she immediately realised was far from appropriate, in view of the prisoner's tale.

'The SS called Hans made me run back towards the main camp, hitting me with his truncheon all the way. He left me in one of the blocks, and I remained there until the camp was liberated, on the

11th of April 1945. For seven months, my job was to take Fleischer and Ebner their dinners. It was at 18.00 precisely, every single day, until the final evening came, on the 10th of April 1945, the eve of the Liberation. Stan, another prisoner, took care of their lunch.'

Alexis thought about the hell Langman and the other child prisoners had endured in the concentration camps. She'd heard the stories of the 'boy-dolls' of Buchenwald, those children persecuted by the paedophile members of the SS and the kapos – the privileged camp inmates. As if the trauma of being separated from their mothers and families, the inhuman living conditions and the cruelty of their gaolers, weren't enough…

'Every evening, when I walked in, they laid down their surgical instruments, next to the body they were working on. Fleischer sat at the large wooden table in his study and worked through his feast while browsing through his mail. As for Ebner, he had to resort to sipping his soup right next to the putrefying bodies.'

Alexis vigorously blew through her nose as if to chase away the terrible smells the story was evoking.

'Over seven months, I witnessed the relationship between Ebner and Fleischer gradually change. But I was only six at the time so it wasn't until later that I came to understand it better. The way Ebner looked at him began to alter. That compassion he'd shown me on the day we met was draining away and … slowly he … how can I put it? … his humanity dried up. At first there was just silence between Fleischer and Ebner, but gradually, gradually, it was replaced by polite and then longer, more animated conversations.

'Then, one evening when I was entering the block carrying the basket of food, which was almost as heavy as me, I caught them laughing, both peering down at one of the dead bodies. They put down their instruments beside the cadaver, as they normally did. But, this time, I saw Fleischer place his hand approvingly on Ebner's back, almost as if he were proud of him. And then they both sat together and shared Fleischer's dinner. Their mood was so joyful, it seemed almost obscene to me: my saviour had been seduced by his torturer.'

LINDA STEINER STUDIED every photo with particular attention, blinking on each occasion before she moved on to the next.

She handed the set back to Emily and shook her head. 'I'm sorry, none of these men looks at all like him.'

Emily put the photos of Linnéa's friends back into her rucksack.

Linda set her cup of coffee down on the kitchen table and rose from her chair.

'I haven't had a chance to go up to the attic yet. It might take some time,' she explained as she passed in front of Emily to climb the set of stairs that led to the next floor. 'I never did get round to sorting things out up there. I really don't know where the photos of Adam might be.'

With Emily behind her, she walked into the laundry room and caught hold of a rope dangling from a trapdoor set into the ceiling. A narrow staircase unfolded. She began to climb the narrow steps, and, once she had reached the attic, extended her fingers into the darkness, searching for the light switch. Emily followed her up.

'We'll begin over there,' she decided, indicating with her finger a pile of boxes scattered under a yellow glass skylight at the other end of the room.

Emily helped her take one of the boxes from the top of the pile and they set it down on the floor. Linda opened it and quickly began delving inside it. Emily noticed two rag dolls and some plastic figures, the spine of a book. Her host closed the flaps of the box and, with

a heavy sigh, moved on to the next one. She pushed the contents of
the next box around with her foot but was clearly no more successful.

Emily's phone rang and she took the call, watching Linda continue her unsentimental and systematic inspection.

Alexis' voice at the other end of the line struggled against a
cacophony of background noise.

'I was contacted by a Buchenwald deportee who knew Ebner in
the camp,' she said. 'Ebner worked with a Horst Fleischer, a Nazi
doctor or scientist who was engaged in medical experiments.'

'Was he doing so of his own free will?'

'No, no, he had no choice in the matter, at first. But he explained
to me how the two men grew closer over the months. It's an almost
perfect illustration of Stockholm syndrome. Are you at Linda
Steiner's?'

'Yes.'

'Has she found the photos?'

'Not yet.'

'Once you do find them, scan them as fast as you can manage. I'm
not sure if they will prove useful, but who knows?'

'What are you thinking we should look for?'

Alexis explained to Emily what she thought might be of interest.
Emily nodded, although she was surprised, and hung up.

Linda was squatting down now, trying to pull another shoe box from
the pile, and setting it down on the floor, with all the delicacy of an
archaeologist on a dig. She took the lid off, so lost in her own thoughts,
she jumped when Emily approached her; it was as if she had completely
forgotten the profiler was there. She pushed the box over towards the
profiler without saying a word, her face a mask. Emily kneeled and
took a paper folder out of the box. Inside was a set of photographs.

The images of Falkenberg in summer were like a window into
another, Eden-like world. The sun shone confidently in an azure sky,
its luminous rays stretching out over the shining sea. Linda must
have hidden herself in one of the fields to spy on Adam: the photos
were taken through a curtain of wild grass.

In the first photo, clearly taken at dawn, you could recognise Karl Svensson's house in the background, then painted blue, and a bare-chested man walking along the beach. Emily quickly moved on to the other images in the folder, but they were of no interest. They'd all been taken from too far away.

Linda brusquely brushed her hair away from her neck. 'I just don't know why these photos make me feel so ill at ease ... It's been almost thirty years, after all,' she said in a hushed voice, watching Emily leaf through her past.

'Maybe because he was the boy you gave your virginity to. Your memory has unconsciously erased the tender recollection of your first time together and replaced it with something more powerful and dark – the trauma of discovering that the boy you loved was in fact a sadist.'

Linda watched the profiler as she began to leaf through a second batch of photos, then her head nodded abruptly, agreeing with Emily, her jaw quivering.

Emily came to a halt, one particular photo in her hand. She had found what Alexis had requested.

She scanned the image onto her phone and immediately for-warded it.

London
November 2013

'WHEN A MAN IS TIRED of London, he is tired of life.'

Adam had only recently adopted Samuel Johnson's maxim. When he had first come to the capital to study, the tentacular city had seemed to swarm all over him. As if it was affixing a label to the back of his head: he was German, Swedish, English, and now a Londoner. And, despite Father's advice, he had found it hard to adapt. To identify who he was here.

Adam leaned against the parapet of the Millennium Bridge. The churning sky was spitting out an unpleasant drizzle carried along by a sharp wind. But things like this no longer spoiled his enjoyment of the place. Following awkward beginnings, the city had become his haven. As much as Sweden had been. He could never admit this to Father, who would have considered it a betrayal. But the city had tamed him, seduced him. He'd grown roots and now enjoyed the anonymity it offered. He'd built himself a life, far away from his mother's influence. And away from Father. In London, he could choose to do whatever pleased him or didn't. It had become his territory, and his alone. And he liked it.

But tonight, for the first time, he felt constrained by London. Tomas Nilsson awaited him in Sweden, and he couldn't cope with this fact.

Adam had always organised his timetable around the imperatives of the hunt and the kidnapping process. On the other hand, he was always reluctant to proceed with the usual ritual of transformation. It was too fastidious and unpleasant. Father didn't appear to realise this. That was why they complemented each other so perfectly: Father craved the hours spent in his laboratory, while Adam much preferred to hunt and capture the victims.

At first, he had panicked at the thought of deviating from Father's strict plans. For three whole decades, he had followed his instructions to a tee. But now … now, Father was dead. He was no longer there to plan things or show Adam the way. And Adam was no longer obliged to be the silent partner. Because the partnership no longer existed.

He turned his head and gazed at the magnificence of St Paul's Cathedral. The elegant construction, rising to one hundred and ten metres, had been built to dominate the city. But hundreds of years later, it looked small next to the more recent buildings, all those giant towers with their heads in the clouds.

A cold shiver rose up the back of his neck and travelled through the length of his body, bristling his hair, as if he had just undressed and stood naked under the autumn drizzle.

London would make a wonderful hunting ground.

He quickly lowered his eyes, ashamed of this sudden surge of desire of which his father would surely have disapproved.

He turned his back on St Paul's, crossed the Millennium Bridge and arrived at the foot of the old, once abandoned, electric power station, now Tate Modern.

'Father, Father, Father,' he chanted quietly as he walked along the banks of the Thames. The word flayed the inside of his mouth. He was bursting with the images and memories that scarred his mind. Father's death had left him disabled. Father had been his 'other me'. The 'other self'. But, strangely, the pain caused by Father's absence…

He squinted, his eyes just a thin line, as if he had heard a suspicious noise.

His head leaned to one side. 'The Other self … the Other … the Other.' Yes, it was better this way. Best now to call him the 'Other'. A word that flowed, no longer scorched his skin.

...And, strangely, the pain caused by the absence of the Other changed into a feeling of intense excitement, a sensation both sexual and sensory.

While he was waiting to be reunited with Tomas Nilsson in Sweden, surely he could find a victim or two here in London, no?

Oh yes ... London would make one hell of a hunting ground...

He licked the raindrops lingering on his lips and hurried along.

OLOFSSON WAS PLAYING with his pen, balancing it between his extended fingers like a majorette's stick. Alexis had just told them Langman's story. She'd swallowed hard at the end of every sentence, as if something was catching in her throat.

Langman must be something of a superman, Olofsson thought. At six years of age, most kids would have wet themselves and swiftly caught a bullet to the back of the head as they attempted to escape.

Olofsson had to admit that the only thing he knew about the camps was from seeing *Schindler's List*. He could still recall the balcony scene with Ralph Fiennes. The character played by Fiennes had really existed. A crazy guy who shot prisoners as if they were rabbits while enjoying his cigarette; it was unbelievable. Hitler had invited every psychopath in the country to eliminate all non-Aryans, the way you trod on spiders. They were seriously crazy guys those SS. Squadrons of serial killers who'd been given the go-ahead to kill at leisure. All Hitler's work. A dirty chapter in history.

'Where have we got to?' Bergström's voice interrupted Olofsson's thoughts, like a nail scratching a window pane.

He brought his pen to his mouth. 'I have fifty-two Adams born in 1970 and 1971.'

'How many in the Bohuslän and Halland regions?'

'Eleven.'

'Start with them.'

Did Bergström think he was retarded?

'That's what I've done, Kommissionar.'

Bergström ignored Olofsson's sarcastic tone of voice. 'So?'

'So, that's why I'm clicking away like a madman with my mouse. Refreshing my inbox. I'm expecting some news any minute now. Two are deceased, that's all I know.'

At that moment, his phone rang. Bergström indicated he should take the call and returned to his office.

Olofsson answered unenthusiastically, his eyes still on his computer screen. But he immediately straightened his posture. Elena, from the census office, whose voice was as sweet as a hand delving down into his pants, had some new information. She said she preferred to communicate it over the phone rather than forwarding it by e-mail. Good choice.

'Well, if we eliminate the two dead ones, we are left with three Adams who moved overseas,' said Elena. 'The first one has been in Australia since 1997, the second in Cyprus since 2007 and the third in Iceland since 2000.'

'Let's set them aside for now,' replied Olofsson, 'although I'll look into the Icelandic one later.'

'So, there are six left. Two live in Stockholm.'

'Tell me about them.'

'Adam Johansson – married, four children; works for an insurance company. Adam Westerberg – married, two children; a hairdresser.'

'Hmm. Neither sounds quite right, but forward me their details anyway.'

The tapping of fingers on the keyboard replaced Elena's erotic voice.

'Done. I'll continue. Adam Clarkson – lives in Malmö, owns a delicatessen; married, three children. Adam Wallen – lives in Västervik; an electrician; married, five children.'

'Bloody hell, shitting kids – our national sport…'

'Why, don't you have any?'

'No.'

She seemed horrified. Sacrilege.

'What about you?' he asked.

'Of course. Three children. Four grandchildren.'

Olofsson's fantasies melted away like snow in the sun.

'And the last two?' he asked sharply.

'What?'

'The final two Adams, Elena.'

'Ah … Then we have Adam Strandberg – lives in Gothenburg; married, two children; journalist.'

'Strandberg, the one from the telly?'

'I think so, yes.'

Olofsson whistled as he rocked his chair back and forth. 'Shit, that's not going to please Bergström … And what about the eleventh?'

'Adam Berg. I still haven't … Oh, there we are. I was waiting to find out his occupation. No wonder; he doesn't have one. How lucky to have independent means. Probably has his dad to thank. Oh, no … he was registered under his mother's name at birth. So sorry, Mr Adam Berg, for assuming that about you. He's a bachelor, no children, no known job; lives in Särö.'

'Will you send on all that information?'

Olofsson hung up without even thanking Elena and rushed into Bergström's office.

HER HEART BEATING WILDLY, Alexis opened the e-mail Emily had just sent her. When the photo appeared on the screen, she couldn't repress a tiny cry of victory. You could clearly see two men in the photograph, identified by Linda Steiner as Erich Ebner and his son, Adam. They were walking along a beach, wearing shorts and sleeveless vests.

Alexis dialled Théodore Langman's number and forwarded the photo.

'Mr Langman, I've just sent you the photo,' she told him.

As he picked up, Alexis could hear Langman speaking to someone called Olivier.

'My son is dealing with it,' he explained to Alexis. 'I'm not sure how to make it work, all this internet stuff, and I have no intention of learning…'

A few moments of silence followed.

'Mr Langman?' Alexis asked.

'I don't … I don't understand.' Langman's halting voice seemed to stumble over a rush of painful memories. 'I don't understand Madame Castells … The man in the photograph … it's not Ebner…'

Again, Alexis had to stifle her excitement. *I knew it*, she thought. *I knew it.*

'Erich Ebner had a tattoo stretching all the way down from his right shoulder and along his arm. Verse by the German poet Theodor Storm. He'd explained to me why, one evening, when he told me I shared a first name with the great man: "So that we never forget that Germany has not always given birth to monsters like the Nazis, but also geniuses, like Storm," he said…'

It sounded as if the old man's tongue was stuck to the roof of his mouth for a moment.

'The man in the photograph is not Ebner…' he continued at last.

'It's Horst Fleischer, isn't it, Mr Langman?'

'Yes, it's Horst Fleischer. The butcher. The torturer.'

EMILY LEANED AGAINST THE CAR DOOR and breathed in a mouthful of glacial air.

She'd been wrong.

She puffed out a cloud of mist, savouring the bite of the cold.

She'd been wrong, because she'd opted for the easy path. A lazy choice that had led to her mistake. A mistake that would have no lasting consequences for the investigation, but an error all the same.

She should have harboured doubts, as had Alexis, Bergström and the young police officer. Not sought out the obvious. There was no way that Erich Ebner, a deportee, a survivor of the hell of the concentration camps, could have become a bloody killer. Erich Ebner, the prisoner of Buchenwald, could not be Erich Ebner, the Swedish citizen.

She should have looked closer at the facts and questioned them, as she usually did. But she'd foolishly simply accepted them, ignoring the evidence by dredging up her theory about Stockholm syndrome, with some measure of intellectual arrogance to boot, she had to acknowledge. And that combination had done the trick: she had accepted her own morally revolting hypothesis.

It was just fortunate that Alexis had been tenacious, resisted her interpretation and corrected the error she was promulgating.

According to Théodore Langman, he had brought along the final dinner to Ebner and Fleischer on the eve of the camp's liberation. So Fleischer must have killed Ebner on the day the camp was rescued – the 11th of April 1945 – and travelled to Sweden using his identity.

Her phone rang. Emily unzipped her parka and pulled it out of the inner pocket.

Bergström's breathless voice buzzed inside her ear. 'We have our culprit, Emily; we have him.'

Adrenaline raced through the profiler's body like a surge of electricity.

'His name is Adam Berg. His name appears on the manifests of a whole load of flights between Gothenburg and London, and he owns a property in Särö, twenty-five kilometres south of Gothenburg and fifteen minutes from Kungsbacka.'

She thought of Linda, still living close to the man who had hurt her and whose name she could barely utter, thirty years later. A man who had no doubt affected the course of her later relationships with men.

'Are you still with Martha Knudsen's daughter?' Bergström asked.

'I've just left her place.'

'Did you find anything out?'

'Nothing.'

The teenager in Linda's photos didn't look like any of Linnéa's friends. Emily had assumed this would be the case; faces change over thirty years, but she'd needed to check.

'OK … Anyway, all will become clearer soon. Olofsson and I will be on the road in ten minutes. I've called Gothenburg, but there won't be any reinforcements available for an hour or so. They're dealing with a hostage situation and a visit from the King. We'll be there in under an hour. Best you go straight to Särö, as you're closer. I'll send you the GPS coordinates.'

Ten minutes later, Emily was parking two hundred metres from Adam Berg's house, on the crest of a small hill.

She checked the map on her phone and stepped out of the car. She slipped her hat on, threw the backpack over her shoulders and began walking briskly up the snow-covered and badly lit street.

Berg's house was at street level, on the left, and the path leading to it was twenty metres away. Emily pulled her binoculars from her bag and observed the house carefully. It was completely dark. No car in the drive. Maybe Berg was in London?

Bergström and Olofsson wouldn't be here for another half-hour. It would be better to get off the street and wait.

'*Hej*, Emily.'

She swivelled around.

It took her a few seconds to recognise the man. She froze, surprised.

'Over here, they call me Adam Berg. But I reckon you'd already guessed that.'

She looked down and saw the gun pointing at her. A 92 Beretta.

'Come, my dear, I'll give you a tour of the property. I'm sure you're dying to see it.'

The light from the three electric torches stripes across the pit.

A perfect rectangle. One metre thirty in length, fifty centimetres in width. Made to measure.

He picks up the spade, gathers earth and spreads it out in the hole. A single shovelful and the legs are already covered; all that sticks out are the toes. Toes as smooth as pebbles, as cold as ice, that make him want to touch them with the tip of his fingers.

Smooth and cold.

He throws another pile of damp earth over the stomach. Some lands just below the thoracic cage, around the navel; the rest slides down the sides. A few more spadefuls and it will all be done.

It had all been child's play.

All of a sudden, he lets go of the spade and brings his muddy gloves up to his ears.

'Just shut up, will you?'

He spits the words out, his jaw frozen with anger.

'No, no, no, no! Stop shouting. Stop!'

He kneels down beside the pit and places his hands against the colourless lips.

'Shh. Shh, I said...'

His nose brushes across the ice-like cheek.

'OK ... OK ... I'll do it ... I'll sing your little song. I'll sing you "Imse Vimse", but you must remain quiet. Is that understood?'

He stands up and shakes dirt from his trousers.

'*Imse Vimse spindel klättrar upp för trä'n…*'

He takes hold of the spade and throws another lot of earth across the torso. It sinks into the wide-open gash running down from the chin to the sternal notch.

'*Ned faller regnet spolar spindeln bort…*'

A spadeful over the face. The earth spills across the forehead, obscuring the hair, falling into the eye sockets.

'*Upp stiger solen torkar bort allt regn, Imse Vimse spindel klättra upp igen.*'

The dirt rains across the marble whiteness of the body to the rhythm of the nursery rhyme.

He packs the final layer of earth tight and smooths it out, then arranges a bunch of brown winter leaves across the top with exaggerated, arrogant artistry. He walks away backwards, his eyes still fixed on the grave, then retraces his steps and kicks a few leaves around with his foot.

He cleans down the spade with his gloved hand, replaces the electric torches in their bag, takes his gloves off, shakes them free of dirt, then one at a time places his tools inside the bag.

Just as he pulls the bag over his shoulder, he hears the chatter of the parakeets. He'd heard somewhere that the exotic birds had escaped from the Shepperton film studios, in Surrey, during the making of Bogart's Oscar-winning 1951 film *The African Queen*. But the truth was, no such bird was used on the set, and the film had actually been shot in the studios at Isleworth. So where had the damned birds come from, then?

He stops for a moment and searches the depths of night for their apple-green plumage. All he can hear is a nearby rustle.

He really needs a second pair of binoculars with night vision. Just can't work by torchlight any more, much too dangerous. He has to get himself better organised and avoid such imprudence.

He pulls one of the torches out of his parka pocket, and, keeping its beam low, gets on his way.

He's just begun a new chapter, he reckons, as he makes his way between the trees. A chapter he has written on his own, for the very first time. And he's already eager to get writing again.

He planned everything with the same rigour the Other taught him, and the whole operation has played out perfectly.

Finding the right prey was easy: there was an embarrassment of choice around. As early as the second night of tracking, he had already selected three families who all met his criteria. For his initial London hunt, he had chosen Andy Meadowbanks. His father brought him up alone, since his wife had left them. Well, 'bringing up' was something of a euphemism: during the daytime, the father spent most of his time drinking in pubs, not even bothering to go pick his kid up from school. In the evening, around eight, he left for the north London club where he worked as a bouncer, without even preparing his kid's dinner or saying goodbye on his way out.

The hunt therefore took a very short time, and proved less pleasurable than Adam had expected. He organised the kidnapping very easily; it was child's play, really. For the rest of the task, he had a specially modified van in his garage, similar to the one they used in Sweden.

Then the unforeseen communion with nature happened. The Other would have gone raving mad to learn he ended up burying his prey. But the exercise proved so exciting, he didn't even feel the slightest guilt.

At first, he wondered how he would manage to conserve the body, until he realised he had no obligation whatsoever to do so.

Here, in London, he only does what he wants to do.

Here, in London, it is he, Adam, who makes the rules.

Home of Adam Berg, Särö
Friday, 24 January 2014, 18.00

EMILY'S NAKED BODY was covered in goosebumps from the initial contact with the ice-cold dissection table. The chill had held her in its grip ever since.

Peter Templeton had his back to her. He was busy preparing things on the metal trolley.

She tried to move her fingers and toes and chase away the pain caused by the straps tightened around her wrists and ankles.

He turned round, a metal disc approximately five centimetres in diameter held between the thumb and the forefinger of his left hand.

His gaze swept over Emily's naked body.

'I bet I can guess what you're thinking: how long it will take them to find me? Am I right?'

His head moved from side to side.

'They have to make it here all the way from Falkenberg. They'll have to search the house. Find the reinforced trapdoor. Blow it up, or whatever way they think of. Or … or maybe they will just give up once they've searched the house and assume I've taken you somewhere else … And then…'

He took a deep breath as he closed his eyes and then exhaled, as his hands drew spirals in front of his face.

'Yes, I'm sure I have plenty of time to deal with you properly.'

He looked into Emily's eyes.

'I see this raises another question in your mind, doesn't it? How exactly is he planning to deal with me?'

He stepped towards the wall, which was covered with sketches. He pointed with his finger to the image of a man raping a stretched-out woman, who was tied to a table as the man cut her throat open. There were two black holes where her eyes had once been.

'Like this, maybe? Or...' His finger spun like a drunken insect and landed on another illustration. A woman, again stretched out, whose breasts had been severed and deposited either side of her head. '...like this...?'

Urine leaked under Emily's backside and along her thighs.

Peter watched as the liquid flowed all the way down to the table's recessed corners.

'Interesting. This must be the first time a woman has peed over herself here. Not quite how I expected it to flow.'

He turned to look at the sketches.

'Actually, I must confess, Emily, that this one is more of a temptation...' His middle finger glided over another drawing. The woman's nipples had been cut away and placed inside her eye sockets.

'I know what you must be thinking: that this is so different to what we'd been doing, the Other and I. Me and Father. True, it is different. But you in particular should know how much one's conditioning holds back one's instincts. And one's inspiration.'

He stared at Emily, observing her feverishly.

'Do you want to know why I was with Linnéa?'

He set the metal disc down on the trolley and picked up a switchblade.

'Because, at the end of the day, I'm just a sentimental sort of guy...' He laid the blade down against Emily's sex and began to carefully shave her pubis. '...Something of a romantic. To meet a woman in London who owned a house right where I was born and spent the most important part of my life was ... was as if the universe was handing me the future on a plate. Such a woman would have to play a crucial part in our work. Naturally.' He brushed the smooth pubis with his fingers.

'When we came face to face in Gothenburg, I was on my way

back from tracking down a possible victim and wasn't in disguise. Despite the darkness of the night and the hood that I wore, she recognised me right away. I reckoned it was a twist of fate – time for me to finally invite her into my world.' His mouth was contorted, expressing his disappointment. 'But it turned out I'd been completely wrong, barking up the wrong tree altogether.'

He took hold of the metal disc again and placed the edge against Emily's arm. The tool cut into the flesh as if it were butter.

A scream rose from Emily's throat. She closed her eyes, visualised the pain, a black stone whose red heart was incandescent, and attempted to banish it as far as she possibly could.

She tried to control her breathing and collected her thoughts.

'A swastika … in honour of your father?' she said.

He shook his head and laughed, still carving. 'You're the one I should have met, Emily. You. Not Linnéa.'

Bile rose in Emily's throat. She focused on the black-and-red stone, and mentally crushed it underfoot. It crumbled under her heel.

'Each boy displayed a branch. They … they were all constituent parts of your work…'

'It was a dismantled swastika. Never actually reassembled. The cross Father had to wear.'

The adrenaline she had managed to release revivified Emily's body, chasing the pain away. So Peter was unaware of his father's true identity. This was something she could definitely take advantage of.

'No, Peter. Horst Fleischer, your father, chose to wear that cross of his own free will.'

Peter's arm froze, suspended over Emily's body.

'What? Who are you talking about? Father was called Erich Ebner.'

She feigned surprise. 'Erich Ebner? No, Peter. Erich Ebner was the German medical student who worked for Horst Fleischer; your actual father was a decorated Nazi officer.'

Peter straightened up and blinked.

Emily continued, trying to keep her voice steady. 'Your father, Horst Fleischer, killed Ebner just as the Buchenwald camp was being liberated. He pretended to be him and fled to Sweden.'

'No. No. You must be wrong.' His words rushed out of his mouth as he brandished the now-bloodstained metal disc. The thin, deadly crest of the blade passed just a few centimetres from Emily's face.

'Father told me about Buchenwald. How it was liberated and he travelled to Sweden and ended up here.'

He turned his back on Emily and stood, legs apart, facing the wall full of drawings.

'Father would have told me. He would have been truthful.'

He turned round and stepped back brusquely towards the dissection table.

Emily spasmed and her whole body began to tremble. She had to calm herself down. She directed her thoughts to the deformed oak tree that rose on Hampstead Heath, close to Kenwood House, like a guard protecting its domain. To the inner strength, the serenity and solidity that stemmed from it. To its twisted roots burrowing into the ground, its unassailable majesty.

Peter's face approached Emily's, his forehead bumping against hers. 'You're lying! You're lying! You're lying!'

'No, Peter,' Emily whispered. 'I'm not lying. I'm telling you the truth. I thought you knew. I'm sorry.'

He moved back, gazing into space, like a lost child. 'No, no, no, no, no. It just isn't possible.'

She had to slow him down. Slow time down. Establish some form of connection between the two of them.

'You're right, Peter. You're right. Maybe I got it wrong. Your father couldn't have hidden the truth from you. Neither would my own father have concealed any truth from me, but my mother…'

'My mother left him … She found herself some aristocrat fool … And I could only see Father during the holidays … I lived for those moments, the times I spent with him … How can you prove what you're saying?'

Of course. She needed some form of proof. She would tell him she had photographs.

'Proof?'

'Proof. About Ebner. Fleischer.'

'I have photos, Peter.'

'Stop. Stop calling me Peter!' he shrieked, almost spitting at her.

Good, Emily thought. *He's reacting to the stimulus.*

'Sorry … Adam … It's just that I thought you preferred to be called Peter…'

He gazed at her, with a look of incomprehension.

'Adam was the one who caused man to become mortal when he ate the fruits of the tree of good and evil; Adam condemned mankind. On the other hand, Peter was the stone on which Jesus built his church and, you, you are the stone on which your father built his work…'

Peter closed and opened his eyes again, shaking his head from side to side, seemingly fighting off a terrible lassitude. 'Where are they, those photos? And what's in them?'

'They're photos of Erich Ebner, when he was a prisoner in Buchenwald,' she lied. 'He had a tattoo covering his right shoulder and arm. Verse written by a German poet, Theodor Storm. Did your father have a tattoo like that, Adam?'

'A tattoo?' Peter's wide-open eyes stared unblinkingly at Emily. 'Where are these photos? Have you got them with you?'

Emily wondered how long it had been since she had been captured. Ten minutes? Quarter of an hour? Half an hour? She could pretend the photographs were in her backpack but, when he failed to locate them, he might…

'It's the Buchenwald Foundation, in Germany, who own them … I'm sorry, Adam, I thought you knew…'

'The Buchenwald Foundation in Germany. Yeah, yeah, I see. I'll look them up.' He nodded a few times and grabbed the scalpel.

'Don't struggle like you did earlier, otherwise I'll start with your eyes.' He leaned over Emily, holding her left breast with one hand and planting his scalpel beside her right areola.

An animal groan rose from Emily's lips. Pain crucified her thoracic cage and began to spread downwards through her whole body.

She had run out of options. Of ways to fight back the monster. She had to distance herself. Move as far as she could from the pain. From her body. From this room.

The blade continued its journey across her breast.

She had to find a place where Templeton could no longer reach her. Her own personal Eden.

Drops of blood splattered across her face. He now held her nipple just in front of her right eye.

She closed her eyes.

Her own personal Eden … Next to her son … her little angel…

Emily felt his tiny mouth, delicate as a half-formed olive tree leaf, alight on her breast. A soft suction, no stronger than the beating of a butterfly's wing. This breast against which he had fallen asleep forever just two months after he had been born. This poisoned breast. She had held him in the hollow of her arms until his small body had gone cold.

My son.

My son … He's big, now. Dear God, how he resembles his father, with that everlasting smile on his lips. I run my hand through his hair. He tries to disengage himself, as teenagers do, embarrassed by this display of maternal affection, his lips curling gently just like his father's. I lay my hand across his smooth cheek. He doesn't flee the caress and speaks to me, with all that energy at the bottom of his eyes, that thirst for life. I watch his lips, the olive-leaf mouth shaping itself like a heart, growing ever more masculine as he grows in years. 'Speak louder, my heart. Speak loud and high. I can't hear you. There's too much noise.'

'Emily, it's Bergström. It's over, Emily. We're here.'

'I can't hear you, Sebastian … Speak louder, my heart … Speak louder…'

'It's Lennart, Emily. It's over. We're taking you to the hospital. You're safe.'

EMILY LAID HER HAND on Alexis'. The trembling subsided, and then came to an end.

Peter was sitting facing them.

The rattling of the handcuffs against the metal table elicited a smile from him.

'Pretty bracelets,' she said.

Alexis gazed at the serene and relaxed features of this man she thought she knew. Seeking out the specific clue that should have acted as a warning, but that she hadn't been able to detect, that she hadn't been willing to see. But there was nothing obvious.

Peter ran his fingers through his beard and moustache. 'Don't you like it, Alexis? It's the Adam Berg style. So I can resemble the photo in my Swedish passport, eh? It will take a bit longer before they grow long enough to imitate the false ones, but time is on my side, isn't it, until the trial comes around?'

He paused, looking at Emily and Alexis in turn.

'Do you know what is the most fun, girls? At least I managed to forever dirty the name of my mother's husband: Templeton.' His handcuffed hands traced evanescent patterns in front of his face. 'It will forever be desecrated by the sheer weight of all those cadavers…' He grimaced with feigned horror. 'I'm sure the shares in his company will suffer badly…'

'Your mother is in remarkable health, Adam,' Emily interrupted him. 'According to the media, she's just signed a lucrative deal with a major British publisher to tell her side of the story. I guess it will be more about her than you.'

Peter's eyes darkened momentarily, then focused on Emily's chest.

'How's your arm, Emily?' His head leaned sideways. 'And your tit?'

Emily took her coat off and hung it over the back of the chair. 'I've been leafing through your photo album, Adam.'

A crooked smile animated his lips. 'Don't belittle me, Emily. It's a diary.'

'Your diary.'

He nodded approvingly. 'I must confess my presentation is a tad school-like. "Prior to the polymerisation", "After",' he mimed mockingly. 'Father would insist the dosages, the impregnation times, the drying process, etc, were all recorded meticulously … A Nazi sense of discipline, I guess.'

Alexis opened her eyes wide.

'What? What do you want me to do? I can't rewrite history. He was on the side of Evil. On the wrong side, full stop. At any rate, he died at the age of ninety-three, after living a very full life. Erich Ebner can't boast the same.'

'Erich Ebner is a hero.'

'A hero? Why, Alexis? Because he was interned in Buchenwald?' Peter burst out laughing.

Alexis was overcome with anger. 'Erich Ebner is a hero because he was involved in the liberation of Buchenwald, Peter. His actions and those of the other prisoners who formed a network of resistance that allowed the liberation of thousands of inmates on the 11th of April 1945 were heroic gestures. It was thanks to these brave men that information about the Nazi plans, the German army, the Allied advance, were communicated to the international resistance. At the risk of their own lives, they concealed a cache of weapons behind a false wall in the coal cellar of Block 50, forced the SS to retreat and freed Buchenwald. So yes, Peter, Erich Ebner is a hero.'

Peter looked up to the sky.

Emily lowered her forearm on the table, as if marking her territory. She could still feel the bad taste of her mistake in her mouth – assuming the nature of the relationship between Ebner and Fleischer was Stockholm syndrome. The reason Ebner had allied himself to his torturer was not due to a form of emotional indifference connecting them. No, there had never been any form of affection binding the prisoner to his gaoler. Never. The apparent submission had actually served to conceal a powerful sense of motivation.

The profiler leaned forward, as if ready to speak to Peter in confidence.

'Erich Ebner was working on something magnificent inside Block 46 – but not the abominable experiments being practised by your father, Sturmbannführer Fleischer. For months he pretended to go along with the psychopathic actions of your father, knee-deep in blood, cutting open still-warm bodies, sleeping at night next to decomposing cadavers, but only one thing motivated Erich Ebner, and one thing alone: to survive, and help his friends in the resistance to prepare the liberation of Buchenwald, by convincing the monster your father was that he truly admired and worshipped him. Thanks to the testimony of Théodore Langman, an ex-prisoner, we've been able to identify a deportee called Stanislas Legendre, who carried Fleischer and Ebner's lunch to the block every day at noon. And, every single day, Ebner would, amongst the meal's leftovers, communicate little bits of information he'd obtained from your father about the organisation of the camp and about Nazi intelligence. Legendre would then pass on this information to the resistance network. Ebner was not your father's victim, nor just a victim, of anyone, Adam. On the contrary, Erich Ebner was one of the heroes who contributed to the liberation of Buchenwald.'

Peter's features were impassive. He briefly lowered his chin, but quickly raised his face again, displaying a broad smile. A plastic smile that carried little emotion. Like any sociopath, Templeton's emotional prism was impossible to decipher because, somewhere deep inside, he was not human.

Emily moved her face closer to his. 'That's why we came to visit you, Adam,' she continued, her voice remote. 'To give you the good news. We know you have no access to TV here and your close neighbours are not into history. Your father was tricked all along.'

Peter leaped towards Emily, his mouth wide open, carnivorous. Emily jumped back, pulling Alexis by the arm.

The two guards caught Peter in full flight and forced him back down into the chair.

Emily indicated to them that she hadn't quite finished. She moved forward, laying her hands on the table.

'Weren't you the one who said you were the sentimental sort, Adam? Which is why you formed a relationship with Linnéa? We would never have found you if you hadn't made the mistake of killing her. Never. Well, like father, like son; your father's "sentimental" side allowed Erich Ebner to become an instrument of peace. Sentimental was your word, but in my view it's inappropriate for describing a sociopath. Personally, I'd say that, just like you, your father was led by his cock.'

Peter shrieked like an animal in agony and the sound bounced off the four walls of the room.

Emily put her coat back on and guided Alexis to the exit.

Home of Emily Roy, Hampstead Village, London
Saturday, 1 February 2014, 16.00

STELLAN DROPPED THE SUITCASE in the entrance hall.

Emily thanked him with a weak smile. Her wounds were healing fast, but the mental impact of the past weeks remained a heavy burden.

Alexis brushed a hand over her back, gazing at her with a look in which gratitude and worry somehow managed to coexist. Emily responded with a series of silent nods, and closed the door behind them as they left.

The two lovers stepped into the taxi taking them to Alexis'. Together, they would begin a new chapter. Despite all the compromises, the arguments and the wounds, some people were better off facing things together.

As soon as the door was closed, Emily rushed to the kitchen and walked out onto the terrace. She slipped her wellies on and stepped into the garden. Right at the end, close to the brick wall, was a patch of earth a square metre in area, bordered by stones.

She kneeled, dug inside the inner pocket of her parka and pulled out the little black box. She opened it and looked deep inside. There was nothing inside the box, but still it felt as if it was full. Full of too much heavy baggage. Images scorching her memories. Souvenirs and thoughts she must detach herself from before she could move on to the next case and avoid drowning.

In her mind she could see the cadavers of Andy Meadowbanks, Cole Halliwell, Logan Mansfield, Tomas Nilsson and Linnéa Blix;

the dozens of other bodies found in Fleischer's and Templeton's cellars; she saw the scars on her arm and breast.

She closed the box.

And then buried it alongside the forty-seven others.

Acknowledgments

During the first year of my son Maximilian's life, as I learned how to be a parent, I discovered that I was once again pregnant, but this time with a book; a book I needed to deliver: *Block 46*. This book would never have seen the light of day without the amazing network of people who have helped me on a daily basis: Mattias, my husband – a wonderful and supportive daddy; Maximilian's grandparents: Odile, Jean-Louis and Britt; his aunts and uncles: Elsa, Cedric, Susan and Lionel; and our Maria. Thank you to all of you for taking such good care of my darling little guy. And thank you too, little guy, for being so adaptable, for your happy mood and your endless smiles, which you have inherited from your dad.

Thanks also to my publisher, my dear Karen Sullivan, for your energy and devotion and for the passion with which you support your authors and their books. I am proud and honoured to become part of the formidable 'Team Orenda'.

All my thanks to my translator, Maxim Jakubowski, who has put all his talents at the service of *Block 46*: we are both now parents of this English version of the book.

Without my French editor, my 'writing fairy', *Block 46* wouldn't be in your hands. At a dinner in London, while my belly was still round, you guided me onto the path where I met Emily, Alexis, Bergström, Stellan and the others. So thanks to you, Lilas Seewald.

Thank you, Stephane Marsan and the dynamic team at

Bragelonne, for having welcomed me amongst you. Your enthusiasm gives me wings.

My most sincere thanks, for your patience and availability, to Behavioral Investigative Advisor, Lee Rainbow, to Crime Scene Investigator, Lars-Ake Nordh, to legal medical expert, Sonya Baylis, to profiler, Carl Sesely and sculptor, Pablo Posada Pernikoff, all experts I bombarded with my questions.

I thank my 'dream team': my parents and my sister, for your conscientious reads and re-reads at any time of day and night, and your constructive criticism. Thanks to my sister Elsa and her keen, psychological eye; to my mother, for ferociously and constantly encouraging me and allowing me to become both a mother and a writer; to my father, the conscience of my words: this book is as much yours as it is mine. I realise this descent into the Buchenwald years and family history was a painful journey for you, more than anyone else; thanks for remaining by my side.

I thank my formidable grandmother, Ginette, for her inexhaustible imagination and her storytelling talents; and my grandfather Lucien: you will always be at my shoulder (the left one, of course, Pappy!).

Thanks to Laetitia Milot: *Block 46* is the continuation of a journey we began together.

Thanks also, from the bottom of my heart, to Jan Andersson for his invaluable contacts in the Swedish police; to Eva Munoz, who spurred my curiosity when advising me about the links between Cartier and history; to Philipp Senge for his translations and information about German language and culture; to Charly Young from the Girls Network, for her formidable help in the making of this English edition; and to the team at Blossom & Co for the professional advice on life and the future of *Block 46*.

I also thank Martine Dupont-Girault, my very first and faithful reader, for her support and encouragement.

Finally, thank you to my husband, Mattias. I thank you for being here. Or rather, just for being. As Lamartine once said, without you, my world would be empty.

I would like to close this book by evoking the 11th of April 1945, the day of the liberation of Buchenwald Concentration Camp by a group of superhumans. Amongst them, my grandfather, Simon Lagunas.

I can't outline here the details about the essential role played by the national and international resistance organisations inside Buchenwald. But let us not forget that, without them, and the men who were part of them, not a single prisoner would have been found alive when the allied forces arrived.

In order not to forget, to assist the survivors and maintain the ties that bind them, the Association Française Buchenwald-Dora et Kommandos was founded in July 1945. After seventy years of existence, it continues to spread the indispensable memory across new generations. Let it be thanked here.

In *Block 46*, I have barely skimmed the surface of the tragic years of deportation, but if you wish to learn more, you can read *L'Enfer Organisé* ('Organised Hell') by Eugen Kogon and *Les Francais à Buchenwald et à Dora* ('The French in Buchenwald and Dora') by Pierre Durand.

I will end by saluting here the memory of the survivors of this hell, of the 56,000 victims who died in Buchenwald as well as the millions of women, children and men who perished in the Nazi camps. NEVER AGAIN.

London, 4 July 2015